有限公司
ng Ltd.

N

Magical and Speedy

倍速

朱倩儀 ◎著

學會 iBT字彙

400魔術英語句極速提升字彙力

精選**1600**個 **TPO**循環字彙 x **400**句長難句 = **iBT 110+**

就是這麼神奇!!! 這樣背才有效率!!!
五大學習特色 N倍速學會 iBT字彙

突破長難句：每例句均為長難句，有助於考生輕鬆讀懂**iBT**、**GRE**、**IELTS** 等學術文章及突破**SAT**和**GRE**雙填空題。

循環必考字彙：精選「**TPO**」閱讀文章內必考字彙，只背重複性出題的字彙。

N倍速字彙學習：每例句以四個字一組，由例句**迅速記憶四個單字**。

同反義詞表：由精選字彙延伸出同反義詞表，只收錄**必考字彙**，過難且 不考的字彙均未收錄。

精選試題：驗收成效且大幅提升考試臨場感。

MP3

作 者 序

現在出國念書是為了達到人生更高目標的一個跳板，或者可說是一段必經之路。而因此 TOEFL 考試對於多數人來說是一項難以跨越的障礙，因為托福考試是以學術為基底，目的是測驗出是否能融入英語系國家的課堂，是否能讀懂必讀閱讀材料，因此準備上又更加的不容易。特別是在單詞的部分。而在閱讀部分取得高分，光有很高的字彙量是不夠的，文章的基礎架構以及句子的結構也都是必要的。但托福字彙依舊是 TOEFL 高分的基礎，不論是在閱讀、聽力、口說以及寫作各方面。這次有幸能夠撰寫這本 TOEFL 字彙書，其包含三大部分。前兩部分涵蓋了從萬惡的 ETS 釋出的托福真題 TPO 中選出的最常見必考字詞。第一部分的每句例句皆是由四個 TPO 常見詞彙組合而成，因此學生們可藉由熟讀一句來記熟此句包含的所有托福詞彙。此外，第二部分的題目篇收錄了 100 題字彙題，幫助學生們做更好的複習與測驗自己是否已經熟悉常考字彙，並且可以在即將到來的 TOEFL 戰場上做良好的發揮。最後一部分為背景知識篇，其以不同的主題做分類並包含托福各類主題，例如地質、藝術等等的主題最常考的背景知識。當然，每位學生的主修以及專長背景都不同，所以提早熟悉各專業必考的基本知識成為準備托福的必要過程之一。

準備托福是一條很艱辛的過程，唯有不放棄堅持到最後的人才是贏家。不用去羨慕稍稍準備就可拿高分的人，因為人家可能早你一步經歷了這一切，準備的過程都是艱辛的，不過想想最後勝利的果實可以讓你如願登上你夢想的學術殿堂，就請笑著堅持著讀完這本書吧！

朱倩儀

編 者 序

托福考試由PBT、CBT到IBT期間經歷了幾次的轉變，更能測出學習者的實際英語使用能力，但唯一不變的是托福考試中的學術字彙，托福字彙考來考去就是那些字，這次有幸經友人介紹請朱老師撰寫了這本書，在選字上從TPO選取常考的動詞、形容詞、名詞和副詞等，從這些字中延伸了同反義字，與坊間書籍和字典相較之下，等同於一本精選字彙書，且汰除了許多太難且不考的字彙，在撰寫上為4個一組的常考字所組成了長難句例句，讀者能讀一句就記住四個字，更能藉由這些句子奠定好學術閱讀的基礎。相信熟讀後會發現新托福閱讀根本不難。此外，若欲準備SAT或GRE的讀者也能藉由本書打好SAT或GRE填空題的基礎，並提升學術英語寫作能力。其中題目篇收錄了100題字彙題提供讀者練習，最後的附錄收錄了學術背景字彙，相信讀者能藉由這些演練於短時間獲取理想成績。

編輯部敬上

目次

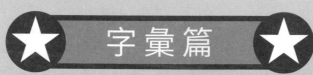

字彙篇

★ 題 目 篇 ★

字彙篇

攻克要點I 必考字彙表

KEY1
Overgrazing 過度放牧 (*n.*)	Primary 主要的 (*a.*)
Extinction 滅絕 (*n.*)	Inhabit 棲息 (*v.*)

KEY2
Adopt 採用 (*v.*)	Protocol 協議 議定書 (*n.*)
Adhere 遵守 依附 (*v.*)	Abandon 拋棄 (*v.*)

KEY3
Absurd 不合理的、荒謬的 (*a.*)	Proponents 支持者 (*n.*)
Bolster 支持、援助 (*n.*)	Abstract 抽象的 (*a.*)

KEY4
Monument 紀念碑 (*n.*)	Property 財產 (*n.*)
Ancient 古老 (*a.*)	Destroy 毀壞 (*v.*)

KEY5
Assume 推測 (*v.*)	Arrange 布置、設置 (*v.*)
Diverse 多樣的 (*a.*)	Uniformity 一致性 (*n.*)

KEY6
Imagine 想像 (*v.*)	Complex 複雜 (*a.*)
Albeit 雖然 (*conj.*)	Comprehensive 全面的、廣泛的 (*a.*)

KEY7

Attempt 嘗試 (*v.*)	Compensate 補償 (*v.*)
Inferiority 不好、劣等 (*n.*)	Consequence 結果 (*n.*)

KEY8

Critical 重要的、關鍵性的 (*a.*)	Depict 描述、描寫 (*v.*)
Adjacent 鄰近的 (*a.*)	Decimate 大量毀滅 (*v.*)

KEY9

Acknowledge 承認 (*v.*)	Ancestor 祖先 (*n.*)
Counsel 勸告、忠告 (*v.*)	Contrive 發明 (*v.*)

KEY10

Pollutants 汙染物質 (*n.*)	Array 排列 (*n.*)
Attest 證實、證明 (*v.*)	Detrimental 有害的 (*a.*)

KEY11

Avid 熱切的 (*a.*)	Characterize 賦予特色 (*v.*)
Enthusiasm 熱情 (*n.*)	Vigorous 精力旺盛的 (*a.*)

KEY12

Inevitable 無可避免的 (*a.*)	Explosion 爆炸 (*n.*)
Collision 碰撞 (*n.*)	Celestial 天空的 (*a.*)

KEY13

Contention 爭論 (*n.*)	Legislation 立法、法律 (*n.*)
Curb 抑制 (*v.*)	Ease 減輕 (*v.*)

KEY14

Emergent 緊急的 (*a.*)	Enlist 謀取、募集 (*v.*)
Entail 承擔起 (*v.*)	Enhance 增加 (*v.*)

KEY15

Grudging 勉強的、不情願的 (a.)	Considered 視為 (v.)
Inauspicious 不吉祥的、不好的 (a.)	Hamper 阻礙 (v.)

KEY16

Lethal 致命的 (a.)	Inhibit 阻礙 (v.)
Giving rise 導致 (v.)	Irrecoverable 無法復原的 (a.)

KEY17

Persist 堅持 (v.)	Nature 自然、本性 (n.)
Penetrate 穿透、看穿 (v.)	Perpetually 永恆地、不斷地 (adv.)

KEY18

Perilous 危險的 (a.)	Territory 領土、版圖 (n.)
Hostile 懷敵意的 (a.)	Paradox 矛盾 (n.)

KEY19

Prominent 卓越的 (a.)	Pristine 原始的 (a.)
Subject 使隸屬、使受到影響 (v.)	Log 伐木 (v.)

KEY20

Preserved 受保育的 (a.)	Annihilated 消滅 (v.)
Probe 調查、探測 (v.)	Decimation 大批殺害、滅絕 (n.)

Unit 1

攻克要點 II 超給力例句

 **KEY 1** ♪ MP3 01

- ✪ Overgrazing 過度放牧 (*n.*)
- ✪ Primary 主要 (*a.*)
- ✪ Extinction 滅絕 (*n.*)
- ✪ Inhabit 棲息 (*v.*)

> Overgrazing was one of the primary factors contributing to the extinction of certain kinds of animals that inhabited around the desert in the northern part of South America.

過度放牧為導致遍布於南美洲北部沙漠特種動物滅絕的其一因素。

KEY 2

- ✪ Adopt 採用 (*v.*)
- ✪ Protocol 協議、議定書 (*n.*)
- ✪ Adhere 遵守、依附 (*v.*)
- ✪ Abandon 拋棄 (*v.*)

> The current citizenship law adopted in the newly-created protocol adheres to the principles of human rights that cannot be abandoned by human beings.

新訂的議定書中採用的公民法律符合人民應有的權益，此權益是人類無法摒棄的。

⭐ KEY 3

- ✪ Absurd 不合理的、荒謬的 (*a.*)
- ✪ Proponents 支持者 (*n.*)
- ✪ Bolster 支持、援助 (*n.*)
- ✪ Abstract 抽象的 (*a.*)

> It has been seen as being so absurd to the nation; however, there are still proponents attempting to be the bolster of those abstract and barely accessible articles.

這行動對國家來說是很愚蠢魯莽的行為，但是還是有支持者嘗試著對這個既抽象又很難理解的條文作援助。

⭐ KEY 4

- ✪ Monument 紀念碑 (*n.*)
- ✪ Property 財產 (*n.*)
- ✪ Ancient 古老 (*a.*)
- ✪ Destroy 毀壞 (*v.*)

> The monument located right behind this property was built for the purpose of remembering the ancient civilization destroyed by the ancestors of the people who are still dwelling in this area.

Unit 1

在這棟建物後的紀念碑是為了紀念被現在還居住在這裡的人們的祖先所毀壞的古老文明。

KEY 5

✪ Assume 推測 (*v.*)
✪ Arrange 布置、設置 (*v.*)
✪ Diverse 多樣的 (*a.*)
✪ Uniformity 一致性 (*n.*)

> I assume that there will be diverse books purposefully arranged but positioned with lacking any uniformity in this brand new library.

我推測在這間新的圖書館內，各式各樣的書籍被有意但卻缺乏一致性地陳列著。

KEY 6

✪ Imagine 想像 (*v.*)
✪ Complex 複雜 (*a.*)
✪ Albeit 雖然 (*conj.*)
✪ Comprehensive 全面的、廣泛的 (*a.*)

> I just could not imagine how complex this test would be, albeit getting a bunch of comprehensive reading materials as preparation references from my friends.

我簡直無法想像這個考試將會有多麼的複雜，雖然已經有從我朋友那邊拿到全面且充分的閱讀資料當作參考。

⭐ KEY 7

- ✪ Attempt 嘗試 (*v.*)
- ✪ Compensate 補償 (*v.*)
- ✪ Inferiority 不好、劣等 (*n.*)
- ✪ Consequence 結果 (*n.*)

Professor Wang attempted to compensate for the shortcomings or feelings of inferiority he had ever made to his girlfriend; however, he got a bad consequence of everything he did.

王教授嘗試著對他曾經對女友所做的不好的缺失或感覺做補償，但是結果並不好。

⭐ KEY 8

- ✪ Critical 重要的、關鍵性的 (*a.*)
- ✪ Depict 描述、描寫 (*v.*)
- ✪ Adjacent 鄰近的 (*a.*)
- ✪ Decimate 大量毀滅 (*v.*)

The critical reason why this country had gone in a flash could be illustrated with the drawings found in this cave, depicting that the attack of an adjacent country fully decimated their defenses.

對於為什麼這個城市會在瞬間就不見，關鍵的原因可以從在這洞穴中發現的畫來做闡釋，這個圖案說明了因為鄰近國家的攻擊完全毀滅了他們的防護。

★ KEY 9

✪ Acknowledge 承認 (*v.*)
✪ Ancestor 祖先 (*n.*)
✪ Contrive 發明 (*v.*)
✪ Counsel 勸告、忠告 (*v.*)

People nowadays are supposed to acknowledge and be thankful for what our ancestors did to make our life even more convenient, like contriving household utensils with stone and counseling us to be respectful to the Earth.

現今的人們應該要承認並感謝我們的祖先所做的任何可以使我們生活更便利的事情，例如發明石製的家用器具，跟對我們提出忠告說要對我們的地球尊敬。

★ KEY 10

✪ Pollutants 汙染物質 (*n.*)
✪ Array 排列 (*n.*)
✪ Attest 證實、證明 (*v.*)
✪ Detrimental 有害的 (*a.*)

The chemical pollutants that this array of plants have been releasing to the land, were attested to be detrimental to the human body, especially our brains and nerve cells.

這一整排工廠排放的化學汙染物被證實對人體會有危害，特別是對人腦以及神經細胞。

★ KEY 11

✪ Avid 熱切的 (*a.*)
✪ Characterize 賦予特色 (*v.*)
✪ Enthusiasm 熱情 (*n.*)
✪ Vigorous 精力旺盛的 (*a.*)

Avid researchers are characterized by enthusiasm for the known and vigorous pursuit to the unknown.

熱切的研究者被賦予對於已知事物的熱誠與熱切對於未知事物的追求。

Unit 1

★ KEY 12

- ✪ Inevitable 無可避免的 (*a.*)
- ✪ Explosion 爆炸 (*n.*)
- ✪ Collision 碰撞 (*n.*)
- ✪ Celestial 天空的 (*a.*)

Scientists just found there will be a huge, inevitable explosion taking place in our solar system, considered a disaster to some of the planets within it, because of the collision between two unknown celestial bodies.

科學家發現將會有一起巨大且無法避免的爆炸，發生在我們的太陽系中，因為兩個未知星體間的碰撞，這個爆炸對一些太陽系裡的星球而言，被視為是一場災難。

★ KEY 13

- ✪ Contention 爭論 (*n.*)
- ✪ Legislation 立法, 法律 (*n.*)
- ✪ Curb 抑制 (*v.*)
- ✪ Ease 減輕 (*v.*)

The Legislative Yuan seems to be in the heated contention about the recently passed legislation that is curbing tax increase to ease peoples' life.

對於最近通過的籍由抑制稅金增加以減輕人民負擔的法案，立法院似乎正處於火熱的爭論當中。

✪ Emergent 緊急的 (*a.*)
✪ Enlist 謀取、募集 (*v.*)
✪ Entail 承擔起 (*v.*)
✪ Enhance 增加 (*v.*)

> This emergent project involves enlisting all the available resources from sponsors and will entail considerable expense to enhance its accessibility.

這個緊急的企劃包含向資助者募集所有可行的資源，且將承擔起龐大的花費負擔來增加它的可行性。

✪ Grudging 勉強的、不情願的 (*a.*)
✪ Considered 視為 (*v.*)
✪ Inauspicious 不吉祥的、不好的 (*a.*)
✪ Hamper 阻礙 (*v.*)

> The man feels grudging handling these problems considered the most inauspicious sign that will hamper the success of this upcoming product.

對於處理這些被視為是不好的，且會阻礙即將問世的商品成功的問題，這男的感到很不情願。

★ KEY 16

✪ Lethal 致命的 (*a.*)
✪ Inhibit 阻礙 (*v.*)
✪ Giving rise to 導致 (*v.*)
✪ Irrecoverable 無法復原的 (*a.*)

> This lethal disease inhibited the function of the child's lung and feet, giving rise to an irrecoverable situation that he has to lie on a bed for the rest of his life.

這個致命的疾病阻礙了這個小孩的肺部和腳的功能，且導致他的餘生都必須躺在床上的這樣的一個無法挽回局面。

★ KEY 17

✪ Penetrate 穿透、看穿 (*v.*)
✪ Perpetually 永恆地、不斷地 (*adv.*)
✪ Persist 堅持 (*v.*)
✪ Nature 自然、本性 (*n.*)

> You can see from stones penetrated with water in great effort constantly and perpetually that we got to persist in what we believe and what we have in nature

你可以從那些日以繼夜滴水穿石中知道，我們必須堅信我們相信的，以及我們天生所擁有的一切。

⭐ KEY 18

- ✪ Perilous 危險的 (*a.*)
- ✪ Territory 領土、版圖 (*n.*)
- ✪ Hostile 懷敵意的 (*a.*)
- ✪ Paradox 矛盾 (*n.*)

> After taking a perilous journey through the hostile territory around the Middle East area, the reporter thinks this world is just a paradox that people have to fight a war for peace.

在他結束了中東的一趟危險的旅程後，這位記者認為這個世界就是個矛盾的存在，因為人們必須依靠戰爭來換取和平。

⭐ KEY 19

- ✪ Prominent 卓越的 (*a.*)
- ✪ Pristine 原始的 (*a.*)
- ✪ Subject 使隸屬、使受到影響 (*v.*)
- ✪ Log 伐木 (*v.*)

This prominent German scientist has proposed that government is supposed to have a well-prepared program to protect this pristine forest that has never been subjected to logging or development.

這位了不起的德國科學家提議，政府應該要有一個完備的計畫來保護這片從未遭受砍伐及開發的原始森林。

★ KEY 20

✪ Preserved 受保育的 (*a.*)
✪ Annihilated 消滅 (*v.*)
✪ Probe 調查、探測 (*v.*)
✪ Decimation 大批殺害、滅絕 (*n.*)

This preserved area has been annihilated with a short time; scientists from around the world are still probing for the cause of the decimation.

這個保育區在短短的時間內就已經被消弭殆盡，而全世界的科學家目前還在持續的探索導致這次滅絕的原因。

Primary	Synonym	Capital/ cardinal/ chief/ dominant
	Antonym	Inessential/ inferior/ minor
Hostile	Synonym	Belligerent/ adverse/ inhospitable
	Antonym	Friendly/ agreeable hospitable
Inhabit	Synonym	Dwell/ live/ reside/ occupy
	Antonym	Depart/ leave/ move
Penetrate	Synonym	Enter/ go through/ infiltrate
	Antonym	Surrender/ yield
Perilous	Synonym	Delicate/ hazardous/ risky
	Antonym	Calm/ safe/ secure
Adhere	Synonym	Comply with/ obey/ follow
	Antonym	Disobey/ ignore/ disregard
Acknowledge	Synonym	Accept/ recognize/ accede
	Antonym	Contradict/ decline/ deny
Absurd	Synonym	Reckless/ foolish/ illogical
	Antonym	Practical/ rational
Inhibit	Synonym	Constrain/ curb
	Antonym	Aid/ allow/ facilitate
Inauspicious	Synonym	Unfortunate/ bad/ baleful
	Antonym	Auspicious/ favorable/ fortunate

Pristine	Synonym	Immaculate/ intact/ natural
	Antonym	Affected/ dirty
Prominent	Synonym	Outstanding/ arresting
	Antonym	Depressed/ common
Destroy	Synonym	Annihilate/ exterminate/ dismantle
	Antonym	Aid/ assist/ construct
Assume	Synonym	Suppose/speculate
	Antonym	Discard/ reject/doubt
Inevitable	Synonym	Irresistible/ unavoidable
	Antonym	Avoidable/ escapable
Enlist	Synonym	Assign/ attract/ admit
	Antonym	Cancel/ discharge/ dismiss
Attest	Synonym	Authenticate/ verify
	Antonym	Conceal/ disprove
Preserved	Synonym	Conserve/ keep/ protect
	Antonym	Abandon/ endanger/ give up
Complex	Synonym	Complicated/ difficult/ convoluted
	Antonym	Simple/ single/ discernible
Annihilate	Synonym	Demolish/ eradicate/ exterminate
	Antonym	Create/ construct/ build

攻克要點 I 必考字彙表

KEY1

Regardless of 不論如何、不管怎樣 (*adv.*)	Chemistry 化學 (*n.*)
Reputation 名聲 (*n.*)	Relatively 相對的 (*adv.*)

KEY2

With respect to 有關於 (*adv.*)	Zenith 頂峰 (*n.*)
Wary 機警的 (*a.*)	Essential 本質的、重要的 (*a.*)

KEY3

Brilliant 聰明的 (*a.*)	Pertinent 相關的 (*a.*)
Manifest (*v.*)	Preeminent 傑出卓越的 (*a.*)

KEY4

Grounds 根據 (*n.*)	Implausible 令人難以相信的 (*a.*)
Arouse 激起 (*v.*)	Domestic 家庭的 (*a.*)

KEY5

Modification 修正 (*n.*)	Abort 停止 (*v.*)
Deviate 脫離軌道 (*v.*)	Expected 預期的 (*a.*)

KEY6

Engulf 捲入、淹沒 (*v.*)	Endangered 瀕臨滅絕的 (*a.*)
Reptile 爬蟲類 (*n.*)	Abundant 充足的 (*a.*)

KEY7

Divest 剝除 (*v.*)	Responsibility 義務、責任 (*n.*)
Delegate 任命 (*v.*)	Take over 接手 (*v.*)

KEY8

Devote 奉獻 (*v.*)	Physics 物理 (*n.*)
Endurance 忍耐力 (*n.*)	Endeavor 努力 (*n.*)

KEY9

Figure out 想出 (*v.*)	Diffuse 擴散 (*v.*)
Dissolve 溶解 (*v.*)	Innovative 創新的 (*a.*)

KEY10

Junction 交叉點 (*n.*)	Hub 中心 (*n.*)
Groundwork 基礎 (*n.*)	Harness 使用 (*v.*)

KEY11

Dwell 居住 (*v.*)	Archaeologist 考古學家 (*n.*)
Explicit 明顯的 (*adv.*)	Groundless 缺乏證據的 (*a.*)

KEY12

Alternative 替代的 (*a.*)	Stimulate 激勵 (*v.*)
Execute 執行 (*v.*)	Ensure 確保 (*v.*)

KEY13

Threshold 門檻 (*n.*)	Pursue 追求 (*v.*)
Prosperous 繁榮的 (*a.*)	Unsurpassed 非常卓越的 (*a.*)

KEY14

Significant 重要的 (*a.*)	Corruption 貪腐 (*n.*)
Disband 解除 (*v.*)	Scrutiny 監視 (*n.*)

Unit 2

KEY15

Architect 建築師 (*n.*)	Impressive 令人印象深刻的 (*a.*)
Adorn 使生色 (*v.*)	Magnificent 華麗的 (*a.*)

KEY16

Run 經營 (*v.*)	Prosperous 繁榮昌盛的 (*a.*)
Involve 包含 (*v.*)	Perseverance 毅力 (*n.*)

KEY17

Designate 指派 (*v.*)	Consequence 結果 (*n.*)
Rival 敵人 (*n.*)	Enormous 廣大的 (*a.*)

KEY18

Basin 盆地 (*n.*)	Engrave 雕刻 (*v.*)
Inscription 題字 碑銘 (*n.*)	Brutal 野蠻的 (*a.*)

KEY19

Struggle 奮鬥 (*v.*)	Adversity 逆境 (*n.*)
Accuse 指控 (*v.*)	Affair 風流事件 (*n.*)

KEY20

Inasmuch as 因為 (*conj.*)	Approved 贊成 (*v.*)
Upset 難過 (*a.*)	Unpleasant 不愉快的 (*a.*)

攻克要點II 超給力例句

⭐ **KEY 1** ♪ MP3 02

✪ Regardless of 不論如何、不管怎樣 (*adv.*)
✪ Chemistry 化學 (*n.*)
✪ Reputation 名聲 (*n.*)
✪ Relatively 相對的 (*adv.*)

> Regardless of the ranking, our Chemistry Department has a good reputation, but the school's science facilities are relatively lacking a bit.

姑且不論排名，我們的化學系擁有好的名聲但是學校的科學設備就相較的缺乏。

⭐ **KEY 2**

✪ With respect to 有關於 (*adv.*)
✪ Zenith 頂峰 (*n.*)
✪ Wary 機警的 (*a.*)
✪ Essential 本質的, 重要的 (*a.*)

Unit 2

With respect to climbing to the zenith of your career, you have to be constantly keeping a wary eye on everything and being energetic to your work- the essential elements to be a successful investor.

有關於你事業的高峰，你必須要時時刻刻的注意身邊的事物並且對你的工作保持熱誠與活力，熱誠與活力就是可以使你成為一位成功投資者的兩個重要因素。

★ KEY 3

✪ Brilliant 聰明的 (*a.*)
✪ Pertinent 相關的 (*a.*)
✪ Manifest (*v.*)
✪ Preeminent 傑出卓越的 (*a.*)

This brilliant 5-year old child impressed the audience with his concise, pertinent answers to the host's questions, manifesting his preeminent capacity of making speech in public.

這位聰穎的五歲孩童，因為他精簡且切中問題核心的回答，展現出他在公眾發表言論之過人的能力，讓在場的觀眾驚嘆不已。

★ KEY 4

✪ Grounds 根據 (*n.*)
✪ Implausible 令人難以相信的 (*a.*)

✪ Arouse 激起 (*v.*)
✪ Domestic 家庭的 (*a.*)

> The grounds he provided to explain why he murdered his wife were implausible and eventually aroused the awareness of the domestic violence.

他所提出有關於他為什麼謀殺他的老婆的理由令人不敢相信，且最後還引起了對於家暴的關注。

★ **KEY 5**

✪ Modification 修正 (*n.*)
✪ Abort 停止 (*v.*)
✪ Deviate 脫離軌道 (*v.*)
✪ Expected 預期的 (*a.*)

> This rough draft of the project needs a few modifications before you submit it, to prevent the project from being aborted because its topics might deviate from its expected gist.

在把這個粗略的草稿交出去之前，必須要對它做一些修正來避免這個計劃因為離題而被終止。

★ **KEY 6**

✪ Engulf 捲入、淹沒 (*v.*)
✪ Endangered 瀕臨滅絕的 (*a.*)

✪ Reptile 爬蟲類 (*n.*)
✪ Abundant 充足的 (*a.*)

Scientists have discovered that the ancient city engulfed by high waves from the hurricane was full of endangered reptiles inhabiting around the large areas of the coastal community abundant with bird life.

科學家發現被颶風吹起的波浪所淹沒的古老城市裡面，在滿布鳥類的海岸邊，群居著瀕臨滅絕的爬蟲類。

★ KEY 7

✪ Divest 剝除 (*v.*)
✪ Responsibility 義務 責任 (*n.*)
✪ Delegate 任命 (*v.*)
✪ Take over 接手 (*v.*)

The former CEO has divested herself most of her responsibilities and already delegated someone to take over all her works.

這個前任的CEO把她自己的職務責任都放出去，並且已經任命其他人來接手她的工作。

KEY 8

- ✪ Devote 奉獻 (*v.*)
- ✪ Physics 物理 (*n.*)
- ✪ Endurance 忍耐力 (*n.*)
- ✪ Endeavor 努力 (*n.*)

> Planning to be standing at the top of this field, this young scientist has been intensely devoting himself to the study of physics in college with his best endurance and endeavor.

計畫要站上這個領域的巔峰，這位年輕的科學家已經非常努力的把他自己奉獻給物理研究。

KEY 9

- ✪ Figure out 想出 (*v.*)
- ✪ Diffuse 擴散 (*v.*)
- ✪ Dissolve 溶解 (*v.*)
- ✪ Innovative 創新的 (*a.*)

> The purpose of this task is to figure out how fast the certain amount of salt and sugar would evenly diffuse and dissolve in water by exploiting this innovative scientific method.

Unit 2

這個任務的目的就是要想出，如何能夠藉由這個新創的科學方法，來快速地將一定量的鹽巴跟糖平均地擴散與溶解在水中。

★ KEY 10

- ✪ Junction 交叉點 (*n.*)
- ✪ Hub 中心 (*n.*)
- ✪ Groundwork 基礎 (*n.*)
- ✪ Harness 使用 (*v.*)

> Situated at the junction of several major rivers in South America, this city has long been a transportation hub with robust groundwork of harnessing water as the source of power to heat homes.

因位處於幾條主要河流的交會處，這個南美的交通中心擁有完整的使用水作為能量來源，來做加熱房子的一個基礎。

★ KEY 11

- ✪ Dwell 居住 (*v.*)
- ✪ Archaeologist 考古學家 (*n.*)
- ✪ Explicit 明顯的 (*adv.*)
- ✪ Groundless 缺乏證據的 (*a.*)

> Mount Olympus has long been well-known for being the dwelling place of the gods even though a few archaeologists explicitly claimed that this statement was groundless.

奧林帕斯山長久以來以作為眾神的居住地而廣為人知，即使一些考古學家清楚地宣稱這項言論是缺乏證據的。

★ KEY 12

- ✪ Alternative 替代的 (*a.*)
- ✪ Stimulate 激勵 (*v.*)
- ✪ Execute 執行 (*v.*)
- ✪ Ensure 確保 (*v.*)

> Research studies into finding alternative energy sources have been stimulated by the funding increase and executed quite smoothly, for the purpose of ensuring the sustainability of the Earth.

為確保地球永續，找尋替代性能源的研究，因研究資金的增加及執行上頗為順利，已大獲鼓舞。

★ KEY 13

- ✪ Threshold 門檻 (*n.*)
- ✪ Pursue 追求 (*v.*)
- ✪ Prosperous 繁榮的 (*a.*)

✪ Unsurpassed 非常卓越的 (*a.*)

Standing at the threshold of a new page of his life, he has to make efforts to pursue the goal he set for making his company the most prosperous and unsurpassed business in Asia.

位處於他人生中嶄新的一頁，他必須努力的去追尋他所設定的目標，來使他的公司成為亞洲最繁盛且最卓越的公司。

★ KEY 14

✪ Significant 重要的 (*a.*)
✪ Corruption 貪腐 (*n.*)
✪ Disband 解除 (*v.*)
✪ Scrutiny 監視 (*n.*)

After the significant report regarding the corruption issue occurring between faculties and governors has been submitted, the university disbanded the committee and started having an intense scrutiny of the members involved.

在報導有關職員與政府之間的重大舞弊之後，這間大學解除了學校的委員會並開始嚴密的監督所有參與的成員。

★ KEY 15

✪ Architect 建築師 (*n.*)
✪ Impressive 令人印象深刻的 (*a.*)
✪ Adorn 使生色 (*v.*)
✪ Magnificent 華麗的 (*a.*)

> The architect's impressive interior designs adorned this church and made this a magnificent achievement.

這位建築師令人印象深刻的室內設計，使這座教堂生色，且成就了一座名勝。

★ KEY 16

✪ Run 經營 (*v.*)
✪ Prosperous 繁榮昌盛的 (*a.*)
✪ Involve 包含 (*v.*)
✪ Perseverance 毅力 (*n.*)

> Running a prosperous business involves a great deal of patience, speed, perseverance, and creativity.

經營成功的事業需要很大的耐心、速度、毅力與創造力。

- ✪ Designate 指派 (*v.*)
- ✪ Consequence 結果 (*n.*)
- ✪ Rival 敵人 (*n.*)
- ✪ Enormous 廣大的 (*a.*)

The lawyer designated to deal with this case said that the suspect already knew the possible consequence of what he had done and prepared to be regarded as being the rival of enormous people in this country.

被指派去處理這個案件的律師指出，嫌疑犯已知道他所做的事情可能會有的結果，且已經準備被視為全民公敵。

★ KEY 18

- ✪ Basin 盆地 (*n.*)
- ✪ Engrave 雕刻 (*v.*)
- ✪ Inscription 題字 碑銘 (*n.*)
- ✪ Brutal 野蠻的 (*a.*)

Research studies indicate that the stone with a strange shape found at the largest basin in South Africa was engraved with Latin inscription by a brutal captain from France.

研究指出這個於南非最大盆地發現，有著奇怪形狀的石頭，是被一位野蠻的法國上校雕刻上拉丁文碑銘的。

★ KEY 19

- ✪ Struggle 奮鬥 (*v.*)
- ✪ Adversity 逆境 (*n.*)
- ✪ Accuse 指控 (*v.*)
- ✪ Affair 風流事件 (*n.*)

> He was struggling with all kinds of adversity taking place in his life, including being accused of having an affair with another woman.

他與在他生命中發生的逆境做搏鬥，其中包含他被指控與其他女性有婚外情。

★ KEY 20

- ✪ Inasmuch as 因為 (*conj.*)
- ✪ Approved 贊成 (*v.*)
- ✪ Upset 難過 (*a.*)
- ✪ Unpleasant 不愉快的 (*a.*)

> Inasmuch as not everyone approved of the events she hosted, she was quite upset and disappointed thinking that everything unpleasant happened to her for no reason.

因為不是所有人都贊成她所舉辦的活動，所以她感到很難過且很失望，並覺得所有不愉快的事情都毫無原因的發生在她身上。

攻克要點III 同義詞一覽表

Approved	Synonym	Accepted/ allowed
	Antonym	Disapproved /refused
Unpleasant	Synonym	Distasteful/ troublesome/ undesirable
	Antonym	Acceptable/ agreeable/ pleasant
Struggle	Synonym	Attempt/ battle/ combat/ conflict
	Antonym	Accord/ agreement/ calm
Adversity	Synonym	Disaster/ catastrophe/ difficulty
	Antonym	Advantage/assistance
Brutal	Synonym	Barbarous/ ferocious
	Antonym	Civilized/ courteous
Enormous	Synonym	Colossal/ excessive/ massive
	Antonym	Little/ miniature
Consequence	Synonym	Reaction/ aftereffect
	Antonym	Cause/ origin/ resource
Prosperous	Synonym	Affluent/ booming/ flourishing
	Antonym	Failing/ impoverished/ disadvantageous
Impressive	Synonym	Extraordinary/ remarkable/ splendid
	Antonym	Common/ insignificant

Disband	Synonym	Destroy/ disperse
	Antonym	Assemble
Stimulate	Synonym	Arouse/ encourage/ inspire
	Antonym	Block/ discourage/ halt
Innovative	Synonym	Contemporary/ ingenious/ inventive
	Antonym	Old/ habitual/ traditional
Explicit	Synonym	Accurate/ correct/ definite
	Antonym	Ambiguous/ equivocal/ imprecise
Devote	Synonym	Assign/ dedicate/ donate
	Antonym	Conceal/ refrain
Wary	Synonym	Attentive/ circumspect/ considerate
	Antonym	Careless/ inattentive/ incautious
Divest	Synonym	Deprive/ dismantle
	Antonym	Maintain/ keep/ offer
Engulf	Synonym	Immerse/ encompass
	Antonym	Neglect/ uncover
Essential	Synonym	Crucial/ imperative / indispensable
	Antonym	Inessential / minor
Pertinent	Synonym	Applicable/ related/ appropriate
	Antonym	Improper/ inappropriate/ irrelevant
Implausible	Synonym	Impossible/ dubious / unconvincing
	Antonym	Believable/ convincing

Unit 2

攻克要點I 必考字彙表

KEY1

Deny 否認 (*v.*)	Vague 模糊的 (*a.*)
Allegation 主張、申述 (*n.*)	Illegal 違法的 (*a.*)

KEY2

Incident 意外 (*n.*)	Critical 重要的 (*a.*)
Campaign 活動、運動 (*n.*)	Uncontrollable 無法控制的 (*a.*)

KEY3

Secure 使…安全 (*v.*)	Supply 供應 (*n.*)
Raid 突襲 (*n.*)	Cease-fire 停火 (*n.*)

KEY4

Dispatch 迅速處理 (*v.*)	Replacement 取代、更換 (*n.*)
Investigate 調查 (*v.*)	Damaged 破壞 (*v.*)

KEY5

Vague 模糊的 (*a.*)	Apparently 明顯的 (*adv.*)
Amuse 開心 被取悅 (*v.*)	Upcoming 即將到來的 (*a.*)

KEY6

Proposal 提議 (*n.*)	Instantly 立即地、馬上地 (*adv.*)
Accompany 伴隨 (*v.*)	Applause 掌聲 (*n.*)

KEY7

Vital 重要的 (*a.*)	Concrete 具體的 (*a.*)
Deal with 處理 (*v.*)	Standardized 標準化的 (*a.*)

KEY8

Incentive 動機 (*n.*)	Method 方法 (*n.*)
Adopt 採用 (*v.*)	Assumption 推測 (*n.*)

KEY9

Accede to 同意 (*v.*)	Settle 使平靜 (*v.*)
Dispute 爭論 (*n.*)	Negotiation 協商 (*n.*)

KEY10

Execute 執行 (*v.*)	Instill 灌輸 (*v.*)
Responsibility 責任 (*n.*)	Affect 影響 (*v.*)

KEY11

Prosecutor 實行者 (*n.*)	Conspire 共謀 (*v.*)
Overthrow 推翻 (*v.*)	Offense 攻擊 (*n.*)

KEY12

Medical 醫學的 (*a.*)	Specify 指定的 (*v.*)
Symptoms 症狀 (*n.*)	Relieve 減輕、解除 (*v.*)

KEY13

Presidential 總統的、首長的 (*a.*)	Announce 發表聲明 (*v.*)
Restrict 限制 (*v.*)	Import 進口 (*n.*)

KEY14

Candidate 候選人 (*n.*)	Modernize 現代化 (*v.*)
Resist 抵抗 (*v.*)	Distribution 分配 (*n.*)

KEY15

Deliberately 故意的 (*adv.*)	Branch 樹枝 (*n.*)
Sip 啜飲 (*n.*)	Straighten up 扶正 (*v.*)

KEY16

Ancient 古老的 (*a.*)	Ladder 階梯 (*n.*)
Gnarled 多節的 (*a.*)	Stem 莖 (*n.*)

KEY17

Rub 摩擦 (*v.*)	Polish 拋光磨亮 (*n.*)
Restore 使回復到 (*v.*)	Original 原來的 (*a.*)

KEY18

Master 熟練 (*v.*)	Instrument 樂器 (*n.*)
Participate 加入 (*v.*)	Opportunity 機會 (*n.*)

KEY19

Pull over 停靠 (*v.*)	Pile 疊 (*n.*)
Neatly 整齊地 (*adv.*)	Fold 摺疊 (*v.*)

KEY20

Lawn 草地 (*n.*)	Routine 例行的 (*a.*)
Lean 倚靠 (*v.*)	Chore 家務雜事 (*n.*)

攻克要點II 超給力例句

 **KEY 1** 🎵 **MP3 03**

✪ Deny 否認 (*v.*)
✪ Vague 模糊的 (*a.*)
✪ Allegation 主張、申述 (*n.*)
✪ Illegal 違法的 (*a.*)

> The speaker denied the vague allegations, claiming that the statement saying that what he has done was illegal and untrue.

這個講者否認這個模糊的申述並宣稱這個說他所做的事都是違法的這個言論不是真的。

KEY 2

✪ Incident 意外 (*n.*)
✪ Critical 重要的 (*a.*)
✪ Campaign 活動；運動 (*n.*)
✪ Uncontrollable 無法控制的 (*a.*)

The incident happening at a critical point in the campaign forces the Britain authorities to consider an airlift if the situation becomes even more uncontrollable in the next few hours.

在這場活動的重要時刻所發生的意外，迫使英國官方考慮，如果接下來幾小時的情況變得無法控制的話，他們將會空運。

★ **KEY 3**

✪ Secure 使⋯安全 (*v.*)
✪ Supply 供應 (n)
✪ Raid 突襲 (*n.*)
✪ Cease-fire 停火 (*n.*)

The American government keeps making efforts to secure a supply line from enemy raids after an agreement to a cease-fire is approved.

在停火協議的通過之後，美國政府繼續努力於使供應線安全，免於敵軍的突襲。

★ KEY 4

- ✪ Dispatch 迅速處理 (*v.*)
- ✪ Replacement 取代、更換 (*n.*)
- ✪ Investigate 調查 (*v.*)
- ✪ Damaged 破壞 (*v.*)

Before dispatching replacement, we have to investigate the possible reasons why all the chairs, books, and tables are all damaged and lost.

在緊急處理更換之前，我們必須要調查所有椅子、書籍跟桌子為什麼都被毀壞或遺失的可能原因。

★ KEY 5

- ✪ Vague 模糊的 (*a.*)
- ✪ Apparently 明顯的 (*adv.*)
- ✪ Amuse 開心 被取悅 (*v.*)
- ✪ Upcoming 即將到來的 (*a.*)

Due to the fact that the speaking you had was too vague and general, the girls, apparently. were not amused and would not join the upcoming party hosted in your apartment.

因為你的演說實在是太模糊又很一般，這些女生很明顯地沒有被取悅，而且也不會參加即將在你公寓舉辦的派對。

Unit 3

★ KEY 6

- ✪ Proposal 提議 (*n.*)
- ✪ Instantly 立即地、馬上地 (*adv.*)
- ✪ Accompany 伴隨 (*v.*)
- ✪ Applause 掌聲 (*n.*)

A proposal outlining how global warming would be controlled in the following years was submitted and instantly voted through, accompanied by enthusiastic applause.

這個描述地球暖化如何在接下來的幾年被控制住的計畫已經被提出，且馬上伴隨著熱烈的掌聲通過。

★ KEY 7

- ✪ Vital 重要的 (*a.*)
- ✪ Concrete 具體的 (*a.*)
- ✪ Deal with 處理 (*v.*)
- ✪ Standardized 標準化的 (*a.*)

People consider standardized education, which could benefit those children who are either below or above average, as a vital, concrete issue to be dealt with.

人們認為標準化教育是個很重要並且要具體被處理的議題，可以有利於不論是高於水平或是低於水平的孩童。

KEY 8

✪ Incentive 動機 (*n.*)
✪ Method 方法 (*n.*)
✪ Adopt 採用 (*v.*)
✪ Assumption 推測 (*n.*)

> There is little or even no incentive to adopt this method due to the fact that the scientific assumption on which the global warming theory is based was questioned by Dr. Chen.

因為以科學推測為基礎的全球暖化理論遭受陳博士的質疑,所以沒有任何動機讓我們採用這個方法。

KEY 9

✪ Accede to 同意 (*v.*)
✪ Settle 使平靜 (*v.*)
✪ Dispute 爭論 (*n.*)
✪ Negotiation 協商 (*n.*)

> These two countries acceded to settle their disputes by negotiation.

這兩個城市同意利用協商的方式來平緩之間的爭論。

KEY 10

⭐ Execute 執行 (*v.*)
⭐ Instill 灌輸 (*v.*)
⭐ Responsibility 責任 (*n.*)
⭐ Affect 影響 (*v.*)

The instructors have the project well executed and hope that their efforts will instill a sense of responsibility in both children and parents and affect their lives.

這些教授者使這個計畫完好的執行,並希望他們的努力可以灌輸家長與小孩責任感,且能夠影響他們的人生。

KEY 11

⭐ Prosecutor 實行者 (*n.*)
⭐ Conspire 共謀 (*v.*)
⭐ Overthrow 推翻 (*v.*)
⭐ Offense 攻擊 (*n.*)

The prosecutors of this gang conspired to overthrow the government, have been regarded as a criminal offense that might directly violate the laws of the country.

這個派別的眾多執行者共謀要推翻政府,這樣的動作被視為是直接違反國家法律的有罪的攻擊。

★ KEY 12

- ✪ Medical 醫學的 (*a.*)
- ✪ Specify 指定的 (*v.*)
- ✪ Symptoms 症狀 (*n.*)
- ✪ Relieve 減輕 解除 (*v.*)

> After receiving the medical treatment from the doctor he specified, the heart diseased patient lets us know that all his symptoms have already been relieved.

在接受了他指派的醫生所給予的醫藥治療後,這位患有心臟疾病的病人讓我們知道他所有的症狀都已經根除了。

★ KEY 13

- ✪ Presidential 總統的、首長的 (*a.*)
- ✪ Announce 發表聲明 (*v.*)
- ✪ Restrict 限制 (*v.*)
- ✪ Import 進口 (*n.*)

> The presidential candidate announced that at least three countries are going to restrict Korean imports to a maximum of twenty percent of their markets.

總統候選人發表聲明,至少有三個國家正準備要抵制韓國進口,達到她們市場的20%。

★ KEY 14

- ✪ Candidate 候選人 (*n.*)
- ✪ Modernize 現代化 (*v.*)
- ✪ Resist 抵抗 (*v.*)
- ✪ Distribution 分配 (*n.*)

One of the candidates recently proposed that he would resist modernizing the distribution of books and fruits.

眾多候選人的其中一位最近計畫要抵制書籍與水果分配的現代化。

★ KEY 15

- ✪ Deliberately 故意的 (*adv.*)
- ✪ Branch 樹枝 (*n.*)
- ✪ Sip 啜飲 (*n.*)
- ✪ Straighten up 扶正 (*v.*)

He deliberately cuts a branch off the tree while the superstar is taking a sip of her coffee and straightening up a painting hung on the wall.

當這位超級巨星正在小啜咖啡，並且扶正掛在牆上的畫時，他故意砍斷樹的樹枝。

★ KEY 16

✪ Ancient 古老的 (*a.*)
✪ Ladder 階梯 (*n.*)
✪ Gnarled 多節的 (*a.*)
✪ Stem 莖 (*n.*)

After walking in a garden full of ancient gnarled trees, he climbed on a ladder, cut the stem on which flowers and leaves grow, and handed it to his girlfriend.

他走進一座種滿多節老樹的花園裡， 攀爬上階梯，截斷長滿花跟葉子的莖，並且把它送給他的女朋友。

★ KEY 17

✪ Rub 摩擦 (*v.*)
✪ Polish 拋光磨亮 (*n.*)
✪ Restore 使回復到 (*v.*)
✪ Original 原來的 (*a.*)

I saw my neighbor taking off her glasses and rubbing it hard and after that, she started using furniture polish to restore her favorite sofa back to its original look.

我看到我的鄰居拿下她的太陽眼鏡用力的摩擦它，然後開始使用家具磨亮劑把她最愛的沙發回復到原來的樣子。

✪ Master 熟練 (*v.*)

✪ Instrument 樂器 (*n.*)

✪ Participate 加入 (*v.*)

✪ Opportunity 機會 (*n.*)

As knowing that mastering a musical instrument takes time, the host gives all the musicians participating in this music discussion course an opportunity to voice their thoughts.

因為知道要駕馭一種樂器很花時間，這位主持人給了所有加入這個音樂討論課程的音樂家機會去表達他們的想法。

✪ Pull over 停靠 (*v.*)

✪ Pile 疊 (*n.*)

✪ Neatly 整齊地 (*adv.*)

✪ Fold 摺疊 (*v.*)

My dad pulled over to the side of the road and found that there were a pile of boxes and neatly folded pants placed in the trash bin.

我爸將車子停靠路旁，發現了放置於垃圾桶內的一疊書跟整齊摺好的褲子。

★ KEY 20

- ✪ Lawn 草地 (*n.*)
- ✪ Routine 例行的 (*a.*)
- ✪ Lean 倚靠 (*v.*)
- ✪ Chore 家務雜事 (*n.*)

My father was sitting on the lawn after carrying out routine maintenance of the vehicle and my mom was leaning against the wall feeling tired after doing household chores.

在做完例行車子維修之後，我爸爸坐在草坪上；然後我媽媽做完家事之後，很累得依靠在牆邊。

Unit 3

Routine	Synonym	Conventional/ ordinary/ periodic
	Antonym	Abnormal/ irregular/ uncommon
Vital	Synonym	Critical/ crucial/ decisive
	Antonym	Inessential/ insignificant/ meaningless
Neat	Synonym	Accurate/ elegant/ immaculate
	Antonym	Careless/dirty/ disorganized
Master	Synonym	Comprehend/ acquire/ grasp
	Antonym	Misinterpret/ misunderstand
Participate	Synonym	Aid/ corporate/ engage in
	Antonym	Hinder/ impede/ obstruct
Standardize	Synonym	Assimilate/ institutionalize / normalize
	Antonym	Disorganize/ mix up/ change
Original	Synonym	Authentic/ initial/ primitive
	Antonym	Last/ derivative
Deliberately	Synonym	Consciously/ purposely / intentionally
	Antonym	Unintentionally/ involuntarily
Resist	Synonym	Prevent/ refuse/ curb
	Antonym	Accept/ allow/ aid
Distribution	Synonym	Delivery/ dissemination/ disposal
	Antonym	Hold/keeping

Restrict	Synonym	Curb/ hamper/ impede
	Antonym	Aid/ allow/ assist
Accede	Synonym	Accept/ assent/ admit/ allow
	Antonym	Decline/ deny/ disagree
Relieve	Synonym	Allay/ alleviate/ comfort
	Antonym	Aggravate/ incite/ agitate
Dispute	Synonym	Bickering/ conflict/ controversy
	Antonym	Accord/ agreement
Conspire	Synonym	Collude/ connive/ cooperate/ cogitate
	Antonym	Neglect/ overlook/ ignore/ disregard
Overthrow	Synonym	Abolish/ conquer/crush
	Antonym	Establish/ institute/ construct
Concrete	Synonym	Detailed/ objective/ specific
	Antonym	General/ indefinite / abstract
Execute	Synonym	Administer/ apply/ enforce/ implement
	Antonym	Miss/ ignore/ disregard
Affect	Synonym	Alter/ change/ influence
	Antonym	Remain/ keep/ hold
Instill	Synonym	Impart/ disseminate/ inject
	Antonym	Leave alone/ take out/ neglect

Unit 3

攻克要點I 必考字彙表

KEY1

Anniversary 周年 (*n.*)

Lower 降低 (*v.*)

In charge 負責 (*adv.*)

Interest 利率 (*n.*)

KEY2

Editor 編輯 (*n.*)

Condemnation 有罪宣告 (*n.*)

Unanimous 無異議的 (*a.*)

Widespread 遍及的 (*a.*)

KEY3

Budget 預算 (*n.*)

Initiative 初步行動 (*n.*)

Prevention 防止 (*n.*)

Inadequate 不足的 (*a.*)

KEY4

Revision 修正 (*n.*)

Insufficient 不足的 (*a.*)

Medications 醫療照顧 (*n.*)

Ensure 確保 (*v.*)

KEY5

Deem 認為 (*v.*)

Equipped 設備 (*v.*)

Outstanding 出眾的 (*a.*)

Prestigious 享有高聲望的 (*a.*)

KEY6

Conference 會議 (*n.*)

Retain 保留 (*v.*)

Traditional 傳統的 (*a.*)

Beforehand 事前先… (*adv.*)

KEY7

Itinerary 旅行指南 (*n.*)

Attorney 律師 (*n.*)

Imprecise 不清楚的 (*a.*)

Faith 信心 (*n.*)

KEY8

Aluminum 鋁 (*n.*)

Abdomen 腹部 (*n.*)

Abundant 富有的 (*a.*)

Intestine 腸 (*n.*)

KEY9

Volcanic 火山的 (*a.*)

Debris 岩屑 (*n.*)

Eruption 爆發 (*n.*)

Avalanche 崩落 (*n.*)

KEY10

Extraordinary 不同凡響的 (*a.*)

Exploitation 開採、利用 (*n.*)

Vast 大的 (*a.*)

Geology 地質學 (*n.*)

KEY11

Archives 檔案 (*n.*)

Crust 殼 (*n.*)

Disclosed 揭露 (*v.*)

Unprecedented 空前的 (*a.*)

KEY12

Waves 波 (*n.*)

Transmit 傳輸 (*v.*)

Frequencies 頻率 (*n.*)

Undulating 波浪的 (*a.*)

KEY13

Polar 極的 (*a.*)

Rotation 旋轉 (*n.*)

Axis 軸 (*n.*)

Perpendicular 直角的 (*a.*)

KEY14

Illumination 闡明 (*n.*)

Controversial 有爭議的 (*a.*)

Viewpoints 觀點 (*n.*)

Epidemic 流行病 (*n.*)

KEY15

Analyze 分析 (*v.*)	Properly 合適地 (*adv.*)
Economically 合算地 (*adv.*)	Feasible 可行的 (*a.*)

KEY16

Rare 罕見的 (*a.*)	Intact 完整的 (*a.*)
Steam 蒸氣 (*n.*)	Originally 起源地 (*adv.*)

KEY17

Mortality 死亡率 (*n.*)	Interior 室內的 (*a.*)
Excess 過度 (*n.*)	Kidney 腎 (*n.*)

KEY18

Autism 自閉症 (*n.*)	Pervasive 相關的 (*a.*)
Developmental 發展性的 (*a.*)	Disorder 失調 (*n.*)

KEY19

Psychological 心理上的 (*a.*)	Phobias 恐懼症 (*n.*)
Characterized 表示有…特色 (*v.*)	Unusually 不常見的 (*adv.*)

KEY20

Criminal 犯罪的 (*a.*)	Propensity 傾向 (*n.*)
Extend 延長到 (*v.*)	Intended 意圖的 (*a.*)

攻克要點 II 超給力例句

★ **KEY 1** 🎵 MP3 04

- ✪ Anniversary 周年 (*n.*)
- ✪ In charge 負責 (*adv.*)
- ✪ Lower 降低 (*v.*)
- ✪ Interest 利率 (*n.*)

> Since Korea is celebrating the one hundredth anniversary of the birth of Emperor Lee, the person in charge of Central Bank decides to lower the interest rates by five percent.

因為韓國正在慶祝李皇帝的百年誕辰，負責中央銀行的人決定要降低利率達5%。

★ **KEY 2**

- ✪ Editor 編輯 (*n.*)
- ✪ Unanimous 無異議的 (*a.*)
- ✪ Condemnation 有罪宣告 (*n.*)
- ✪ WIdespread 遍及的 (*a.*)

The new editor of Daily Pennsylvania states that the unanimous vote in the condemnation of the killings happening in Brooklyn has already been nationally widespread.

賓州日報的新編輯說道，發生在布魯克林受譴責的殺人案消息遍及全美，嫌犯的有罪宣告已經無異議投票通過。

⭐ KEY 3

✪ Budget 預算 (*n.*)
✪ Prevention 防止 (*n.*)
✪ Initiative 初步行動 (*n.*)
✪ Inadequate 不足的 (*a.*)

We can tell from this year's budget for AIDS prevention that probably the government's initiative to help AIDS patients has been inadequate.

我們可以從今年防禦AIDS的預算中得知，可能政府幫助AIDS病患的初步行動目前為止是不足的。

KEY 4

✪ Revision 修正 (*n.*)
✪ Medications 醫療照顧 (*n.*)
✪ Insufficient 不足的 (*a.*)
✪ Ensure 確保 (*v.*)

> Our government needs to make a revision of how we take care of our elders due to the fact that supplies of food and medications are insufficient and to ensure that all of them are safely settled down.

由於食物與醫療的不足，我們的政府必須要對如何照顧老人做出修正，並且得確保所有的人都可以被安全的安置好。

KEY 5

✪ Deem 認為 (*v.*)
✪ Outstanding 出眾的 (*a.*)
✪ Equipped 設備 (*v.*)
✪ Prestigious 享有高聲望的 (*a.*)

> School of Education is deemed as one of the outstandingly equipped and prestigious schools in this university.

教育學院被認為是這個大學裡設備完善並且享譽盛名的學院之一。

Unit 4

✪ Conference 會議 (*n.*)
✪ Traditional 傳統的 (*a.*)
✪ Retain 保留 (*v.*)
✪ Beforehand 事前先… (*adv.*)

Right in the conference, researchers are proposing that nowadays Taiwan still retains the traditional ways of celebrating Lunar Chinese New Year and people are used to having everything prepared beforehand.

會議中，研究者指出現今台灣依舊保留傳統慶祝農曆新年的方式，而且還說到人們習慣在事前都把所有事情都先準備好。

✪ Itinerary 旅行指南 (*n.*)
✪ Imprecise 不清楚的 (*a.*)
✪ Attorney 律師 (*n.*)
✪ Faith 信心 (*n.*)

The copy of the itinerary in which their honeymoon locations are listed seems imprecise, so they decide to discuss with an attorney they have enough faiths in.

因為記載蜜月地點的旅程指南的本子寫得不清楚，所以他們決定要跟他們信賴的律師討論。

★ KEY 8

- ✪ Aluminum 鋁 (*n.*)
- ✪ Abundant 富有的 (*a.*)
- ✪ Abdomen 腹部 (*n.*)
- ✪ Intestine 腸 (*n.*)

> Aluminum is the most abundant metallic element in the Earth's crust and has been found to be fatal to human bodies, especially abdomen that contains a twenty feet long small intestine.

鋁是地殼中最多的金屬元素，且被發現對人體有致命性，特別是對存有二十呎長的小腸的腹部。

★ KEY 9

- ✪ Volcanic 火山的 (*a.*)
- ✪ Eruption 爆發 (*n.*)
- ✪ Debris 岩屑 (*n.*)
- ✪ Avalanche 崩落 (*n.*)

> Volcanic eruptions and debris avalanches always accompany other natural disasters, such as earthquake and tsunami.

火山爆發跟岩屑崩落通常會伴隨著其他的自然災害，像是地震跟海嘯。

Unit 4

☼ Extraordinary 不同凡響的 (*a.*)
☼ Vast 大的 (*a.*)
☼ Exploitation 開採 利用 (*n.*)
☼ Geology 地質學 (*n.*)

> With its extraordinary size and power, the Great Smoky Mountains is believed to be the vast storehouse of national resources, and the exploitation in the mountain relies on two factors: knowledge of geology and advances in technology.

大煙山擁有驚人的巍壯與力量，所以被視為是自然資源的一大儲藏所，而山林的開採仰賴兩個因素：地質知識與新進的科技。

☼ Archives 檔案(*n.*)
☼ Disclosed 揭露 (*v.*)
☼ Crust 殼 (*n.*)
☼ Unprecedented 空前的 (*a.*)

> The frozen archives have been disclosed gradually and give scientists unprecedented views of the history of earth's crust.

被冰封的檔案漸漸地揭露，並且帶給科學家對於地殼歷史前所未有的視角。

★ KEY 12

- ✪ Waves 波 (*n.*)
- ✪ Frequencies 頻率 (*n.*)
- ✪ Transmit 傳輸 (*v.*)
- ✪ Undulating 波浪的 (*a.*)

> Sounds waves, like other types of frequencies, are transmitting in an undulating manner.

聲波就像是其他的頻率一樣，能以波浪的方式傳播。

★ KEY 13

- ✪ Polar 極的 (*a.*)
- ✪ Axis 軸 (*n.*)
- ✪ Rotation 旋轉 (*n.*)
- ✪ Perpendicular 直角的 (*a.*)

> The reason why the Sun always appears in the polar regions of the Moon is that the Moon's axis of rotation is almost perpendicular to the surface of its orbit around the Sun.

太陽總是出現在月球的極區的原因是，因為月亮的旋轉軸幾乎跟它繞著太陽轉的軌道呈現直角。

✪ illumination 闡明 (*n.*)
✪ Viewpoints 觀點 (*n.*)
✪ Controversial 有爭議的 (*a.*)
✪ Epidemic 流行病 (*n.*)

> The presidential candidate's illuminations of her viewpoints on a number of controversial issues, regarding epidemic prevention, left many supporters in confusion.

這位總統候選人對於一些有爭議性議題的闡明，像是流行病的預防，讓很多支持者感到疑惑。

KEY 15

✪ Analyze 分析 (*v.*)
✪ Properly 合適地 (*adv.*)
✪ Economically 合算地 (*adv.*)
✪ Feasible 可行的 (*a.*)

> The ways used to deal with global warming need to be analyzed thoroughly to see which method could be properly adopted and more economically feasible.

處理全球暖化的方法需要被仔細地分析過，才可以知道什麼樣的方法可以被採用，且在經濟上是比較可行的。

★ KEY 16

✪ Rare 罕見的 (*a.*)
✪ Intact 完整的 (*a.*)
✪ Steam 蒸氣 (*n.*)
✪ Originally 起源地 (*adv.*)

> It is rare to find such an old, intact American steam engine, which is not originally from America but from England.

這個古老又完好無缺，且又是英國產而非美國產的美國蒸汽引擎是很罕見的。

★ KEY 17

✪ Mortality 死亡率 (*n.*)
✪ Interior 室內的 (*a.*)
✪ Excess 過度 (*n.*)
✪ Kidney 腎 (*n.*)

> Over eighty research studies on the mortality of engineers and interior designers, about thirty found excess risk of death from kidney cancer and heart diseases.

在超過八十項研究關於工程師與室內設計師的死亡率的報告中，大約三十項報告發現過高的致死危機來自腎癌與心臟疾病。

★ KEY 18

✪ Autism 自閉症 (*n.*)
✪ Pervasive 相關的 (*a.*)
✪ Developmental 發展性的 (*a.*)
✪ Disorder 失調 (*n.*)

> Over two millions of people in China nowadays have autism or some other forms of pervasive developmental disorder.

在中國大陸，超過兩百萬的人口現今患有自閉症，或是其他相關形式的發展性失調。

★ KEY 19

✪ Psychological 心理上的 (*a.*)
✪ Phobias 恐懼症 (*n.*)
✪ Characterized 表示有…特色 (*v.*)
✪ Unusually 不常見的 (*adv.*)

> According to the psychological studies, many doctors claimed that people with a lot of phobias may be characterized as having unusually high stress levels.

根據心理學研究指出，很多的醫生宣稱擁有很多恐懼症的人可能被標籤為有很多不常見的高壓力。

★ KEY 20

- ✪ Criminal 犯罪的 (*a.*)
- ✪ Propensity 傾向 (*n.*)
- ✪ Extend 延長到 (*v.*)
- ✪ Intended 意圖的 (*a.*)

Scientists said that the criminal propensities of the family may extend over several generations because children may be forced to do what they are not intended to do by their parents.

科學家指出犯罪習慣是會傳到下一代的，因為小孩會被他們的大人逼迫去做他們不想要做的事。

攻克要點III 同義詞一覽表

Inadequate	Synonym	Deficient/ scarce/ incompetent
	Antonym	Abundant/ adequate
Extend	Synonym	Broaden/ enlarge/ expand
	Antonym	Abbreviate/ abridge
Psychological	Synonym	Cognitive/ mental
	Antonym	Physical/ corporeal
Unanimous	Synonym	Consistent/ unified
	Antonym	Divided/ split
Pervasive	Synonym	Common/ inescapable/ prevalent
	Antonym	Rare/ scarce/ uncommon
Insufficient	Synonym	Deficient/ faulty./ inadequate
	Antonym	Adequate/ enough/ sufficient
Mortality	Synonym	Fatality/ deadliness
	Antonym	Immortality
Rare	Synonym	Scarce/ limited
	Antonym	Common/ frequent
Intact	Synonym	Flawless/ perfect/ unblemished
	Antonym	Broken/ damaged /flawed
Proper	Synonym	Appropriate/ decent
	Antonym	Improper/ inappropriate/ unfitting

Feasible	Synonym	Achievable/ attainable/
	Antonym	Implausible/ impractical
Prestigious	Synonym	Distinguished/ esteemed/ prominent
	Antonym	Common/ insignificant/ ordinary
Controversial	Synonym	Contentious/ disputed/ questionable
	Antonym	Certain/ definite
Imprecise	Synonym	Estimated/ uncertain/ surmised
	Antonym	Definite/ precise/ accurate
Retain	Synonym	Cling to/ maintain/ preserve
	Antonym	Abandon/ disperse/ dispossess
Transmit	Synonym	Carry/ convey/ disseminate
	Antonym	Hold/ keep
Disclose	Synonym	Acknowledge/ admit/ confess
	Antonym	Conceal/ cover
Unprecedented	Synonym	Extraordinary/ miraculous/
	Antonym	Bad/ common/ ordinary
Vast	Synonym	Ample/ boundless/ enormous
	Antonym	Bounded/ calculable
Abundant	Synonym	Bountiful/ copious/ ample
	Antonym	Depleted/ insufficient

Unit **5**

攻克要點I 必考字彙表

KEY1

Cores 核心 (*n.*)	Hollow 空心的、中空的 (*a.*)
Glaciers 冰河 (*n.*)	Slope 斜波 (*n.*)

KEY2

According to 根據 (*adv.*)	Slaves 奴隸 (*n.*)
Underlying 可能的 (*a.*)	Emancipation 解放 (*n.*)

KEY3

Fog 霧 (*n.*)	Enshroud 隱蔽 (*v.*)
Evaporate 蒸發 (*v.*)	Exceptional 異常的 (*a.*)

KEY4

Prestigious 聲望很高的 (*a.*)	Evolution 進化 (*n.*)
Explosions 爆炸 (*n.*)	Galaxy 銀河 (*n.*)

KEY5

Stimulate 激勵 (*v.*)	Alternative 替代的 (*a.*)
Strenuous 發憤的 (*a.*)	Experiment 實驗 (*n.*)

KEY6

Temperate 溫和的 (*a.*)	Situate 位處於 (*v.*)
Celsius 攝氏 (*n.*)	Escape 逃離 (*v.*)

KEY7

Thrive 繁榮 (*v.*)	Guarantee 保證 (*v.*)
Religious 宗教的 (*a.*)	Tolerance 忍受 (*n.*)

KEY8

Thrive 繁榮 (*v.*)	Guarantee 保證 (*v.*)
Religious 宗教的 (*a.*)	Tolerance 忍受 (*n.*)

KEY9

Heredity 遺傳 (*n.*)	Ancestors 祖先 (*n.*)
Descendants 後代 (*n.*)	Genes 基因 (*n.*)

KEY10

Commission 指派任務 (*v.*)	Retarded 延緩的 (*a.*)
Surveillance 監視 (*n.*)	Analyze 分析 (*v.*)

KEY11

Abundant 富足的 (*a.*)	Isolated 隔絕的 (*a.*)
self-sustaining 自給自足的 (*a.*)	Feasible 可行的 (*a.*)

KEY12

Internal 內部 (*a.*)	Organs 器官 (*n.*)
Mass 質量 (*n.*)	Significant 重要的 (*a.*)

KEY13

Mystery 神秘 (*n.*)	Genre 流派 類型 (*n.*)
Incline 傾向於 (*v.*)	Literary 文學 (*n.*)

KEY14

Impact 衝擊 (*n.*)	Fertility 生產 (*n.*)
Commit 忠誠的 (*a.*)	Association 關聯性 (*n.*)

KEY15

Overwhelmingly 壓倒性地 (*adv.*)	Commence 開始 (*v.*)
Achieve 達成 (*v.*)	Capabilities 能力 (*n.*)

KEY16

Candor 真誠 (*n.*)	Scandal 醜聞 (*n.*)
Attempt 試圖 (*v.*)	Camouflage 偽裝 (*v.*)

KEY17

Refuse 拒絕 (*v.*)	Obey 遵守 (*v.*)
Mandating 強制的 (*a.*)	Segregation 隔離 (*n.*)

KEY18

Strike 襲擊 (*v.*)	Predict 預測 (*v.*)
Vital 重要的 (*a.*)	Volcanic 火山的 (*a.*)

KEY19

Unique 獨一的 (*a.*)	Trait 特色 (*n.*)
Rotate 旋轉 (*v.*)	Dive 潛 (*v.*)

KEY20

Backbone 脊椎 (*n.*)	Distinguishing 可區分的 (*a.*)
Anatomical 解剖上的 (*a.*)	Vertebrates 有脊椎動物 (*n.*)

攻克要點II 超給力例句

⭐ KEY 1   🎵 MP3 05

- ✪ Cores 核心 (*n.*)
- ✪ Hollow 空心的、中空的 (*a.*)
- ✪ Glaciers 冰河 (*n.*)
- ✪ Slope 斜波 (*n.*)

The article says that scientists are collecting ice cores by diving a hollow tube deep into the miles thick ice sheets of glaciers, a large body of ice moving slowly down a slope or valley.

文章說，科學家正嘗試將中空的管子鑽入冰河（一大片的冰滑落斜坡或山谷）幾哩深，以收集冰核。

⭐ KEY 2

- ✪ According to 根據 (*adv.*)
- ✪ Slaves 奴隸 (*n.*)
- ✪ Underlying 可能的 (*a.*)
- ✪ Emancipation 解放 (*n.*)

According to the book discussing the role of slaves played in the nation's history, we know that one underlying cause of the Civil War was for the emancipation of all slaves in the South.

根據這本描述奴隸在美國歷史上所扮演的角色的書，我們可以知道造成南北戰爭的可能的因素是因為南部所有奴隸的解放。

★ KEY 3

✪ Fog 霧 (*n.*)
✪ Enshroud 隱蔽 (*v.*)
✪ Evaporate 蒸發 (*v.*)
✪ Exceptional 異常的 (*a.*)

Since the temperature is getting higher, by mid-morning, the fog that has enshrouded this village just evaporates and the land covered with an exceptional amount of snow appears right in front of us.

因為氣溫逐漸升高，接近中午的時候，之前掩蓋村莊的霧氣都已經蒸發了，而且被超大量的雪所覆蓋的土地也探出頭來了。

★ KEY 4

✪ Prestigious 聲望很高的 (*a.*)
✪ Evolution 進化 (*n.*)

✪ Explosions 爆炸 (*n.*)
✪ Galaxy 銀河 (*n.*)

> Some prestigious scientists believe that the evolution of the universe basically depends on a series of explosions, which is also essential in the formation of galaxy and planets.

一些享譽盛名的科學家相信，宇宙的進化基本上是基於一系列的爆炸，這些爆炸也就是銀河跟星球形成的必備要素。

★ **KEY 5**

✪ Stimulate 激勵 (*v.*)
✪ Alternative 替代的 (*a.*)
✪ Strenuous 發憤的 (*a.*)
✪ Experiment 實驗 (*n.*)

> The funding increase has stimulated those research studies on finding alternative energy sources, making scientists perform a more strenuous work on their experiment.

研究資金的增加激勵了替代能源的研究，並且使科學家們更加努力的去做實驗。

Unit 5

★ KEY 6

- ✪ Temperate 溫和的 (*a.*)
- ✪ Situate 位處於 (*v.*)
- ✪ Celsius 攝氏 (*n.*)
- ✪ Escape 逃離 (*v.*)

Situated close to the Atlantic Ocean, France has a temperate climate with temperatures ranging from fifteen to thirty Celsius degrees so that people from Greenland and Alaska would escape a cold polar region by vacationing down south.

法國因為靠近大西洋，而擁有溫和的氣候，且平均氣溫介於攝氏15到30度，以致於格林蘭和阿拉斯加的民眾願意逃離寒冷的極地地區，而往南度假。

★ KEY 7

- ✪ Thrive 繁榮 (*v.*)
- ✪ Guarantee 保證 (*v.*)
- ✪ Religious 宗教的 (*a.*)
- ✪ Tolerance 忍受 (*n.*)

Many businesses were thrived while he was the Prime Minister of Britain because the constitution guarantees religious tolerance; that is why people decided to settle down in England.

當他是英國總理的時候，很多的企業因為憲法保證宗教寬容而繁榮昌盛，這也就是為什麼人們會選擇安身於英國。

★ KEY 8

✪ Primary 主要的 (*a.*)
✪ Infections 傳染 (*n.*)
✪ Pathogen 病原體 (*n.*)
✪ Invasion 侵犯 (*n.*)

Primary causes of lung cancer can include infections, the establishment of a pathogen in its host after invasion, or exposure to chemical toxins such as insecticides.

造成肺癌的主要原因為傳染（因為病毒入侵造成病原體建立在宿主身體裡），或是長期暴露於化學毒素中，例如殺蟲劑。

★ KEY 9

✪ Heredity 遺傳 (*n.*)
✪ Ancestors 祖先 (*n.*)
✪ Descendants 後代 (*n.*)

✪ Genes 基因 (*n.*)

> Heredity, known as the transmission of some qualities from ancestors to descendants through the genes, maybe one of the deciding factors in why some individuals become clinically obese.

遺傳，特質藉著基因由祖先傳給後代，可能是有些人為何會有病學上的肥胖的主因。

⭐ KEY 10

✪ Commission 指派任務 (*v.*)
✪ Retarded 延緩的 (*a.*)
✪ Surveillance 監視 (*n.*)
✪ Analyze 分析 (*v.*)

> He was commissioned by our instructor to figure out the ways to better educate retarded children, such as developing a surveillance system to track records and further analyzing every action they perform in the lab.

他被我們的指導者交代說要想出可以更好教育遲緩兒的方法，例如發展一個監看系統來記錄並分析他們在實驗室裡所做的每一個動作。

KEY 11

✪ Abundant 富足的 (*a.*)
✪ Isolated 隔絕的 (*a.*)
✪ self-sustaining 自給自足的 (*a.*)
✪ Feasible 可行的 (*a.*)

> Abundant supplies of water and foods on this isolated island would make the establishment of a self-sustaining community much more feasible.

這個與世隔絕的島嶼上有著豐富的水與食物的供應，這使得建造自給自足的社區更加可行。

KEY 12

✪ Internal 內部 (*a.*)
✪ Organs 器官 (*n.*)
✪ Mass 質量 (*n.*)
✪ Significant 重要的 (*a.*)

> Exercising would be the best way to protect our internal organs and keep them working properly because it increases bone mass and is extremely significant to keep healthy and strong bones.

運動可能是保護並使我們的內部器官功能適當的被使用的最好的方法，因為運動增加我們骨頭的質量，且使骨頭更加的強壯。

★ KEY 13

- ✪ Mystery 神秘 (*n.*)
- ✪ Genre 流派 類型 (*n.*)
- ✪ Incline 傾向於 (*v.*)
- ✪ Literary 文學 (*n.*)

His favorite book, a classic of the mystery genre, inclined him toward a literary career.

他最喜歡的書(神秘類的經典書籍) 驅使他朝向文學的事業。

★ KEY 14

- ✪ Impact 衝擊 (*n.*)
- ✪ Fertility 生產 (*n.*)
- ✪ Commit 忠誠的 (*a.*)
- ✪ Association 關聯性 (*n.*)

Even though we have already known the potential impact of age on a woman's fertility, scientists committed to fertility research claim that this is the first time a strong association has been found between age and male fertility.

即使我們已經知道了年紀對於女人生產力的可能影響，致力於生育力研究的科學家們指出。這是第一次年紀與男性生產力有了強力的關聯性。

★ KEY 15

- ✪ Overwhelmingly 壓倒性地 (*adv.*)
- ✪ Commence 開始 (*v.*)
- ✪ Achieve 達成 (*v.*)
- ✪ Capabilities 能力 (*n.*)

The study overwhelmingly indicates that a critical period does exist by which second language learning must be commenced, for achieving native-like capabilities.

學說壓倒性地指出，為了能夠達到像是母語人士的能力，第二語言的學習應該要在關鍵期就開始。

★ KEY 16

- ✪ Candor 真誠 (*n.*)
- ✪ Scandal 醜聞 (*n.*)
- ✪ Attempt 試圖 (*v.*)
- ✪ Camouflage 偽裝 (*v.*)

The idol is having an interview in which she spoke with candor about the recent scandal; however, folks feel she is still attempting to hide something, just as how snakes camouflage in the sand or rocks.

這個偶像在訪問中真誠的說出有關最近的醜聞，然而人們仍然覺得她只是在試圖掩蓋一些東西，就像是蛇偽裝在沙子或是岩石中。

Unit 5

⭐ KEY 17

- ✪ Refuse 拒絕 (*v.*)
- ✪ Obey 遵守 (*v.*)
- ✪ Mandating 強制的 (*a.*)
- ✪ Segregation 隔離 (*n.*)

Five days after Montgomery civil rights activist Rosa Parks refused to obey the city's rules mandating segregation on buses, black residents launched a bus boycott.

在人民權利爭取者羅斯帕克拒絕遵守隔離政策五天後，黑人居民發起了巴士杯葛。

⭐ KEY 18

- ✪ Strike 襲擊 (*v.*)
- ✪ Predict 預測 (*v.*)
- ✪ Vital 重要的 (*a.*)
- ✪ Volcanic 火山的 (*a.*)

There will be something happening to strike us according to the records that allow researchers to predict the impact of vital events from volcanic eruptions to global warming.

根據讓研究者從火山爆發到全球暖化的影響的紀錄中去預測重要事件，將會有一些事情發生且襲擊我們。

★ KEY 19

✪ Unique 獨特的 (*a.*)
✪ Trait 特色 (*n.*)
✪ Rotate 旋轉 (*v.*)
✪ Dive 潛 (*v.*)

A unique trait to owls is that they can rotate their heads and necks as much as 270 degrees and to blue whales is that they can dive down really deep into the ocean for long periods of time.

貓頭鷹獨特的特色是他們的頭跟脖子可旋轉達到270度，而藍鯨獨特的特色是牠們可以潛到很深的海底而且待很長的時間。

★ KEY 20

✪ Backbone 脊椎 (*n.*)
✪ Distinguishing 可區分的 (*a.*)
✪ Anatomical 解剖上的 (*a.*)
✪ Vertebrates 有脊椎動物 (*n.*)

Animals possessing a backbone as a distinguishing anatomical feature are known as vertebrates, including mammals, birds, reptiles, amphibians, and fishes.

擁有脊椎這樣結構上可易區分的特色的動物可被視為有脊椎動物，包含哺乳類、鳥類、爬蟲類、兩棲類以及魚類。

Unit 5

攻克要點III 同義詞一覽表

Escape	Synonym	Depart/ disappear/ dodge
	Antonym	Arrive/ confront/ encounter
Stimulate	Synonym	Arouse/ encourage/ inspire/
	Antonym	Block/ discourage/ halt
Unique	Synonym	Exclusive/ rare/ particular/
	Antonym	Common/ normal/ ordinary
Strike	Synonym	Affect/influence/ inspire
	Antonym	Dissuade
Predict	Synonym	Anticipate/ envision/ foresee/ calculate
	Antonym	Discredit / disbelieve
Refuse	Synonym	Decline/ protest/ turn down
	Antonym	Accept/ allow
Obey	Synonym	Adhere to/ comply/ embrace
	Antonym	Decline/ deny
Trait	Synonym	Attribute/ character/ feature
	Antonym	Normality/ usualness
Attempt	Synonym	Pursue/ seek/ solicit
	Antonym	Forget/ neglect
Candor	Synonym	Directness/ fairness/ frankness
	Antonym	Deceit/ dishonesty
Camouflage	Synonym	Conceal/ cover up/ obscure
	Antonym	Reveal/ uncover

Commence	Synonym	Begin/ inaugurate/ initiate/
	Antonym	Close/ conclude/end
Impact	Synonym	Brunt/ impression/ significance
	Antonym	Unimportance
Committed	Synonym	Devoted /pledged
	Antonym	Disloyal/ unfaithful
Incline	Synonym	Bend/ prefer/ impel
	Antonym	Discourage/ prevent/ dissuade
Internal	Synonym	Constitutional/ domestic/
	Antonym	External/ outer
Significant	Synonym	Impotent/ Momentous/ consequential
	Antonym	Dull/ inconsequential/ insignificant
Underlying	Synonym	Elemental/ beginning/ rudimental
	Antonym	Advanced
Unshroud	Synonym	Expose/ uncover/
	Antonym	Cover /mask
Strenuous	Synonym	Arduous/ demanding/ exhausting
	Antonym	Easy/ trivial

6
★ Unit ★

攻克要點 I 必考字彙表

KEY1

Tremble 發抖 (*v.*)	Abruptly 突然的、陡峭的 (*adv.*)
Deforms 解體 (*v.*)	Vertically 垂直地 (*adv.*)

KEY2

Deem 認為 (*v.*)	Vigorous 精力旺盛的、健壯的 (*a.*)
Patriotic 有愛國心的 (*a.*)	Vibrant 震動的、響亮的、戰慄的 (*a.*)

KEY3

Vomit 嘔吐 (*v.*)	Disgorge 吐出、流出 (*v.*)
Consume 消耗 (*v.*)	Diarrhea 腹瀉 (*n.*)

KEY4

Wary of 當心的、警惕留心的 (*a.*)	Aggressive 侵略的、好鬥的 (*a.*)
Investors 投資者 (*n.*)	Defensive 防備的、防禦性的 (*a.*)

KEY5

Epicenter 震央 (*n.*)	Earthquake 地震 (*n.*)
Magnitude 震度 (*n.*)	Extensive 擴大的、廣泛的 (*a.*)

KEY6

Equation 相等、等式 (*n.*)	Equality 相等 (*n.*)
Equivalence 相同、等價 (*n.*)	Quantitatively 定量地 (*adv.*)

KEY7

Eternal 永恆的、無窮的 (*a.*)	Succession 連續 (*n.*)
Citizens 市民、公民 (*n.*)	Cease 停止 (*v.*)

KEY8

Reveal 透露、表明 (*v.*)	Inhabitant 居民、住戶 (*n.*)
Essentially 實質上、本質上 (*adv.*)	Devoid of 全無的、缺乏 (*a.*)

KEY9

Operating 操作 (*n.*)	Apparatus 設備、器具 (*n.*)
Surgical 外科的、手術上的 (*a.*)	Strength 力量、實力 (*n.*)

KEY10

Appall 驚恐 (*v.*)	Misconduct 錯誤處置 (*n.*)
Tackle 處理 (*v.*)	Vote 投票 (*v.*)

KEY11

Definitely 一定地 (*adv.*)	Cherish 珍惜 (*v.*)
Gain 獲取 (*v.*)	Donate 捐贈 (*v.*)

KEY12

Fictional 虛構的、小說的 (*a.*)	Chronicle 載入編年史 (*v.*)
Historical 歷史上的 (*a.*)	Assassination 暗殺、行刺 (*n.*)

KEY13

Groan 呻吟、嘆息 (*v.*)	Grim 冷酷的、殘忍的 (*a.*)
Destroy 破壞 (*v.*)	Extinct 滅絕的 (*a.*)

KEY14

Lack 缺乏、欠缺 (*n.*)	Handicap 加障礙於、妨礙 (*v.*)
Cure 治癒 (*n.*)	Virus 病毒 (*n.*)

KEY15

Murderer 謀殺者 (*n.*)	Deliberately 刻意地 (*adv.*)
Hostile 懷敵意的 (*a.*)	Intruder 入侵者 (*n.*)

KEY16

Speculate 深思、推測 (*v.*)	Continental 大陸的、洲的 (*a.*)
Plate 板塊 (*n.*)	Hotspot 熱點 (*n.*)

KEY17

Competitor 競賽 (*n.*)	Household 家庭的 (*a.*)
Fashion 方式 (*n.*)	Retain 保持 (*v.*)

KEY18

Establish 建造 (*v.*)	Humanitarian 人道主義者 (*n.*)
Determined 決心的、堅決的 (*a.*)	Imprison 限制、監禁 (*v.*)

KEY19

Industrial 工業的、產業的 (*a.*)	Ideology 意識形態、觀念學 (*n.*)
Cooperation 合作、協力 (*n.*)	Spread 散佈、傳播 (*v.*)

KEY20

Imply 暗示、意味 (*v.*)	Imperceptible 不能感知的、細微的 (*a.*)
Meter 公尺 (*n.*)	Coast 海岸 (*n.*)

攻克要點 II 超給力例句

★ KEY 1 ♪ MP3 06

- ✪ Tremble 發抖 (*v.*)
- ✪ Abruptly 突然的、陡峭的 (*adv.*)
- ✪ Deforms 解體 (*v.*)
- ✪ Vertically 垂直地 (*adv.*)

> Earthquake performs shaking or trembling of the earth that could be either volcanic or tectonic in origin and may cause tsunami to be generated when the seafloor abruptly deforms and vertically displaces the overlaying water.

地震（搖晃與震動）有可能是火山或是板塊造成的，而且當海床突然解體且垂直取代覆蓋的水體，還有可能會造成海嘯的發生。

★ KEY 2

- ✪ Deem 認為 (*v.*)
- ✪ Vigorous 精力旺盛的、健壯的 (*a.*)
- ✪ Patriotic 有愛國心的 (*a.*)
- ✪ Vibrant 震動的、響亮的、戰慄的 (*a.*)

Deemed as a vigorous, patriotic person who runs enormous local offices, he soon becomes a leader but feels like rather overwhelmed working in the vibrant environment of the big city.

這位被認為是個精力旺盛、富有愛國心,且經營多家公司的人,很快的成為了領導者,但卻越覺得在令人感到戰慄的大城市裡努力很有壓力。

★ KEY 3

✪ Vomit 嘔吐 (*v.*)
✪ Disgorge 吐出、流出 (*v.*)
✪ Consume 消耗 (*v.*)
✪ Diarrhea 腹瀉 (*n.*)

Vomiting, the process of disgorging the contents of the stomach through the mouth, sometimes happens when a person intentionally consumes a large amount of food and then vomits or has diarrhea, for the purpose of avoiding weight gain.

嘔吐,一種胃裡的東西從嘴巴流出的過程,時常發生在為了減重而刻意地吃太多,然後發生嘔吐或是腹瀉的狀況。

★ KEY 4

✪ Wary of 當心的、警惕留心的 (*a.*)

✪ Aggressive 侵略的、好鬥的 (*a.*)

✪ Investors 投資者 (*n.*)

✪ Defensive 防備的、防禦性的 (*a.*)

> The business owner wary of aggressive investors would be more likely to believe defensive investors, but are less likely to make any mistakes.

提防激進投資者的企業家比較相信防備心較強且較少犯錯的投資者。

★ **KEY 5**

✪ Epicenter 震央 (*n.*)

✪ Earthquake 地震 (*n.*)

✪ Magnitude 震度 (*n.*)

✪ Extensive 擴大的、廣泛的 (*a.*)

> A large number of buildings in Tokyo, Japan, from as far as eighteen miles from the epicenter of the earthquake measuring 8.5 magnitudes, suffered extensive damage.

大量的日本東京建築物，甚至遠至地震震央十八英里外，測出震度8.5級的震度，而遭受大規模的災害。

★ **KEY 6**

✪ Equation 相等、等式 (*n.*)

✪ Equality 相等 (*n.*)

✪ Equivalence 相同、等價 (*n.*)
✪ Quantitatively 定量地 (*adv.*)

Equation is usually a formal statement of the equality or equivalence of mathematical or logical expressions, such as A + B = C, or an expression representing a chemical reaction quantitatively by means of chemical symbols.

等式被視為是數學上或是邏輯表達上相等概念的一種表達方式，例如 A＋B＝C，或者是一種藉由化學符號量化化學反應的表達方式。

⭐ **KEY 7**

✪ Eternal 永恆的、無窮的 (*a.*)
✪ Succession 連續 (*n.*)
✪ Citizens 市民、公民 (*n.*)
✪ Cease 停止 (*v.*)

It was not until the end of the Civil War that the eternal succession of wars between opposing groups of citizens ceased in the United States of America.

直到南北戰爭結束，美國人民兩派間無止境的戰爭才得以結束。

⭐ **KEY 8**

✪ Reveal 透露、表明 (*v.*)

✪ Inhabitant 居民、住戶 (*n.*)

✪ Essentially 實質上、本質上 (*adv.*)

✪ Devoid of 全無的、缺乏 (*a.*)

> According to the recently revealed studies about Moon, it stated that there may be no underwater supplies that could be used for lunar inhabitants due to the possible fact that the interior Moon is essentially devoid of water.

根據最近發表的有關月亮的研究，因為事實顯示月球內部實質上是缺乏水資源的，所以月球上可能沒有可供居住用的地下水。

 **KEY 9**

✪ Operating 操作 (*n.*)

✪ Apparatus 設備、器具 (*n.*)

✪ Surgical 外科的、手術上的 (*a.*)

✪ Strength 力量、實力 (*n.*)

> The hospital's operating rooms are full of the latest medical apparatus that could be especially helpful for doctors to save people and increase surgical strength and experiences.

醫院的手術室擺滿了最新的醫療器材，其特別對醫生救人，以及增加手術經驗與實力有幫助。

KEY 10

✪ Appall 驚恐 (*v.*)
✪ Misconduct 錯誤處置 (*n.*)
✪ Tackle 處理 (*v.*)
✪ Vote 投票 (*v.*)

> Nowadays, a large number of people in Korea were appalled about the misconduct of their president on tackling the scandal even though they had voted for her.

現在大多數的韓國人民對於他們總理處理緋聞的錯誤方式感到很驚恐，縱使他們在之前的選舉是投給她的。

★ KEY 11

✪ Definitely 一定地 (*adv.*)
✪ Cherish 珍惜 (*v.*)
✪ Gain 獲取 (*v.*)
✪ Donate 捐贈 (*v.*)

> The audience of The Ellen Show definitely cherishes every opportunity they gain to win free flight tickets and free presents donated by other organizations.

《艾倫秀》的觀眾們非常珍惜有機會可以贏得其他組織所捐贈的免費機票及禮物。

★ KEY 12

✪ Fictional 虛構的、小說的 (a.)
✪ Chronicle 載入編年史 (v.)
✪ Historical 歷史上的 (a.)
✪ Assassination 暗殺、行刺 (n.)

> Even though the movie is partially fictional, it still chronicles some historical events of the assassination of Abraham Lincoln.

雖然這部電影有部分是虛構的,但是這部電影還是有照著編年史的形式來敘述亞伯拉罕·林肯的行刺事件。

★ KEY 13

✪ Groan 呻吟、嘆息 (v.)
✪ Grim 冷酷的、殘忍的 (a.)
✪ Destroy 破壞 (v.)
✪ Extinct 滅絕的 (a.)

> I can hear the groaning sounds from the land of our planet while looking at the grim chart that shows nearly sixty percent of the Earth's natural forests and wild lives have already been destroyed and extinct, according to the World Resource Institute.

當我看著這個殘酷的圖表上顯示著根據World Resource Institute的調查,近六成地球上的自然森林及野生動物已經被破壞且滅絕,我可以聽到從我們的土地傳來的嘆息聲。

⭐ KEY 14

- ✪ Lack 缺乏、欠缺 (*n.*)
- ✪ Handicap 加障礙於、妨礙 (*v.*)
- ✪ Cure 治癒 (*n.*)
- ✪ Virus 病毒 (*n.*)

> Researchers and scientists have been handicapped in finding a cure for SARS, AIDS, and Ebola virus due to a lack of funding by the academy.

由於缺乏來自科學院的資金支持，研究員和科學家在關於治癒 SARS、AIDS以及伊波拉病毒方面的研究受到了阻礙。

⭐ KEY 15

- ✪ Murderer 謀殺者 (*n.*)
- ✪ Deliberately 刻意地 (*adv.*)
- ✪ Hostile 懷敵意的 (*a.*)
- ✪ Intruder 入侵者 (*n.*)

> The murderer who deliberately kills the poor little girl has the hostile towards foreigners, especially white people, this is attributable to the fight he once had with the whites while he was in Africa.

蓄意謀殺小女孩的謀殺者對於外來者懷有惡意，特別是對於白人，因為當他還在非洲的時候，他曾經跟白人入侵者有過鬥爭。

★ KEY 16

✪ Speculate 深思、推測 (*v.*)
✪ Continental 大陸的、洲的 (*a.*)
✪ Plate 板塊 (*n.*)
✪ Hotspot 熱點 (*n.*)

Most scientists speculate that volcanos located away from the edges of continental plates are the cause but the studies state that hotspot of lava rising from deep in the Earth might be the actual cause.

大部分的科學家推測說遠離大陸板塊邊緣的火山是主因，但是研究指出從地球深處上升的熔岩熱點可能才是真正的主因。

★ KEY 17

✪ Competitor 競賽 (*n.*)
✪ Household 家庭的 (*a.*)
✪ Fashion 方式 (*n.*)
✪ Retain 保持 (*v.*)

This game asks competitors to remember a list of twenty household items in a minute; as a result, team A gets the items faster and retains the items in mind longer than other teams, by means of listing the given items in an organized fashion.

這個遊戲要求應賽者要在一分鐘內記住表單上的二十件家用物品，結果A組藉由把這些物品做有組織性的排列，而成為最快完成且在心裡記住這些物品最久的隊伍。

★ KEY 18

- ✪ Establish 建造 (*v.*)
- ✪ Humanitarian 人道主義者 (*n.*)
- ✪ Determined 決心的、堅決的 (*a.*)
- ✪ Imprison 限制、監禁 (*v.*)

This castle was established by a group of Humanitarians who were determined to create a settlement for those imprisoned in the Philadelphia jails.

這座城堡由一群人道救援者所造，他們決心要為被監禁於費城監獄的人創建一個可安身立命的地方。

★ KEY 19

- ✪ Industrial 工業的、產業的 (*a.*)

✪ Ideology 意識形態、觀念學 (*n.*)
✪ Cooperation 合作、協力 (*n.*)
✪ Spread 散佈、傳播 (*v.*)

> The industrial machinery, style of work, and ideology of nonviolence and freely given cooperation in United States were spread originally from England, the world's most industrial country in eighteens.

在美國，工業化的機器、工作型態、以及反暴力和合作這樣的意識形態，最剛開始是從英國這個在十七世紀是世界上最工業化的國家傳播過來的。

![KEY 20]

✪ Imply 暗示、意味 (*v.*)
✪ Imperceptible 不能感知的、細微的 (*a.*)
✪ Meter 公尺 (*n.*)
✪ Coast 海岸 (*n.*)

> After reading the study, an expert implies that a tsunami, imperceptible at sea, can grow up to several meters or more in height near the coast, due to its shoaling effect.

這位專家在讀完這份研究之後，暗示因為淺灘效應，海嘯是無法被注意到的，且會在沿海升高幾公尺甚至更高。

Deform	Synonym	Contort/ impair/ mangle
	Antonym	Aid/ assist/ repair
Cure	Synonym	Alleviate/ ameliorate/ relieve
	Antonym	Damage/ destroy
Abrupt	Synonym	Blunt/ crude/ discourteous
	Antonym	Calm/ leisurely
Vigorous	Synonym	Active/ brisk/ dynamic
	Antonym	Apathetic/ delicate / dull
Patriotic	Synonym	Loyal/ nationalistic
	Antonym	Traitorous
Spread	Synonym	Disperse/ spray/ stretch
	Antonym	Collect/ compress
Consume	Synonym	Absorb/ deplete/ devour
	Antonym	Obtain/ accumulate
Aggressive	Synonym	Combative/ contentious/ intrusive
	Antonym	Calm/ easy-going
Defensive	Synonym	Averting/ conservative/ opposing
	Antonym	Unwary/ unwatchful
Extensive	Synonym	Broad/ comprehensive/ expanded
	Antonym	Exclusive/ limited

Equivalence	Synonym	Agreement/ alikeness/ conformity
	Antonym	Difference/ disagreement/ Dissimilarity
Cease	Synonym	Break off/ desist/ discontinue
	Antonym	being/ carry on/ complete
Eternal	Synonym	Abiding/ boundless/ continual
	Antonym	Bounded/ ceased/ ephemeral
Devoid of	Synonym	Vacant/ weaken/ drained
	Antonym	Energized/ full
Strength	Synonym	Concentration/ effectiveness /
	Antonym	Inactivity/ weakness
Imperceptible	Synonym	Gradual/ inaudible / indistinguishable
	Antonym	Apparent/ conspicuous/evident
Tackle	Synonym	Engage in/ deal with / undertake
	Antonym	Abstain/ end/ dodge
Chronicle	Synonym	Narrate/ recite/ describe
	Antonym	Unorganized
Historical	Synonym	Actual/ archival/ factual/
	Antonym	False/ imaginary
Grim	Synonym	Bleak/ cruel/ ghastly
	Antonym	Bright/ cheerful/ comforting

7 Unit

攻克要點I 必考字彙表

KEY1

Heal 治療、痊癒 (*v.*)

Maintain 維持 (*v.*)

Resistance 抵抗、反抗 (*n.*)

Adjust 調整 (*v.*)

KEY2

Remain 維持 (*v.*)

Beneficial 好處的 (*a.*)

Immune 免疫的、不受影響的 (*a.*)

Bacteria 細菌 (*n.*)

KEY3

Colony 殖民地 (*n.*)

Impending 迫切的 (*a.*)

Composer 作家、作曲家 (*n.*)

Ruin 毀壞 (*v.*)

KEY4

Revolutionize 徹底改革 (*v.*)

Apparatus 儀器、器具 (*n.*)

Innovative 創新的、改革的 (*a.*)

Diagnose 診斷 (*v.*)

KEY5

Incurable 不能醫治的 (*a.*)

Abuse 濫用、虐待 (*n.*)

Insanity 精神錯亂 (*n.*)

Addicted to 上癮的 (*a.*)

KEY6

Suffer 受痛苦 (*v.*)

Virtually 實質上地 (*adv.*)

Insomnia 失眠 (*n.*)

Stress 壓力 (*n.*)

KEY7

Prior to 在前、居先 (*preposition*)

Instigate 唆使、煽動 (*v.*)

Fuel 燃料 (*n.*)

Reduction 削減 (*n.*)

KEY8

Intense 緊張的、強烈的 (*a.*)

Terrain 地帶、地形 (*n.*)

Conducive 有助的、有益的 (*a.*)

Elevation 海拔、提高 (*n.*)

KEY9

Hostage 人質、抵押品 (*n.*)

Alive 活潑的、活著的 (*a.*)

Notorious 惡名昭彰的 (*a.*)

Intercept 攔截、截斷 (*v.*)

KEY10

Tsunamis 海嘯 (*n.*)

Propagate 繁殖、增值 (*v.*)

Inversely 相反地、增值地 (*adv.*)

Length 長度、全長 (*n.*)

KEY11

Hypothesis 假設 (*n.*)

Predictions 預言、預報 (*n.*)

Approaching 接近 (*a.*)

Catastrophic 災難的 (*a.*)

KEY12

Lumber 笨重的、無用的 (*a.*)

Character 個性、天性 (*n.*)

Lure 引誘 (*v.*)

Prey 被掠食者、犧牲者 (*n.*)

KEY13

Cave 洞穴 (*n.*)

Luminescent 發光的 (*a.*)

Fungus 菌類、蘑菇 (*n.*)

Squid 烏賊 (*n.*)

KEY14

Malfunction 故障 (*n.*)

Accused 被指控 (*v.*)

Lynch 處以私刑 (*v.*)

Mob 暴民、暴徒 (*n.*)

KEY15

Anorexia 厭食 (n.)	Prolong 延長、拖延 (v.)
Nutrients 營養物 (n.)	Malnutrition 營養失調、營養不良 (n.)

KEY16

Recommend 推薦 (v.)	Procedure 程序、過程 (n.)
Enrollment 登記 (n.)	Manageable 易控制的、易管理的 (a.)

KEY17

Mangled 亂砍、損毀 (v.)	Anonymous 沒署名的 (a.)
Spread 散佈 (v.)	Torso 軀幹 (n.)

KEY18

Portrait 肖像 (n.)	Depict 描述、描繪 (v.)
Manifestation 顯示、證明 (n.)	Maternal 母親的 (a.)

KEY19

Techniques 技巧、技法 (n.)	Signs 記號、標誌 (n.)
Manipulate 操作、利用 (v.)	Commands 命令、指令 (n.)

KEY20

Masterpieces 傑作、名著 (n.)	Architectures 建築相關理論、樣式、學說及風格 (n.)
Sculpture 雕塑 (n.)	Myth 神話、虛構的人事 (n.)

攻克要點II 超給力例句

★ KEY 1   ♪ MP3 07

- ✪ Heal 治療、痊癒 (*v.*)
- ✪ Resistance 抵抗、反抗 (*n.*)
- ✪ Maintain 維持 (*v.*)
- ✪ Adjust 調整 (*v.*)

> After getting healed from Ebola infection, he adjusts his eating habits due to the realization of the importance of maintaining a healthy balance of good and bad bacteria and destroying infected cells that may cause harmful effects to human body. Now he is having a high degree of resistance to any type of illnesses.

在從伊波拉病毒感染中痊癒後，因為知道維持身體裡好菌、壞菌平衡以及殺死受感染的細胞的重要性，所以他調整了他的飲食習慣，而現在他對於任何疾病都有很強的抵抗力。

★ KEY 2

- ✪ Remain 維持 (*v.*)
- ✪ Immune 免疫的、不受影響的 (*a.*)
- ✪ Beneficial 好處的 (*a.*)
- ✪ Bacteria 細菌 (*n.*)

Not only is remaining a healthy balance in the intestines important in developing mature immune system, but also taking certain medications that can stimulate the growth of beneficial bacteria in human body plays an important role in keeping you away from disease, according to Scientific America.

根據《科學人雜誌》，不僅維持腸道健康平衡有助於免疫系統發展之外，使用可促進身體好菌成長的特定藥物也對於遠離疾病很重要。

★ KEY 3

✪ Colony 殖民地 (*n.*)
✪ Composer 作家、作曲家 (*n.*)
✪ Impending 迫切的 (*a.*)
✪ Ruin 毀壞 (*v.*)

Under the period of being a colony of Japan, from 1895 to 1945, many writers and composers still went on writing some of the greatest books and songs of all time even though they were facing impending financial ruin in World War II.

在日本殖民的1895年到1945年期間，即使在二次世界大戰時受到很急迫的財政上的破壞，許多作家與作曲家仍然創作出很多很棒的書籍與歌曲。

- ✪ Revolutionize 徹底改革 (*v.*)
- ✪ Innovative 創新的、改革的 (*a.*)
- ✪ Apparatus 儀器、器具 (*n.*)
- ✪ Diagnose 診斷 (*v.*)

Hundreds of innovations in different fields have been launched, such as computer, the one revolutionizing the business and financial worlds, and innovative medical apparatus, designed to aid in diagnosing and monitoring medical conditions.

近期推出很多的創新發明，像是徹底改革商業與財政世界的電腦，以及被設計用來幫助診療及監控醫療狀況之極具創新的醫療器材。

KEY 5

- ✪ Incurable 不能醫治的 (*a.*)
- ✪ Insanity 精神錯亂 (*n.*)
- ✪ Abuse 濫用、虐待 (*n.*)
- ✪ Addicted to 上癮的 (*a.*)

After knowing that his incurable insanity in drug abuse requires spending the rest of his life in a hospital, I end up realizing how important it is to know why and how a person would become addicted to drugs.

在知道了他藥物濫用的瘋狂狀態是無法治癒的，且他往後的人生要被囚禁在醫院裡時，我終於了解知道一個人是為什麼及如何染上藥癮的重要性。

★ KEY 6

- ✪ Suffer 受痛苦 (*v.*)
- ✪ Insomnia 失眠 (*n.*)
- ✪ Virtually 實質上地 (*adv.*)
- ✪ Stress 壓力 (*n.*)

> The young woman has been suffering from insomnia virtually twenty five years because of the extreme stress from her boss.

因為她的老闆給她過多壓力的關係，這位年輕的女士實際上已經深受失眠之苦二十年了。

★ KEY 7

- ✪ Prior to 在前、居先 (preposition)
- ✪ Instigate 唆使、煽動 (*v.*)
- ✪ Fuel 燃料 (*n.*)
- ✪ Reduction 削減 (*n.*)

> It would be possible to return to pre-settlement landscapes, existing prior to European contact, with instigating burning and fuel reduction through forest thinning.

透過森林間伐，利用燃燒及縮減燃料把土地回復到歐洲人接觸前的樣子，是有可能的。

★ KEY 8

- ✪ Intense 緊張的、強烈的 (*a.*)
- ✪ Terrain 地帶、地形 (*n.*)
- ✪ Conducive 有助的、有益的 (*a.*)
- ✪ Elevation 海拔、提高 (*n.*)

> The expert said that high rainfall amounts, intense winter storms, and steep terrain areas are all conducive to land sliding, which is also found to be especially high in the median range of elevation.

專家說高降雨量、強烈的冬季風暴以及陡峭的地形都會促成土石流，且其也被發現特別容易發生於中海拔的地區。

★ KEY 9

- ✪ Hostage 人質、抵押品 (*n.*)
- ✪ Alive 活潑的、活著的 (*a.*)
- ✪ Notorious 惡名昭彰的 (*a.*)

✪ Intercept 攔截、截斷 (*v.*)

The government believes the two hostages are still alive in that someone intentionally intercepted the talking between these two notorious leaders in this record.

政府方面相信這兩位人質還依舊活著，因為有人在這卷錄音中刻意打斷了這兩位惡名昭彰的領導者的對話。

KEY 10

✪ Tsunamis 海嘯 (*n.*)
✪ Propagate 繁殖、增值 (*v.*)
✪ Inversely 相反地、增值地 (*adv.*)
✪ Length 長度、全長 (*n.*)

Scientists claimed that the possible reason why a tsunamis not only propagates at high speeds, but also travels great distances with limited energy losses is that the rate at which a wave loses its energy is inversely related to its wave length.

科學家指出海嘯為什麼能夠在高速下快速地增值增量，且其海浪能夠移動很長的距離卻只有很少的能量損失，其原因為海浪的能量損失與波長呈現相反關係。

KEY 11

✪ Hypothesis 假設 (*n.*)
✪ Predictions 預言、預報 (*n.*)
✪ Approaching 接近 (*a.*)
✪ Catastrophic 災難的 (*a.*)

> They use the hypothesis to generate predictions that approaching catastrophic events might happen only to one or more mountains in Asia.

他們用假設法推出預言，並指出在亞洲的幾座山區可能即將發生災難事件。

KEY 12

✪ Lumber 笨重的、無用的 (*a.*)
✪ Character 個性、天性 (*n.*)
✪ Lure 引誘 (*v.*)
✪ Prey 被掠食者、犧牲者 (*n.*)

> He, in spite of having a lumbering sort of character, is quite effective as a trainer who knows how all animals lure their preys.

他雖然天生駑鈍，但做為一位知道所有動物是如何引誘獵物的訓練師還蠻成功的。

Unit 7

✪ Cave 洞穴 (*n.*)
✪ Luminescent 發光的 (*a.*)
✪ Fungus 菌類、蘑菇 (*n.*)
✪ Squid 烏賊 (*n.*)

We could see inside the cave deep down the Pacific Ocean without a flashlight due to the fact that there are full of luminescent fungus and squid.

因為這裡遍布會發光的菌類與烏賊，所以我們可以不用手電筒就很深入的看到這個位處於太平洋底部的洞穴。

✪ Malfunction 故障 (*n.*)
✪ Accused 被指控 (*v.*)
✪ Lynch 處以私刑 (*v.*)
✪ Mob 暴民、暴徒 (*n.*)

The malfunction of this machine that the accused murders were in charge of might be the primary reason why he was lynched by many aggressive mobs in this village.

這個被指控的謀殺犯所負責的機器故障部分，有可能是為什會他會被這個村莊裡許多激進的暴徒處以私刑的原因。

★ KEY 15

- ✪ Anorexia 厭食 (*n.*)
- ✪ Prolong 延長、拖延 (*v.*)
- ✪ Nutrients 營養物 (*n.*)
- ✪ Malnutrition 營養失調、營養不良 (*n.*)

> The model, having anorexia, a prolonged disorder of eating due to inadequate or unbalanced intake of nutrients, has to be hospitalized because of malnutrition.

這位模特兒患有厭食症，一種因為營養的攝取不足與不平衡而造成的飲食長期失調，所以營養失調的她必須被迫住院。

★ KEY 16

- ✪ Recommend 推薦 (*v.*)
- ✪ Procedure 程序、過程 (*n.*)
- ✪ Enrollment 登記 (*n.*)
- ✪ Manageable 易控制的、易管理的 (*a.*)

> We recommend applying for your top universities as early as possible to keep the enrollment procedures in a manageable level.

為了可以讓登記的程序可以達到最好管理的狀態，我們推薦越早申請妳的前幾志願學校越好。

Unit 7

- ✪ Mangled 亂砍、損毀 (*v.*)
- ✪ Anonymous 沒署名的 (*a.*)
- ✪ Spread 散佈 (*v.*)
- ✪ Torso 軀幹 (*n.*)

> The news reporter said that mangled body parts of an anonymous woman were found completely spread in this square with head on the swing, torso in a tree, and a leg in a fountain.

記者報導指出,這個無名女屍被毀損的屍塊散佈在這個廣場上,頭在鞦韆上、軀幹在樹上,以及腳在噴泉裡。

- ✪ Portrait 肖像 (*n.*)
- ✪ Depict 描述、描繪 (*v.*)
- ✪ Manifestation 顯示、證明 (*n.*)
- ✪ Maternal 母親的 (*a.*)

> The portrait of a mother and her children, the most famous on in this museum, depicts the very manifestation of maternal love.

這個博物館裡最著名的畫作,一位母親與她的孩子的肖像畫,描述了母愛的顯現。

★ KEY 19

- ✪ Techniques 技巧、技法 (*n.*)
- ✪ Signs 記號、標誌 (n,)
- ✪ Manipulate 操作、利用 (*v.*)
- ✪ Commands 命令、指令 (*n.*)

> Elephants have long been taught some hand signs and techniques to manipulate drawing tools and to understand some spoken commands.

大象長久被指導一些手勢以及操作繪畫工具，並且了解一些口語指令的技巧。

★ KEY 20

- ✪ Masterpieces 傑作、名著 (*n.*)
- ✪ Architectures 建築相關理論、樣式、學說及風格 (*n.*)
- ✪ Sculpture 雕塑 (*n.*)
- ✪ Myth 神話、虛構的人事 (*n.*)

> Masterpieces of architectures, literature, sculpture, painting and more are mostly inspired by myths and mythological characters.

建築、文學、雕塑、繪畫及更多方面的傑作主要都是受到神話及神話虛構人物所激發而有靈感的。

攻克要點III 同義詞一覽表

Hypothesis	Synonym	Assumption/ supposition
	Antonym	Fact/ reality/ truth
Maintain	Synonym	Continue/ cultivate/ keep
	Antonym	Abandon/ discontinue
Adjust	Synonym	Accommodate/ alter/ adapt
	Antonym	Disarrange/ disorganize/ disorder
Beneficial	Synonym	Benign/ constructive/ favorable
	Antonym	Disadvantageous/ harmful/ injurious
Impending	Synonym	Approaching/ imminent
	Antonym	Gone/ past/ distant
Ruin	Synonym	Bankrupt/decimate/demolish
	Antonym	Aid/ assist/ construct
Catastrophic	Synonym	Calamitous/ disastrous/ fatal
	Antonym	Advantageous/ fortunate
Prediction	Synonym	Forecast/ indicator
	Antonym	Proof/ reality
Addicted to	Synonym	Accustomed/ hooked/ obsessed
	Antonym	Disinclined/ independent
Suffer	Synonym	Deteriorate/ endure
	Antonym	Soothe/ please/ calm

Prolonged	Synonym	Continued/ delayed/ extended
	Antonym	Shorten
Instigate	Synonym	Abet/ incite
	Antonym	Deter/ discourage/ dissuade
Reduction	Synonym	Contraction/ cutback/ devaluation
	Antonym	Increase/ enlargement
Intense	Synonym	Acute/ bitter/ excessive
	Antonym	Gentle/ bland
Conducive	Synonym	Helpful/ contributive/ useful
	Antonym	Useless/ worthless
Luminescent	Synonym	Bright/ effulgent/ fluorescent
	Antonym	Dull/ Obscured
Intercept	Synonym	Ambush/ interrupt / cut off
	Antonym	Allow/ free
Manipulate	Synonym	Employ/ manage/ operate
	Antonym	Destroy
Propagate	Synonym	Inseminate/ multiply/ proliferate
	Antonym	Decease/ deplete
Anonymous	Synonym	Nameless/ unidentified
	Antonym	Known/ named

Unit 7

攻克要點I 必考字彙表

KEY1

Legally 法律上合法地 (*adv.*)

Discrepancy 矛盾、差異 (*n.*)

Maturity 成熟、完備 (*n.*)

Wisdom 智慧、學識 (*n.*)

KEY2

Mathematically 數學上地 (*adv.*)

Anatomically 解剖學上地 (*adv.*)

Medial 中間的、普通的 (*a.*)

Stabilize 使穩定 (*v.*)

KEY3

Mental 精神的、心理的 (*a.*)

Consecutive 連續的、始終一貫的 (*a.*)

Physical 身體的 (*a.*)

Menstrual 月經的、每月一次的 (*a.*)

KEY4

Metabolism 新陳代謝 (*n.*)

Digestion 消化力、領悟 (*n.*)

Organism 生物、有機體 (*n.*)

Glucose 葡萄糖 (*n.*)

KEY5

Chief 主要的 (*a.*)

Metropolis 大都市、首府、重要中心 (*n.*)

Capital 首都的、重要的 (*a.*)

Ambitious 野心勃勃的 (*a.*)

KEY6

Meticulous 一絲不苟的、精確的 (*a.*)	Anxious 憂慮的、渴望的 (*a.*)
Accurate 準確的 (*a.*)	Consist of 包含、組成 (*v.*)

KEY7

Parasites 寄生蟲 (*n.*)	Migrate 遷移 (*v.*)
Host 主人 (*n.*)	Reproduce 繁殖、生殖 (*v.*)

KEY8

Reflex 反射、反映 (*n.*)	Salivate 分泌唾液 (*v.*)
Analyze 分析 (*v.*)	Associate 使有聯繫 (*v.*)

KEY9

Victim 受害人、犧牲品 (*n.*)	Restrain 抑制、約束 (*v.*)
Verdict 裁決、判斷 (*n.*)	Suspect 可疑分子 (*n.*)

KEY10

Regardless of 不管、不顧 (*preposition*)	Refract 使折射 (*v.*)
Temperature 溫度 (*n.*)	Redirect 使改變方向 (*v.*)

KEY11

Ritual 宗教儀式 (*n.*)	Defined 清晰的 (*a.*)
Prior to 之前 (*preposition*)	Worship 尊敬、禮拜 (*n.*)

KEY12

Century 世紀、百年 (*n.*)	Reduce 減少、降低 (*v.*)
Rubble 粗石、碎磚 (*n.*)	Routine 例行的 (*a.*)

Unit 8

KEY13

Rudimentary 基本初步的、尚未發展完全的 (*a.*)	Prehistoric 史前的 (*a.*)
Regiment 嚴密管制、把…編成大團 (*v.*)	Contrive 策畫、圖謀 (*v.*)

KEY14

Sacred 宗教的、不可侵犯的 (*a.*)	Candidates 候選人 (*n.*)
Electorate 有選舉權者 (*n.*)	Secular 世俗的 (*a.*)

KEY15

Savage 野蠻的、兇猛的 (*a.*)	Domesticated 被馴服了的 (*a.*)
Liberate 解放、使自由 (*v.*)	Ally 同盟國 (*n.*)

KEY16

Immigrant 移民 (*n.*)	Scatter 散播、分散 (*v.*)
Scrutiny 監視、仔細檢查 (*n.*)	Humanitarian 人道主義的 (*a.*)

KEY17

Mental 內心的、心理的 (*a.*)	Behavior 行為 (*n.*)
Phenomena 現象 (*n.*)	Sensation 感覺、知覺 (*n.*)

KEY18

Serendipitous 偶然發現的 (*a.*)	Committed 忠誠的 (*a.*)
Relevant 相關的 (*a.*)	Expect 期待 (*v.*)

KEY19

Severe 嚴厲的 (*a.*)	Uncompromising 不妥協的、不讓步的 (*a.*)
Afterward 之後 (*adv.*)	Torture 折磨、拷問 (*v.*)

KEY20

Systematized 使系統化 (*v.*)	Efficiency 效率、效能 (*n.*)
Sharpen 使尖銳、加重 (*v.*)	Blade 刀身、葉片 (*n.*)

攻克要點II 超給力例句

 **KEY 1** ♪ **MP3 08**

- ✪ Legally 法律上合法地 (*adv.*)
- ✪ Maturity 成熟、完備 (*n.*)
- ✪ Discrepancy 矛盾、差異 (*n.*)
- ✪ Wisdom 智慧、學識 (*n.*)

Even though people are legally considered reaching the maturity at the age of eighteen in almost all Asian countries, the discrepancy is still there. Maturity and wisdom are regarded as necessities to run a company.

即使幾乎在所有亞洲國家的法律上，年齡達到十八歲的就算是認可上的成熟，但還是有差異存在。成熟與智慧是被視為經營企業的必需品。

KEY 2

- ✪ Mathematically 數學上地 (*adv.*)
- ✪ Medial 中間的、普通的 (*a.*)
- ✪ Anatomically 解剖學上地 (*adv.*)
- ✪ Stabilize 使穩定 (*v.*)

Unit 8

Mathematically, ten is the medial number between five and fifteen; anatomically, the part located in the medial part of the knee structure, stabilizing the knee when a person is in an upright position, is called anterior cruciate ligament.

以數學上來說，十是五跟十五的中間數；在解剖學上來說，當人們站立的時候，膝關節中間用來穩定膝蓋的部分，被稱作為前十字韌帶。

⭐ KEY 3

- ✪ Mental 精神的、心理的 (*a.*)
- ✪ Physical 身體的 (*a.*)
- ✪ Consecutive 連續的、始終一貫的 (*a.*)
- ✪ Menstrual 月經的、每月一次的 (*a.*)

Anorexic girls might have some mental and physical disorders, say, having an extreme fear of gaining weights or missing at least half a year consecutive menstrual periods.

有厭食症的女生有可能會有心理與身體上的不協調症狀出現，包含極度害怕體重增加，或者是會有至少連續半年沒有月經來。

⭐ KEY 4

- ✪ Metabolism 新陳代謝 (*n.*)
- ✪ Organism 生物、有機體 (*n.*)

✪ Digestion 消化力、領悟 (*n.*)
✪ Glucose 葡萄糖 (*n.*)

> Metabolism can refer to all chemical reactions that occur in living organisms, such as digestion and transport of substances into or between different cells. For example, the glucose hydrolyzed from starch by your body is metabolized and used for energy.

新陳代謝就是指生物體內發生的化學反應，像是消化，或是物質於兩種不同的細胞間相互運輸。舉例來說，澱粉在你體內水解後的葡萄糖，會被新陳代謝，然後用於增加能量。

★ KEY 5

✪ Chief 主要的 (*a.*)
✪ Capital 首都的、重要的 (*a.*)
✪ Metropolis 大都市、首府、重要中心 (*n.*)
✪ Ambitious 野心勃勃的 (*a.*)

> The chief or capital city of a country, region, or state is called Metropolis, normally the largest city of that area. such as Los Angeles, Tokyo, Paris, and New York, where ambitious people from all over the world come to make their marks.

一個國家、地區、或是洲的主要城市被稱作是首府，通常是那個地區最大的城市，像是洛杉磯、東京、巴黎以及紐約，且通常是來自世界各地充滿雄心的人們來發展的地方。

✪ Meticulous 一絲不苟的、精確的 (*a.*)
✪ Anxious 憂慮的、渴望的 (*a.*)
✪ Accurate 準確的 (*a.*)
✪ Consist of 包含、組成 (*v.*)

Professor Martin, a meticulous researcher who is anxious about doing everything in an extremely accurate and exact fashion, assigns a task that consists of more than three hundreds questions with terribly detailed instructions for each question.

馬丁博士是個做事一絲不苟，且總是焦慮地對於所做的每件事都要十分精確，並使用一定的方式去完成的研究員，出了包含超過三百題問題的一個任務，且每一題都附上極詳細的指示。

✪ Parasites 寄生蟲 (*n.*)
✪ Migrate 遷移 (*v.*)
✪ Host 主人 (*n.*)
✪ Reproduce 繁殖、生殖 (*v.*)

Scientists speculate parasites that can migrate within the human body normally stay in their hosts for an extended period and reproduce at a faster rate than their hosts.

科學家推測可以在人體內游移的寄生蟲，通常會在寄主的身體內停留很長一段時間，且會比牠們寄主繁殖的速率更快。

★ **KEY 8**

✪ Reflex 反射、反映 (*n.*)
✪ Salivate 分泌唾液 (*v.*)
✪ Analyze 分析 (*v.*)
✪ Associate 使有聯繫 (*v.*)

The concept Ian Pavlov is famous for is the Conditional Reflex, presenting that dogs would salivate when food presents. He further analyzed how the dogs associated the sound with the presentation of food.

使Ian Pavlov有名的概念就是條件反射，其表示當食物出現時，狗會分泌唾液。他嘗試去分析狗是如何把聲音與食物的出現做連結。

★ **KEY 9**

✪ Victim 受害人、犧牲品 (*n.*)
✪ Restrain抑制、約束 (*v.*)
✪ Verdict 裁決、判斷 (*n.*)

Unit 8

✪ Suspect 可疑分子 (*n.*)

The victim's family members could not restrain their emotions upon hearing the verdict because the suspects were going to be arrested and taken to the city jail.

一聽到判決的時候，受害人的家屬便無法克制他們的情緒，因為嫌疑人就要被拘留且帶往監獄。

⭐ **KEY 10**

✪ Regardless of 不管、不顧 (preposition)
✪ Refract 使折射 (*v.*)
✪ Temperature 溫度 (*n.*)
✪ Redirect 使改變方向 (*v.*)

Regardless of how large the space is, sound waves traveling straightforward may be refracted because of the difference in temperatures and redirected toward the ground.

不論這個空間有多大，直直往前的聲波有可能會因為遇到不同的溫度而折射，並可能改向而朝向地面。

⭐ **KEY 11**

✪ Ritual 宗教儀式 (*n.*)
✪ Defined 清晰的 (*a.*)
✪ Prior to 之前 (preposition)

✪ Worship 尊敬、禮拜 (*n.*)

The aim of performing these rituals is to remove specifically defined uncleanliness before proceeding to particular activities, especially prior to the worship of a deity.

實行這個宗教儀式的目的是，要在進行特定活動之前洗除掉被特別認定為不乾淨的東西，特別是在對神禮拜之前。

★ KEY 12

✪ Century 世紀、百年 (*n.*)
✪ Reduce 減少、降低 (*v.*)
✪ Rubble 粗石、碎磚 (*n.*)
✪ Routine 例行的 (*a.*)

During the Osaka earthquake at the end of the twentieth century, many buildings were reduced to nothing, but a pile of rubble and then praying has become a routine activity since then.

二十世紀末發生的阪神大地震，許多的建物在一夕之間變成了大量的碎石，從此祈禱成為了例行活動。

★ KEY 13

✪ Rudimentary 基本初步的、尚未發展完全的 (*a.*)

✪ Prehistoric 史前的 (*a.*)

✪ Regiment 嚴密管制、把…編成大團 (*v.*)

✪ Contrive 策畫、圖謀 (*v.*)

The rudimentary shelters standing out along this river bank were assumed to be built by prehistoric people who probably had taken regimented constructing training contrived by people from other village.

在河岸邊的基本避難所被推測為史前人所建造的，而且這些人有可能有接受過來自其他村莊的人所謀畫的嚴密管制的建造訓練。

⭐ KEY 14

✪ Sacred 宗教的、不可侵犯的 (*a.*)

✪ Candidates 候選人 (*n.*)

✪ Electorate 有選舉權者 (*n.*)

✪ Secular 世俗的 (*a.*)

There is the sacred belief existing between candidates and the electorate, even though the election itself is a secular work.

候選人與選民之間存有神聖的信仰，縱使選舉本身就是件很世俗的事。

⭐ KEY 15

✪ Savage 野蠻的、兇猛的 (*a.*)

✪ Domesticated 被馴服了的 (*a.*)

✪ Liberate 解放、使自由 (*v.*)

✪ Ally 同盟國 (*n.*)

> Those savage concentration camps built during the World War II were known as the symbol of not being domesticated and were not liberated by the allies until the end of the war.

那些在第二次世界大戰中所建立的野蠻集中營被認為是未被馴服的象徵，且直到戰爭結束才被同盟國解放。

★ KEY 16

✪ Immigrant 移民 (*n.*)

✪ Scatter 散播、分散 (*v.*)

✪ Scrutiny 監視、仔細檢查 (*n.*)

✪ Humanitarian 人道主義的 (*a.*)

> A large number of immigrants from China were scattered among ten different countries and are still under scrutiny from humanitarian organizations.

來自中國大量的移民被分散到十個不同的國家，且現在還在人道組織的監視下。

★ KEY 17

✪ Mental 內心的、心理的 (*a.*)

✪ Behavior 行為 (*n.*)

Unit 8

✪ Phenomena 現象 (*n.*)
✪ Sensation 感覺、知覺 (*n.*)

> Cognitive Psychology is the study of mental processes, their effects on human behaviors and some other phenomena, such as sensation, memory, learning, and more.

認知心理學主要是有關心智歷程的研究，以及其對於人的行為的影響和其他的現象，例如感知、記憶、學習之類的。

★ KEY 18

✪ Serendipitous 偶然發現的 (a)
✪ Committed 忠誠的 (*a.*)
✪ Relevant 相關的 (*a.*)
✪ Expect 期待 (*v.*)

> For the sake of enjoying the serendipitous encounter to good books, I am committed to running a bookshop because I believe that we all have experienced the serendipity of relevant information arriving just when we were least expecting it.

為了能夠享受到與好書來個不期而遇，我非常致力於經營書店，因為我相信我們都有過，當我們不期待能夠遇到相關資訊的時候，在找的東西就出現了的經驗。

★ KEY 19

☼ Severe 嚴厲的 (*a.*)
☼ Uncompromising 不妥協的、不讓步的 (*a.*)
☼ Afterward 之後 (*adv.*)
☼ Torture 折磨、拷問 (*v.*)

> Professor Morgan is such a severe, uncompromising educator who normally locks the door upon the bell ringing and won't let anyone in afterward, just as how the hot weather in San Diego tortures people.

摩根教授就是個很嚴厲且不妥協的教育家，他是個在鐘一響就立刻關上門，且之後不讓任何人進來的人，就像是聖地牙哥的天氣如何折磨人們一樣。

★ KEY 20

☼ Systematized 使系統化 (*v.*)
☼ Efficiency 效率、效能 (*n.*)
☼ Sharpen 使尖銳、加重 (*v.*)
☼ Blade 刀身、葉片 (*n.*)

> Studies state that a systematized schedule could be helpful in increasing efficiency at work because it sharpens your mind, just as how you sharpen the blade of your knife frequently for the purpose of cutting things off sharply.

研究指出，有系統的行程能夠促進工作效率，因為它使你的心變得敏銳，這就像是你為了能夠銳利地切斷某物，而使刀片變得尖銳一樣。

Systematize	Synonym	Arrange/ array
	Antonym	Confuse/ destroy
Efficiency	Synonym	Adeptness/ effectiveness
	Antonym	ignorance
Sharpen	Synonym	Hone/ grind
	Antonym	Blunt/ dull
Severe	Synonym	Uncompromising/ stern
	Antonym	Compromising/ amenable
Torture	Synonym	Abuse/ injure
	Antonym	Comfort/ appease
Uncompromising	Synonym	Stubborn/ determined/
	Antonym	Irresolute/ flexible
Serendipitous	Synonym	Occasional/ spontaneous
	Antonym	Deliberate / planned
Committed	Synonym	Act/ execute/ perpetrate
	Antonym	Leave/ neglect
Relevant	Synonym	Appropriate/admissible / applicable
	Antonym	Improper/inapplicable
Expect	Synonym	Anticipate/ forecast
	Antonym	Disregard/ disbelieve
Mental	Synonym	Intellectual/ psychological
	Antonym	Physical

Behavior	Synonym	Action/ demeanor/
	Antonym	Cessation/ inactivity
Scatter	Synonym	Disperse/ discard/ distribute
	Antonym	Collect/ gather
Contrive	Synonym	Invent/ design/ fabricate
	Antonym	Destroy/ discourage
Domesticate	Synonym	Tame/ habituate / naturalize
	Antonym	Disjoin/ abandon
Ally	Synonym	Associate/ colleague
	Antonym	Detractor / enemy
Sacred	Synonym	Disperse/ discard/ distribute
	Antonym	Collect/ gather
Secular	Synonym	Civil/ materialistic
	Antonym	Holy/ religious
Rudimentary	Synonym	Basic/ fundamental/ elemental
	Antonym	Complex/ intricate/ sophisticated
Meticulous	Synonym	Detailed/ accurate/ conscientious
	Antonym	Imprecise/careless

Unit 8

攻克要點I 必考字彙表

KEY1

Transplantation 移植 (*n.*)	Organ 器官 (*n.*)
Donor 捐贈者 (*n.*)	Revolution 革命 (*n.*)

KEY2

Advent 出現、到來 (*n.*)	Access 接近 (*n.*)
Agile 靈活的、輕快敏捷的 (*a.*)	Alter 改變 (*v.*)

KEY3

Consequential 結果的、相因而生的、重要的 (*a.*)	Commemorate 紀念 (*v.*)
Devoted to 專心於 (*v.*)	Conviction 定罪、堅信 (*n.*)

KEY4

Apart from 遠離、除…之外 (*preposition*)	Essential 本質的、必要的、重要的 (*a.*)
Reconciliation 和解、順從 (*n.*)	Divergent 分歧的 (*a.*)

KEY5

Scheme 方案 (*n.*)	Comparable 可比較的 (*a.*)
Scant of 缺乏的 (*a.*)	Deviate 脫離、使脫軌 (*v.*)

KEY6

Corroborate 使堅固、確證 (*v.*)	Particle 粒子、極小量 (*n.*)

Consist of 構成 (*v.*)	Converge 聚合、集中於一點 (*v.*)

KEY7

Elaborate 闡述 (*v.*)	Eccentric 奇怪的 (*a.*)
Efface 忘去、抹卻 (*v.*)	Elusive 難以捉摸的 (*a.*)

KEY8

Divest 剝奪 (*v.*)	Ephemeral 短暫的、短命的 (*a.*)
Equilibrium 平衡、均衡 (*n.*)	Creatures 生物 (*n.*)

KEY9

Dissipate 失散、驅散消散 (*v.*)	Eradicate 根絕、滅絕 (*v.*)
Erratic 不穩定的、奇怪的 (*a.*)	Tribe 部落、部族 (*n.*)

KEY10

Encapsulate 壓縮、形成膠囊、概述 (*v.*)	Drastic 激烈的 (*a.*)
Consider 考慮、認為 (*v.*)	Discard 拋棄、解雇 (*v.*)

KEY11

Fertile 肥沃的、能生產的 (*a.*)	Contaminate 毒害、汙染 (*v.*)
Flee 消失、逃避 (*v.*)	Fabricate 製造、偽造、杜撰 (*v.*)

KEY12

Investigation 研究、調查 (*n.*)	Excavate 挖掘 (*v.*)
Extant 現存的、未毀的 (*a.*)	Extraneous 無關係的、外來的 (*a.*)

KEY13

Exceedingly 非常地、極度地 (*adv.*)	Formidable 強大的、艱難的 (*a.*)
Expanse 寬闊的區域 (*n.*)	Exploit 開採、開發 (*v.*)

KEY14

Extol 吹捧、稱讚 (*v.*)	Get accustomed to 習慣於 (*v.*)
Escalate 逐步擴大 (*v.*)	Expose 使暴露、揭穿 (*v.*)

KEY15

Heed 注意、留心 (*n.*)	Fluctuate 使起伏、動搖 (*v.*)
Handy 便利的、容易取得的 (*a.*)	Flexible 柔軟的、靈活的 (*a.*)

KEY16

Hire 雇用 (*v.*)	Prefer 較喜歡 (*v.*)
Haphazard 偶然的、隨便的 (*a.*)	Genuinely 真誠地 (*adv.*)

KEY17

Identical 完全相似的 (*a.*)	Idiosyncrasy 特質、特性 (*n.*)
Diligent 勤勉的 (*a.*)	Inert 惰性的 (*a.*)

KEY18

Indispensable 不可或缺的 (*a.*)	Trait 特色、品質 (*n.*)
Inflate 使得意、使驕傲 (*v.*)	Infirm 柔弱的、虛弱的 (*a.*)

KEY19

Incursion 入侵 (*n.*)	Induce 勸誘、導致、促使 (*v.*)
Indigenous 本地的、固有的 (*a.*)	Severe 嚴厲的、劇烈的 (*a.*)

KEY20

Imposing 氣勢宏偉的、莊嚴的 (*a.*)	Inaccessible 難接近的 (*a.*)
Implausible 難信的、不像真實的 (*a.*)	Ruin 毀壞 (*v.*)

攻克要點 II 超給力例句

★ **KEY 1** ♪ **MP3 09**

✪ Transplantation 移植 (*n.*)
✪ Organ 器官 (*n.*)
✪ Donor 捐贈者 (*n.*)
✪ Revolution 革命 (*n.*)

> Transplantation is the revolution of modern medicine that performs transferring an organ from a donor to a recipient.

移植是現代醫學的一大革命，其把器官從捐贈者的身上轉移到另一個人身上。

★ **KEY 2**

✪ Advent 出現、到來 (*n.*)
✪ Access 接近 (*n.*)
✪ Agile 靈活的、輕快敏捷的 (*a.*)
✪ Alter 改變 (*v.*)

Unit 9

The advent of Internet provides folks with an access to instant events taking place in this world, fostering people to have an agile mind and making them alter the way they perceive this world.

網路的出現提供民眾一個可以接觸到這世界上立即發生的事件的管道，也訓練人們有一顆靈敏的心，並讓他們改變了他們看世界的方式。

★ KEY 3

✪ Consequential 結果的、相因而生的、重要的 (*a.*)
✪ Commemorate 紀念 (*v.*)
✪ Devoted to 專心於 (*v.*)
✪ Conviction 定罪、堅信 (*n.*)

It's such a consequential day today that people all around the world are so ready for commemorating those who are devoted to achieving their convictions of peace.

今天是如此重要的一天，全世界的人民都準備好要紀念那些致力於達成他們所堅信的和平的人。

★ KEY 4

✪ Apart from 遠離、除…之外 (**preposition**)
✪ Essential 本質的、必要的、重要的 (*a.*)

✪ Reconciliation 和解、順從 (*n.*)
✪ Divergent 分歧的 (*a.*)

> Apart from simply imparting knowledge, it is extremely essential for an educator to instruct students the importance of reaching reconciliation when they encounter divergent options and ideas.

除了只是傳遞知識之外，對於一位教育家來說，當他們遇到意見分歧時，教導學生如何達到和解也是很重要的。

★ KEY 5

✪ Scheme 方案 (*n.*)
✪ Comparable 可比較的 (*a.*)
✪ Scant of 缺乏的 (*a.*)
✪ Deviate 脫離、使脫軌 (*v.*)

> The scheme presented for redeveloping the city center is not comparable to the best one due to scant of feasibility and deviating from the theme and the original purposes of the competition.

這個中心城市重新發展的方案無法與最好的那個相比，因為它缺乏可行性，並且脫離主題和這個比賽的最初目的。

Unit 9

✪ Corroborate 使堅固、確證 (*v.*)
✪ Particle 粒子、極小量 (*n.*)
✪ Consist of 構成 (*v.*)
✪ Converge 聚合、集中於一點(*v.*)

The experiment corroborates the prediction that these particles consisting of the particular materials will converge on the central point in high temperature.

研究證實以下的預測：這些由特定物質組成的粒子會在高溫下聚合到中心點。

★ **KEY 7** ◄

✪ Elaborate 闡述 (*v.*)
✪ Eccentric 奇怪的(*a.*)
✪ Efface忘去、抹卻 (*v.*)
✪ Elusive 難以捉摸的 (*a.*)

This chart elaborates an eccentric way of how our ancestors effaced unpleasant memories, yet it has been regarded as an elusive action for us nowadays.

這個表闡述我們的祖先是如何以支怪的方式抹去不好的回憶，但是這對我們現今來說，已經被認為是個模糊難懂的動作。

★ KEY 8

✪ Divest 剝奪 (*v.*)
✪ Ephemeral 短暫的、短命的 (*a.*)
✪ Equilibrium 平衡、均衡 (*n.*)
✪ Creatures 生物 (*n.*)

> Creatures are divested of all their rights to live on the land, making us realize that victory is just ephemeral and we have to seek the equilibrium between environmental sustainability and economic growth.

生物被剝奪居住在這片土地上的權力這件事，讓我們理解到勝利是短暫的，以及我們必須要尋找環境永續與經濟成長之間的平衡點。

★ KEY 9

✪ Dissipate 失散、驅散消散(*v.*)
✪ Eradicate 根絕、滅絕 (*v.*)
✪ Erratic 不穩定的、奇怪的 (*a.*)
✪ Tribe 部落、部族 (*n.*)

> In order to dissipate all people's fears and anxiety, the government attempts to eradicate the erratic way of punishing raped women that has existed in this tribe for hundreds of years.

Unit 9

為了要驅散民眾的害怕與焦慮，政府嘗試著去根除這個已經存於這個部落幾百年的，用來懲罰強暴婦女的怪異的方式。

★ KEY 10

✪ Encapsulate 壓縮、形成膠囊、概述 (*v.*)
✪ Drastic 激烈的 (*a.*)
✪ Consider 考慮、認為 (*v.*)
✪ Discard 拋棄、解雇 (*v.*)

> The article encapsulates the drastic protest taking place about twenty six years ago when people considered liberty the belief that human beings cannot discard.

這篇文章簡述這個發生在約莫二十六年前的激烈抗爭，當時人民視自由為一種身為人不能拋棄的信仰。

★ KEY 11

✪ Fertile 肥沃的、能生產的 (*a.*)
✪ Contaminate 毒害、汙染 (*v.*)
✪ Flee 消失、逃避 (*v.*)
✪ Fabricate 製造、偽造、杜撰 (*v.*)

After knowing that this fertile land had been contaminated by chemical waste, thousands of people fled this area yet the information; however, was found fabricated.

在知道這個肥沃的土地已經被化學廢棄物污染了之後，數千民民眾逃離這塊土地，但是卻發現這個消息是杜撰的。

★ KEY 12

- ✪ Investigation 研究、調查 (*n.*)
- ✪ Excavate 挖掘 (*v.*)
- ✪ Extant 現存的、未毀的 (*a.*)
- ✪ Extraneous 無關係的、外來的 (*a.*)

Through detailed investigation, the reason why this buried vase, excavated by a fisherman few years ago, is extant is that it was made from extraneous materials.

經過詳細的調查之後，這個被一位漁夫幾年前挖掘出的花瓶還現存著的原因為這個花瓶是由外來的物質所製成的。

★ KEY 13

- ✪ Exceedingly 非常地、極度地 (*adv.*)
- ✪ Formidable 強大的、艱難的 (*a.*)
- ✪ Expanse 寬闊的區域 (*n.*)

✪ Exploit 開採、開發 (*v.*)

The emperor is exceedingly in love with his wife, so he assigns a formidable task to his slaves saying that they have to find a broad expanse of land that can be exploited by his wife to plant roses.

這位國王非常愛他的老婆，並且分派了一個艱難的任務給他的奴隸，要尋找一片寬廣且可以讓他老婆種植玫瑰的土地。

★ KEY 14

✪ Extol 吹捧、稱讚 (*v.*)
✪ Get accustomed to 習慣於 (*v.*)
✪ Escalate 逐步擴大 (*v.*)
✪ Expose 使暴露、揭穿 (*v.*)

The business man, whom everyone extols as a symbol of success, says that the reason why the revenue and growth of his company can be escalated is that he gets accustomed to exposing himself in challenges out of his comfort zone.

這個每個人都稱讚且視為成功的象徵的商人說到，為什麼他的公司各項收益以及成長可以快速擴大，是因為他習慣把他自己暴露於舒適圈外的挑戰之下。

★ **KEY 15**

✪ Heed 注意、留心 (*n.*)
✪ Fluctuate 使起伏、動搖 (*v.*)
✪ Handy 便利的、容易取得的 (*a.*)
✪ Flexible 柔軟的、靈活的 (*a.*)

> You can take heed of how fluctuating your body temperature is by using this handy and flexible machine that can accommodate its size according to your body temperature.

你可以藉由使用這個便利、彈性空間大且可以隨著你的體溫改變他的大小的機器,來仔細留意你的體溫有多容易變動不穩。

★ **KEY 16**

✪ Hire 雇用 (*v.*)
✪ Prefer 較喜歡 (*v.*)
✪ Haphazard 偶然的、隨便的 (*a.*)
✪ Genuinely 真誠地 (*adv.*)

> My boss notices that the recently hired employee prefers to put host of notes in folders in a haphazard fashion and that is why he genuinely recommends her use tags to identify each folder.

我的老闆最近發現這個剛被雇用的員工比較喜歡隨便的把大量的筆記塞進資料夾裡,這就是為什麼老闆真誠地推薦這位員工用標記的方式來定位每一個資料夾。

✪ Identical 完全相似的 (*a.*)
✪ Idiosyncrasy 特質、特性 (*n.*)
✪ Diligent 勤勉的 (*a.*)
✪ Inert 惰性的 (*a.*)

> They have an identical idiosyncrasy that they will be rather diligent if working in an inert working atmosphere.

他們擁有完全相同的特質，就是如果他們在一個惰性且無生命的工作環境下，他們會比較用功專心。

✪ Indispensable 不可或缺的 (*a.*)
✪ Trait 特色、品質 (*n.*)
✪ Inflate 使得意、使驕傲 (*v.*)
✪ Infirm 柔弱的、虛弱的 (*a.*)

> Flattering is an indispensable trait for a salesman who needs to inflate customers' infirm mind to the sky.

對於需要使顧客不確定的心得意到飛上天的銷售員來說，奉承諂媚是個不可或缺的特色。

★ KEY 19

✪ Incursion 入侵 (*n.*)
✪ Induce 勸誘、導致、促使 (*v.*)
✪ Indigenous 本地的、固有的 (*a.*)
✪ Severe 嚴厲的、劇烈的 (*a.*)

> The incursion of enemy troops with no reasons induces indigenous people to launch a severe protest that has never happened in this country.

敵軍毫無理由的入侵導致本地民眾發起了一個在這國家從沒發生過的劇烈抗爭。

★ KEY 20

✪ Imposing 氣勢宏偉的、莊嚴的 (*a.*)
✪ Inaccessible 難接近的 (*a.*)
✪ Implausible 難信的、不像真實的 (*a.*)
✪ Ruin 毀壞 (*v.*)

> This imposing star made an inaccessible impression on people after she had committed an implausible crime that could ruin her career.

在她犯下了一個令人難以相信且會毀掉她事業前程的罪後，這個氣勢強大的明星給民眾一種難以接近的印象。

Unit 9

攻克要點III 同義詞一覽表

Imposing	Synonym	Impressive / commanding / grandiose
	Antonym	Inferior / insignificant
Inaccessible	Synonym	Distant/ impassable / unattainable
	Antonym	Accessible/ approachable
Implausible	Synonym	Dubious / inconceivable/ unreasonable
	Antonym	Creditable/ convincing
Ruin	Synonym	Devastate / destroy/ bankrupt
	Antonym	Repair/ construct
Indigenous	Synonym	Native/ domestic/ primitive
	Antonym	Alien/ foreign
Induce	Synonym	Encourage/ bring about/ motivate
	Antonym	Destroy/ discourage
Inflate	Synonym	Exaggerate / boost/ escalate
	Antonym	Abridge/ diminish
Indispensable	Synonym	Necessary/ crucial / essential
	Antonym	Additional / inessential
Identical	Synonym	Equal/ exact/ indistinguishable
	Antonym	Different/ dissimilar
Diligent	Synonym	Hardworking/ assiduous
	Antonym	Ignorant/ inattentive

Inert	Synonym	Immobile/ motionless
	Antonym	Active/ mobile
Haphazard	Synonym	Aimless/ arbitrary / careless
	Antonym	Careful/ definite / deliberate
Prefer	Synonym	Adopt/ promote / choose
	Antonym	Reject/ refuse
Flexible	Synonym	Adaptable / adjustable
	Antonym	Inflexible / resistant
Fluctuate	Synonym	Vacillate/ change/
	Antonym	Remain/continue
Extol	Synonym	Acclaim/ applaud/ commend
	Antonym	Blame/ castigate/ condemn
Escalate	Synonym	Increase/ expand/ intensify
	Antonym	Decline/ diminish
Formidable	Synonym	Dangerous/ intimidating / dreadful
	Antonym	Unimportant/ unthreatening
Exploit	Synonym	Abuse/employ/ manipulate
	Antonym	Misuse
Excavate	Synonym	Scrape/ shovel/ uncover
	Antonym	Cover/ fill

Unit 9

10 ★ Unit ★

攻克要點I 必考字彙表

KEY1

Inherent 固有的、與生俱來的 (*a.*)

Initiate 開始 (*v.*)

Ingenuity 智巧 (*n.*)

Instructive 有益的、有教育性的 (*a.*)

KEY2

Instantaneous 即時的、同時發生的 (*a.*)

Integral 整體的、必須的 (*a.*)

Intricate 複雜的、錯縱的 (*a.*)

Invaluable 無價的 (*a.*)

KEY3

Jettison 投棄 (*v.*)

Justify 證明合法、替…辯護 (*v.*)

Intrinsic 本身的、固有的 (*a.*)

Escalation 逐步上升、逐步擴大 (*n.*)

KEY4

Initially 最初地 (*adv.*)

Jolt 震搖、顛簸 (*n.*)

Matter 事件、原因、物質 (*n.*)

Subsequent 後來的、併發的 (*a.*)

KEY5

Inherent 固有的、與生俱來的 (*a.*)

Expression 表達、措辭 (*n.*)

Mimic 模仿 (*v.*)

Intriguing 吸引人的、有趣的 (*a.*)

KEY6

Meticulously 一絲不苟地、極細心地 (*adv.*)	Manipulate 操作、利用 (*v.*)
Mandatory 命令的、強制的 (*a.*)	Lucrative 有利益的、獲利的 (*a.*)

KEY7

Constantly 不斷地、時常地 (*adv.*)	Alter 改變 (*v.*)
Manifest 表明、證明 (*v.*)	Malleable 有延展性的 (*a.*)

KEY8

Legitimacy 合法、合理、正統 (*n.*)	Unreachable 不能得到的 (*a.*)
Objective 目的 (*n.*)	Milestone 里程碑、劃時代的事件 (*n.*)

KEY9

Obsession 迷住 (*n.*)	Peculiar 奇特的、特殊的 (*a.*)
Notwithstanding 儘管、還是 (*adv.*)	Misunderstanding 誤解 (*n.*)

KEY10

Oblige 強制、束縛 (*v.*)	Monitor 監控、監視 (*v.*)
Innumerable 無數的、數不清的 (*a.*)	Monotonous 單調的、無變化的 (*a.*)

KEY11

Maintain 維修、保養 (*v.*)	Minutely 仔細地、微小地 (*adv.*)
myriad 無數 (*n.*)	Minuscule 極小的 (*a.*)

KEY12

Nature 自然、天性 (*n.*)	Unique 獨特的 (*a.*)
Noticeable 引人注目的 (*a.*)	Obscure 含糊的、難解的 (*a.*)

KEY13

Nearly 幾乎 (*adv.*)

On the contrary 相反地 (*conj.*)

Mundane 現世的、世俗的 (*a.*)

Pacify 使平靜、安慰 (*v.*)

KEY14

Permeate 瀰漫、滲透滲入 (*v.*)

Offset 彌補 (*v.*)

Patch 補釘 (*n.*)

Imperfection 不完美、瑕疵 (*n.*)

KEY15

Overview 概要 (*n.*)

Penetrate 滲透、穿入 (*v.*)

Outcome 結果、後果 (*n.*)

Territory 版圖、領地 (*n.*)

KEY16

Tide 潮汐 (*n.*)

Perceptible 可察覺的、可感覺的 (*a.*)

Periodic 週期的、定期的 (*a.*)

Differ 不一致、不同 (*v.*)

KEY17

Landlord 房東、地主 (*n.*)

Parcel out 分配 (*v.*)

Pledge 保證、抵押、發誓 (*n.*)

Outermost 最外邊的、離中心最遠的 (*a.*)

KEY18

Evidently 顯然、明顯的 (*adv.*)

Ornament 裝飾 (*v.*)

Paradox 似是而非的論點 (*n.*)

Opaque 不透明的、含糊的 (*a.*)

KEY19

Peak 山頂、高峰 (*n.*)

Omit 忽略 (*v.*)

Allow 允許 (*v.*)

Permit 許可、容許 (*v.*)

KEY20

Outbreak 爆發、暴動 (*n.*)

Ongoing 前進的、進行的 (*a.*)

Options 選擇 (*n.*)

Instantaneously 即時的、同時發生地 (*adv.*)

攻克要點 II 超給力例句

★ KEY 1　♪ MP3 10

✪ Inherent 固有的、與生俱來的 (*a.*)
✪ Ingenuity 智巧 (*n.*)
✪ Initiate 開始 (*v.*)
✪ Instructive 有益的、有教育性的 (*a.*)

> Her inherent character of ingenuity of making her
> initiate her new career with an instructive meaning is in
> teaching aboriginal children how to make paper flowers.

她與生俱來的機靈及靈活的天性使她開創了她教導原住民小孩如何製作紙花這樣富有教育意義的新事業。

★ KEY 2

✪ Instantaneous 即時的、同時發生的 (*a.*)
✪ Intricate 複雜的、錯縱的 (*a.*)
✪ Integral 整體的、必須的 (*a.*)
✪ Invaluable　無價的 (*a.*)

Unit 10

The procedure of performing instantaneous rescue is intricate, so that is why emergency rescue personnel and salvage apparatus are integral parts and regarded as invaluable assets to all people.

要做到即時救援的步驟是很複雜的，所以這就是為什麼緊急救援人員跟救助器材是整體不可或缺，且被視為對於人民來說是無價的資產。

★ KEY 3

✪ Jettison 投棄 (*v.*)
✪ Intrinsic 本身的、固有的 (*a.*)
✪ Justify 證明合法、替…辯護 (*v.*)
✪ Escalation 逐步上升、逐步擴大 (*n.*)

This jettisoned plan, of which people did not perceive the intrinsic value, literally justifies that an escalation in wages could improve productivity and efficiency at work.

這個被拋棄且沒有人了解到其中固有價值的計畫，確切地證明工資的提高可以增進工作的生產力與效率。

★ KEY 4

✪ Initially 最初地 (*adv.*)
✪ Matter 事件、原因、物質 (*n.*)
✪ Jolt 震搖、顛簸 (*n.*)

✪ Subsequent 後來的、併發的 (*a.*)

> She did not get shocked when initially noticing this matter, but it gave her quite a jolt after she knew the beginning and the subsequent development of it.

他在最開始注意到這件事情時並沒有被嚇到,但當他知道這件事的起因以及之後的發展後,卻給了他一個很大的震撼。

★ KEY 5

✪ Inherent 固有的、與生俱來的 (*a.*)
✪ Mimic 模仿 (*v.*)
✪ Expression 表達、措辭 (*n.*)
✪ Intriguing 吸引人的、有趣的 (*a.*)

> His inherent ability, of mimicking people's action and facial expressions, makes him an intriguing person.

他天生善於模仿他人動作與臉部表情的能力,使他成為一位很有趣的人。

★ KEY 6

✪ Meticulously 一絲不苟地、極細心地 (*adv.*)
✪ Manipulate 操作、利用 (*v.*)
✪ Mandatory 命令的、強制的 (*a.*)
✪ Lucrative 有利益的、獲利的 (*a.*)

You have to meticulously manipulate public opinions because firstly, it is mandatory and secondly, it may affect the forthcoming presentation about running a lucrative business.

你必須要非常細心地去操作公眾言論，因為第一，這是必須的；第二，這些言論有可能會影響到接下來的一個可以獲利的企業經營簡報。

⭐ KEY 7

✪ Constantly 不斷地、時常地 (*adv.*)
✪ Alter 改變 (*v.*)
✪ Manifest 表明、證明 (*v.*)
✪ Malleable 有延展性的 (*a.*)

Constantly altering thoughts manifests that he is a malleable person rather than a stiff person.

時常改變想法顯示他是個有延展性的人，而不是一個腦袋不靈活的人。

⭐ KEY 8

✪ Legitimacy 合法、合理、正統 (*n.*)
✪ Unreachable 不能得到的 (*a.*)
✪ Objective 目的 (*n.*)

✪ Milestone 里程碑、劃時代的事件 (*n.*)

> The legitimacy of this action that has been regarded as an unreachable objective is now a historical milestone of our country.

這個曾經被視為是無法達成的目的的動作，其合法性是我們國家歷史上的一個里程碑。

★ KEY 9

✪ Obsession 迷住 (*n.*)
✪ Peculiar 奇特的、特殊的 (*a.*)
✪ Notwithstanding 儘管、還是 (*adv.*)
✪ Misunderstanding 誤解 (*n.*)

> Her obsession with coding makes her a peculiar person in the school; notwithstanding, her parents have a slight misunderstanding over the reasons why she chose to study technology rather than literature.

她對於編碼的癡迷使他在學校裡成為一名很特殊的人物，然而她的爸媽對於她為什麼選擇念科技而不是文學有一點小誤解。

✪ Oblige 強制、束縛 (*v.*)
✪ Monitor 監控、監視 (*v.*)
✪ Innumerable 無數的、數不清的 (*a.*)
✪ Monotonous 單調的、無變化的 (*a.*)

> He is obliged to monitor innumerable bicycles parked in this space, which is the most monotonous work he has even done in his life.

他被強制去監視停在這個區域中數不盡輛數的腳踏車，他覺得這工作是他目前人生中做過最單調無聊的一個工作了。

★ **KEY 11** ◀

✪ Maintain 維修、保養 (*v.*)
✪ Minutely 仔細地、微小地 (*adv.*)
✪ myriad 無數 (*n.*)
✪ Minuscule 極小的 (*a.*)

> The engineer maintains the turbines minutely and finds out a myriad of minuscule places needed to be repaired instantly.

這位工程師仔細的保養這個渦輪，並且發現有數不盡的細小地方需要立即地修復。

★ KEY 12

✪ Nature 自然、天性 (*n.*)
✪ Unique 獨特的 (*a.*)
✪ Noticeable 引人注目的 (*a.*)
✪ Obscure 含糊的、難解的 (*a.*)

> Everyone has their unique nature that makes a person noticeable in the crowd; nevertheless, some people are still obscure to who they actually are and what uniqueness they own.

每個人都有他獨特且可以使一個人在人群中受人注目的天性，然而有很多人始終對於他們到底是誰以及他們擁有甚麼樣的獨特性感到很模糊。

★ KEY 13

✪ Nearly 幾乎 (*adv.*)
✪ Mundane 現世的、世俗的 (*a.*)
✪ On the contrary 相反地 (*conj.*)
✪ Pacify 使平靜、安慰 (*v.*)

> Nearly everyone feels that they are in a mundane world, having a mundane life and reading books full of mundane contents; on the contrary, everything mundane still pacifies your life.

幾乎每個人都覺得他們現處於一個世俗的世界，過著世俗的生活，讀著充滿世俗內容的書籍；但相反地，每件世俗的事情仍然使你的人生感到平靜。

KEY 14

✪ Permeate 瀰漫、滲透滲入 (*v.*)
✪ Patch 補釘 (*n.*)
✪ Offset 彌補 (*v.*)
✪ Imperfection 不完美、瑕疵 (*n.*)

> Water has permeated through patches of the wall for a couple of days, so he asks the property agent to pull down the prices to offset the imperfection.

水經由牆上的補釘部分滲透進來，所以他向房仲要求降低價錢來彌補這個瑕疵。

KEY 15

✪ Overview 概要 (*n.*)
✪ Outcome 結果、後果 (*n.*)
✪ Penetrate 滲透、穿入 (*v.*)
✪ Territory 版圖、領地 (*n.*)

This slide is basically an overview demonstrating what the outcome would be if enemy troops keep penetrating our territory.

這個投影片基本上來說，是個概述如果敵軍軍隊一直滲透到我們的領地會有甚麼後果發生。

★ **KEY 16**

✪ Tide 潮汐 (*n.*)
✪ Periodic 週期的、定期的 (*a.*)
✪ Perceptible 可察覺的、可感覺的 (*a.*)
✪ Differ 不一致、不同 (*v.*)

The movement of tides, the periodic rise and fall of the sea level in the given time, is perceptible, which, in this face, differs from tsunami.

潮汐運動，也就是一定時間內海平面週期性上升下降，是可以察覺的，並且可以此來區分其與海嘯的不同。

★ **KEY 17**

✪ Landlord 房東、地主 (*n.*)
✪ Pledge 保證、抵押、發誓 (*n.*)
✪ Parcel out 分配 (*v.*)
✪ Outermost 最外邊的、離中心最遠的 (*a.*)

Unit 10

Even though the landlord gives the pledge that this land will not be parceled out by a dozen or so small buyers, the family still decides to move to the outermost district of the city to ensure safety.

縱使地主給出承諾說，這塊土地不會被十幾位買家所分購，這家人決定為了確保安全，還是要搬到這個城市最外圍的區域。

★ KEY 18

✪ Evidently 顯然、明顯的 (*adv.*)
✪ Paradox 似是而非的論點 (*n.*)
✪ Ornament 裝飾 (*v.*)
✪ Opaque 不透明的、含糊的 (*a.*)

Everyone can tell it's evidently a paradox that the owner spent so much money ornamenting rather than improving the quality of the food, and the explanation he provided was deliberately opaque.

每個人都知道這個主人花很多錢在裝飾而不是優化食物的品質，很明顯是個矛盾的事情，且他對於此事刻意地提出模糊的解釋。

★ KEY 19

✪ Peak 山頂、高峰 (*n.*)
✪ Allow 允許 (*v.*)
✪ Omit 忽略 (*v.*)
✪ Permit 許可、容許 (*v.*)

> At the peak of her beauty career, she does not allow herself to omit any tiny piece of work even if her boss permits tiny mistakes.

正處事業頂峰的她，即使她的老闆允許小錯誤，她也不允許她自己忽略工作上任何細微的部分。

★ KEY 20

✪ Outbreak 爆發、暴動 (*n.*)
✪ Options 選擇 (*n.*)
✪ Ongoing 前進的、進行的 (*a.*)
✪ Instantaneously 即時的、同時發生地 (*adv.*)

> As an outbreak of hostilities interrupted the ongoing construction, the government had no options but to instantaneously crush the rebellion.

因為反對勢力大舉入侵正在進行中的施工工程，政府沒有其他選擇，只好立即地殲滅掉這些叛源。

Outbreak	Synonym	Crash/ disruption/ sudden happening
	Antonym	Calmness/ completion
Ongoing	Synonym	Continuous/ current/ growing
	Antonym	Intermittent
Instantaneous	Synonym	Immediate/ spontaneous / rapid
	Antonym	Delayed
Permit	Synonym	Authorize/ accept/ empower
	Antonym	Deny/ disallow
Omit	Synonym	Exclude/ bypass/ delete/ discard
	Antonym	Heed/ attend
Evident	Synonym	Apparent/ indisputable/ conspicuous
	Antonym	Doubtful/ dubious
Opaque	Synonym	Blurred/ gloomy/ impenetrable
	Antonym	Luminous/ bright/ intelligent
Lucrative	Synonym	Productive/ advantageous/ fruitful
	Antonym	Unprofitable
Pledge	Synonym	Guarantee/ promise/ swear
	Antonym	Break/ disavow/disobey
Periodic	Synonym	Intermittent/ occasional
	Antonym	Constant/ infrequent

Penetrate	Synonym	Pierce/ permeate/ puncture
	Antonym	Surrender/ yield
Minuscule	Synonym	Microscopic/ insignificant / minute
	Antonym	Enormous/ huge
Mundane	Synonym	Banal/ ordinary/
	Antonym	Abnormal/ uncommon
Innumerable	Synonym	Countless/ myriad
	Antonym	Calculable/ limited
Perceptible	Synonym	Noticeable/ obvious/ detectable
	Antonym	Hidden/ imperceptible
Monotonous	Synonym	Dreary/ boring/ repetitious/ dull
	Antonym	Bright/lively
Pacify	Synonym	Ameliorate/ mitigate
	Antonym	Aggravate/ agitate
Intriguing	Synonym	Interesting/ alluring/ appealing
	Antonym	Unexciting
Inherent	Synonym	Basic/ hereditary /implicit
	Antonym	Acquired/ extra
Malleable	Synonym	Pliable/adaptable/ flexible
	Antonym	Rigid/ inflexible

攻克要點I 必考字彙表

KEY1

Comply with 遵守、服從 (*v.*)	Preordain 預先注定、命運來源 (*v.*)
Preeminent 超群的、卓越的 (*a.*)	Compose 組成、構成 (*v.*)

KEY2

Accept 接受 (*v.*)	Premise 前提 (*n.*)
Loan 貸款 (*n.*)	Predicament 困境 (*n.*)

KEY3

Portion 部分 (*n.*)	Manuscript 手稿、原稿 (*n.*)
Prominent 卓越的、顯著的 (*a.*)	Pinnacle 巔峰、最高點 (*n.*)

KEY4

Predominantly 主要地 (*adv.*)	Preclude 預先排除、預防 (*v.*)
Postulate 假設 (*v.*)	Source 來源 (*n.*)

KEY5

Precision 精確度 (*n.*)	Potential 有潛力的、可能的、潛在的 (*a.*)
Ambiguity 不明確、含糊 (*n.*)	Preceding 上述的、在前的 (*a.*)

KEY6

Potent 有力的、有說服力的 (*a.*)	Posit 斷定 (*v.*)

Widespread 廣布的、普及的 (*a.*)	Trend 趨勢、流行 (*n.*)

KEY7

Plausible 似乎有理的、似是而非的 (*a.*)	Phenomenon 現象 (*n.*)
Breathe 呼吸 (*v.*)	Pore 孔 (*n.*)

KEY8

Artificial 人造的 (*a.*)	Pigment 色素 (*n.*)
Phenomenal 非凡的 (*a.*)	Pervasive 普及的、遍布的 (*a.*)

KEY9

Persistent 堅持的、持續的 (*a.*)	Inquisitive 好奇的 (*a.*)
Miraculous 奇蹟的、不可思議的 (*a.*)	Piece 連接、接上 (*v.*)

KEY10

Pertinent 相關的 (*a.*)	Radical 激進的、根本的 (*a.*)
Pronounced 明顯的 (*a.*)	Prosperous 繁榮的 (*a.*)

KEY11

Provoke 激怒、招惹 (*v.*)	Malicious 懷惡意的 (*a.*)
Propel 推進、驅使 (*v.*)	Pursue 追求、追趕 (*v.*)

KEY12

Proponent 支持者 (*n.*)	Prowess 實力、才智 (*n.*)
Protrude 突出、伸出 (*v.*)	Emergent 緊急的、浮現的 (*a.*)

KEY13

Prohibitive 禁止的、抑制的 (*a.*)	In order to 為了 (*ph.*)
Prolifically 多產地、豐富地 (*adv.*)	Assure 向…保證、使放心 (*v.*)

KEY14

Prolong 延長、拖延 (*v.*)

Program 程式化、規劃 (*v.*)

Ruinous 招致破壞的 (*a.*)

Preserve 保護、保存 (*v.*)

KEY15

Protect 保護 (*v.*)

Pristine 原始的、質樸的 (*a.*)

Remaining 剩餘的、剩下的 (*a.*)

Priority 優先 (*n.*)

KEY16

Primitive 原始的 (*a.*)

Presumable 可推測的 (*a.*)

Prevalent 普遍的、流行的 (*a.*)

Remarkable 卓越的、顯著的、非凡的 (*a.*)

KEY17

Reputation 聲譽、名譽 (*n.*)

Drastic 激烈的 (*a.*)

Historic 歷史上重要的、歷史性的 (*a.*)

Residual 剩餘的、殘餘的 (*a.*)

KEY18

Readily 容易地、快捷地 (*adv.*)

Ramifications 分支 (*n.*)

Comprehensible 可理解的 (*a.*)

Rather than 而不是 (*conj.*)

KEY19

Refuse 拒絕 (*v.*) 廢物、殘渣 (*n.*)

Adorn 使裝飾、使生色 (*v.*)

Refined 精緻的、精確的、優雅的 (*a.*)

Refreshing 清爽的 (*a.*)

KEY20

Relatively 相對地、比較而言 (*adv.*)

Regulate 管理、為…制定規章 (*v.*)

Urgent 急迫的、緊急的 (*a.*)

Reinforce 增強、加固 (*v.*)

攻克要點II 超給力例句

★ **KEY 1** 🎵 **MP3 11**

✪ Comply with 遵守、服從 (*v.*)
✪ Preordain 預先注定、命運來源 (*v.*)
✪ Preeminent 超群的、卓越的 (*a.*)
✪ Compose 組成、構成 (*v.*)

> Her life seems to comply with the preordained path of being a playwright due to her preeminent composing and writing abilities.

她的人生似乎遵守了註定好的命運，因為她卓越的作曲跟寫作能力，她成為一個劇作家。

★ **KEY 2**

✪ Accept 接受 (*v.*)
✪ Premise 前提 (*n.*)
✪ Loan 貸款 (*n.*)
✪ Predicament 困境 (*n.*)

> People do not accept the premise that a loan of money could pull our government out of the economical predicament.

人民不接受借款可以使我們的政府脫離經濟困境這樣的一個前提。

⭐ KEY 3

✪ Portion 部分 (*n.*)
✪ Manuscript 手稿、原稿 (*n.*)
✪ Prominent 卓越的、顯著的 (*a.*)
✪ Pinnacle 巔峰、最高點 (*n.*)

A portion of the manuscripts belonging to the prominent scholar has well been preserved, regarded as what made him reach the pinnacle of his instructing career.

屬於這位傑出學者的手稿部分被完好的保存著，且其被認為是使他達到他教學事業巔峰的東西。

⭐ KEY 4

✪ Predominantly 主要地 (*adv.*)
✪ Preclude 預先排除、預防 (*v.*)
✪ Postulate 假設 (*v.*)
✪ Source 來源 (*n.*)

That this language is used predominantly in this district may possibly preclude the development of other dialects that experts postulate as the sources of all languages used in this area.

這個語言在這個地區盛行，很有可能預先排除了其他方言發展，而專家認為方言是這個區域中所有語言的來源。

Unit 11

 **KEY 5**

- ✪ Precision 精確度 (*n.*)
- ✪ Potential 有潛力的、可能的、潛在的 (*a.*)
- ✪ Ambiguity 不明確、含糊 (*n.*)
- ✪ Preceding 上述的、在前的 (*a.*)

> Your report is lack of precision because there might be potential ambiguity happening if you just say the point is mentioned in the preceding paragraph.

你的報告缺乏準確性，因為你如果只說這個論點已經在之前的段落中敘述過了，有可能會有敘述不明確的情況發生。

KEY 6

- ✪ Potent 有力的、有說服力的 (*a.*)
- ✪ Posit 斷定 (*v.*)
- ✪ Widespread 廣布的、普及的 (*a.*)
- ✪ Trend 趨勢、流行 (*n.*)

> It's definitely a potent study positing that the latest trend in accessory fashion would be widespread from East Asia to Western countries.

這個很有說服力的研究斷定飾品的流行趨勢會從東亞到西方國家廣泛普及。

KEY 7

✪ Plausible 似乎有理的、似是而非的 (*a.*)
✪ Phenomenon 現象 (*n.*)
✪ Breathe 呼吸 (*v.*)
✪ Pore 孔 (*n.*)

> It is plausible that the phenomenon of how your skin breathes is just as how moisture passes through the pores in the surface of a leaf.

你的皮膚呼吸就像是水分如何透過葉面的細孔滲透這樣的現象似乎是合理的。

KEY 8

✪ Artificial 人造的 (*a.*)
✪ Pigment 色素 (*n.*)
✪ Phenomenal 非凡的 (*a.*)
✪ Pervasive 普及的、遍布的 (*a.*)

> The color created by mixing artificial and natural pigments up is phenomenal, and the way to create it is pervasive, especially in tropical counties, such as Mexico and Brazil.

由混和人造與自然色素創造出來的色素十分出色，而且製造的方法遍及熱帶國家，像是墨西哥與巴西。

KEY 9

✪ Persistent 堅持的、持續的 (*a.*)
✪ Inquisitive 好奇的 (*a.*)
✪ Miraculous 奇蹟的、不可思議的 (*a.*)
✪ Piece 連接、接上 (*v.*)

> The persistent questioning has been lasting for an hour in this conference in that people are so inquisitive about how this miraculous way of piecing a bridge from just hundreds of poles could form such a solid building.

研討會中的發問持續一小時之久而不間斷，因為人們對於這樣不可思議，只使用幾百根竿子連接橋便可以建出這樣堅固的建物感到好奇。

KEY 10

✪ Pertinent 相關的 (*a.*)
✪ Radical 激進的、根本的 (*a.*)
✪ Pronounced 明顯的 (*a.*)
✪ Prosperous 繁榮的 (*a.*)

> Pertinent comments are raised regarding how the radical changes would bring about a pronounced improvement in establishing a prosperous city.

有關一些根本上的改變如何能於建造一個繁榮城市時帶來顯著的進步，這樣的言論已被提出。

✪ Provoke 激怒、招惹 (*v.*)
✪ Malicious 懷惡意的 (*a.*)
✪ Propel 推進、驅使 (*v.*)
✪ Pursue 追求、追趕 (*v.*)

> She was provoked by the malicious words saying that she has no ability to go to college, which then propels her to pursue a life of research.

她被說她沒有能力進大學這樣的惡意言論給激怒，其促使她去追求走上研究之路。

✪ Proponent 支持者 (*n.*)
✪ Prowess 實力、才智 (*n.*)
✪ Protrude 突出、伸出 (*v.*)
✪ Emergent 緊急的、浮現的 (*a.*)

> Proponents consider this as his prowess that he can hang on to a piece of rock protruding from the cliff face in such an emergent condition.

支持者認為可以在這樣緊急的時刻緊緊抓住由懸崖突出的岩石，是他的英勇才智。

Unit 11

 **KEY 13**

✪ Prohibitive 禁止的、抑制的 (*a.*)
✪ In order to 為了 (*conj.*)
✪ Prolifically 多產地、豐富地 (*adv.*)
✪ Assure 向…保證、使放心 (*v.*)

> Rising fruit and vegetable prices is prohibitive, said
> government, in order to prolifically grow fruits and
> assure farmers' right.

政府表示為了大量的生產水果以及確保農民的權益，抬高水果與蔬菜價格是被禁止的。

⭐ **KEY 14**

✪ Prolong 延長、拖延 (*v.*)
✪ Ruinous 招致破壞的 (*a.*)
✪ Program 程式化、規劃 (*v.*)
✪ Preserve 保護、保存 (*v.*)

> This scheme is prolonged due to the fact that ruinous
> weather condition is programmed to reform the capital
> cities and preserve the ancient temples.

此計劃是用於改善首都以及保存古廟宇，因為破壞性的氣候狀況而延後。

✪ Protect 保護 (*v.*)
✪ Remaining 剩餘的、剩下的 (*a.*)
✪ Pristine 原始的、質樸的 (*a.*)
✪ Priority 優先 (*n.*)

We are supposed to put protecting the world's remaining pristine forests in our top priority.

我們應該要把保護世界上剩餘的原始森林當作我們的第一優先。

✪ Primitive 原始的 (*a.*)
✪ Prevalent 普遍的、流行的 (*a.*)
✪ Presumable 可推測的 (*a.*)
✪ Remarkable 卓越的、顯著的、非凡的 (*a.*)

To live a primitive lifestyle is prevalent nowadays, such as camping, and the presumable reason why it is popular among families may be because children can learn the remarkable way of living.

過著原始的生活方式像是露營，在現今來說是很普遍的，且為什麼這樣的生活方式在家庭間很熱門其可能的原因為小孩子可以學到非凡卓越的生活方式。

KEY 17

✪ Reputation 聲譽、名譽 (*n.*)
✪ Historic 歷史上重要的、歷史性的 (*a.*)
✪ Drastic 激烈的 (*a.*)
✪ Residual 剩餘的、殘餘的 (*a.*)

> The reputation of this historic store has been ruined by this drastic explosion assumed to be terrorist attack, and there is still residual oil spread all over the floor.

這間歷史上重要的商店聲譽被這次推測為是恐怖攻擊的轟炸給摧毀了，而且還有殘餘的油漬遍布地上。

KEY 18

✪ Readily 容易地、快捷地 (*adv.*)
✪ Comprehensible 可理解的 (*a.*)
✪ Ramifications 分支 (*n.*)
✪ Rather than 而不是 (*conj.*)

> Even though this story is readily comprehensible, I would choose to follow all the ramifications of the plot rather than scan and then directly skip to the conclusion.

雖然這個故事可以很快速地被理解，我還是會選擇遵照故事情節的所有分支而不是掃過去然後直接跳到結局。

★ KEY 19

- ✪ Refuse 拒絕 (*v.*) 廢物、殘渣 (*n.*)
- ✪ Refined 精緻的、精確的、優雅的 (*a.*)
- ✪ Adorn 使裝飾、使生色 (*v.*)
- ✪ Refreshing 清爽的 (*a.*)

This group of people regards the sort of interior design as refuse, while another group deems this refined work as adorned with refreshing decoration.

這群人認為這樣類型的室內設計根本是垃圾，然而其他的人卻認為這是個精緻的作品，因為其使用耳目一新的裝飾。

★ KEY 20

- ✪ Relatively 相對地、比較而言 (*adv.*)
- ✪ Urgent 急迫的、緊急的 (a)
- ✪ Regulate 管理、為…制定規章 (*v.*)
- ✪ Reinforce 增強、加固 (*v.*)

Relatively speaking, it is a lot urgent to strictly regulate the army for the sake of reinforcing our defense against attacks.

相對來說，去嚴格的管理我們的軍隊來達到鞏固我們防線免於受到攻擊是更加地緊急。

Reinforce	Synonym	Strengthen/ boost/ bolster
	Antonym	Hinder/ diminish
Regulate	Synonym	Manage/ organize/ coordinate
	Antonym	Damage/ mismanage
Urgent	Synonym	Compelling/ crucial
	Antonym	Inessential/ needless
Inquisitive	Synonym	Curious/ inquiring/ impertinent
	Antonym	Incurious/ indifferent
Refined	Synonym	Cultured/ civilized/ cultivated
	Antonym	Imprecise/ uncultured
Adorn	Synonym	Decorate / beautify / embellish
	Antonym	Disfigure / spoil/ deform
Refreshing	Synonym	Fresh/ invigorating / revitalizing
	Antonym	Boring/ depressing
Comprehensible	Synonym	Understandable/ coherent / explicit
	Antonym	Ambiguous/ equivocal
Precede	Synonym	Anticipate/ predate/ presage
	Antonym	End/ finish

Residual	Synonym	Continuing/ enduring / lingering
	Antonym	Essential/ necessary
Pristine	Synonym	Primeval/ immaculate/intact
	Antonym	Affected
Priority	Synonym	First concern/ preference
	Antonym	Inferiority
Prolong	Synonym	Extend/ continue/ lengthen
	Antonym	Abbreviate / cease/ expedite
Preserve	Synonym	Conserve/ maintain/ keep/ perpetuate
	Antonym	Abandon/ endanger/ halt
Ruinous	Synonym	Disastrous/devastating/ calamitous
	Antonym	Harmless/ fortunate
Propel	Synonym	Drive/ push/ thrust
	Antonym	Discourage/ dissuade/ repress
Provoke	Synonym	Evoke/ stimulate/ arouse
	Antonym	Deter/prevent
Malicious	Synonym	Hateful/ malevolent/ malignant
	Antonym	Aiding/ assisting/ decent
Pertinent	Synonym	Relevant/ suitable/ applicable
	Antonym	Improper/ inapplicable
Prosperous	Synonym	Thriving/ affluent/ flourishing
	Antonym	Destitute/ impoverished

攻克要點I 必考字彙表

KEY1

Reluctantly 不情願地 (*adv.*)	Admit 承認 (*v.*)
Constant 持續的、堅決的 (*adv.*)	Recur 再發生、復發 (*v.*)

KEY2

Replica 複製品、複寫 (*n.*)	Reputation 名聲、名譽 (*n.*)
Delicate 細緻的、微妙的 (*a.*)	Symmetry 對稱、調和 (*n.*)

KEY3

Scrape 刮、擦 (*v.*)	Scatter 散播、散佈 (*v.*)
Gargantuan 巨大的、龐大的 (*a.*)	Screen 隔離 (*v.*)

KEY4

Scorn 輕蔑、奚落 (*n.*)	Carry 攜帶 (*v.*)
Score 大量、許多 (*n.*)	Scorching 灼熱的、激烈的 (*a.*)

KEY5

Scented 有氣味的 (*a.*)	Scope 範圍、廣度 (*n.*)
Samples 樣品 (*n.*)	Save for 除了 (*preposition*)

KEY6

Satisfied 感到滿足的 (*a.*)	Scented 有氣味的 (*a.*)
Roam 漫步、漫遊 (*v.*)	Fanciful 想像的、奇怪的 (*a.*)

KEY7

Realm 領域、界 (*n.*)

Rudimentary 基本的、初步的 (*a.*)

Profound 深奧的 (*a.*)

Sacred 宗教的、不可侵犯的 (*a.*)

KEY8

Roundabout 繞圈子的、不直接 了當的 (*a.*)

Roughly 概略地、粗糙地 (*adv.*)

Rupture 破裂、斷開 (*n.*)

Execute 執行 (*v.*)

KEY9

Robust 強健的、結實的 (*a.*)

Rotate 旋轉 (*v.*)

Role 角色 (*n.*)

Cumbersome 累贅的、麻煩 的、沉重的 (*a.*)

KEY10

Rigorous 嚴格的、苛刻的 (*a.*)

Revival 再生、復活 (*n.*)

Distinguished 卓越的、著名的 (*a.*)

Resilient 彈回的、迅速恢復精力 的 (*a.*)

KEY11

Retrieve 重新得到、收回 (*v.*)

Anonymous 匿名的 (*a.*)

International 國際的 (*a.*)

Retain 保持、保留 (*v.*)

KEY12

Acquire 取得、獲得 (*v.*)

Sought-after 很吃香的、受歡迎 的 (*a.*)

Sophistication 複雜、精密 (*n.*)

Meaningful 有意義的 (*a.*)

KEY13

Myriad 大量的、無數的 (*a.*)

Solitary 獨居的、孤獨的 (*a.*)

Solicit 請求、乞求 (*v.*)

Sink 沉入 (*v.*)

KEY14

Reckon 估計、認為、猜想 (*v.*)	Shield 保護、遮蔽 (*v.*)
Solicitation 懇請、懇求 (*n.*)	Skeptical 懷疑性的 (*a.*)

KEY15

Snap 咬斷、拉斷 (*v.*)	Segment 分割 (*n.*)
Sank 沉入 (*v.*)	Shallow 淺的 (*a.*)

KEY16

Singularity 奇異、奇妙 (*n.*)	Spectator 觀眾、目擊者 (*n.*)
Speculate 推測 (*v.*)	Shiver 顫抖 (*v.*)

KEY17

Switch 主換、切換 (*v.*)	Principally 原理的、原則的 (*adv.*)
Concentrate 集中、集結 (*v.*)	Showcase 陳列 (*v.*)

KEY18

Exceedingly 極端的 (*adv.*)	Severe 嚴厲的 (*a.*)
Sedentary 久坐的 (*a.*)	Secreted 分泌的 (*a.*)

KEY19

Scrutiny 仔細檢查、監視 (*n.*)	Aesthetic 美學的 (*a.*)
Sculpture 雕刻 (*n.*)	Spectacular 驚人的 (*a.*)

KEY20

Establish 創立 (*v.*)	Aid 幫助 (*v.*)
Subjected to 使…遭受 (*v.*)	Abuse 侮辱、虐待 (*n.*)

攻克要點II 超給力例句

★ KEY 1　♪ MP3 12

- ✪ Reluctantly 不情願地 (*adv.*)
- ✪ Admit 承認 (*v.*)
- ✪ Constant 持續的、堅決的 (*adv.*)
- ✪ Recur 再發生、復發 (*v.*)

> The downcast facial expression she had while reluctantly admitting to the truth constantly recurs throughout my mind.

她不情願承認這個事實時的悲哀表情一直在我腦海中反覆浮現。

★ KEY 2

- ✪ Replica 複製品、複寫 (*n.*)
- ✪ Reputation 名聲、名譽 (*n.*)
- ✪ Delicate 細緻的、微妙的 (*a.*)
- ✪ Symmetry 對稱、調和 (*n.*)

> The replica of the Eiffel Tower she made approximately two years ago has received an exceptional reputation for sophistication and its delicate symmetry.

她大約兩年前做的艾菲爾鐵塔的複製品，因為精細與細緻的對稱，贏得很好的聲譽。

⭐ KEY 3

- ✪ Scrape 刮、擦 (*v.*)
- ✪ Scatter 散播、散佈 (*v.*)
- ✪ Gargantuan 巨大的、龐大的 (*a.*)
- ✪ Screen 隔離 (*v.*)

> The fragments of scraped wood and glasses scattered due to the gargantuan explosion have screened off part of the room.

因為巨大爆炸而四射的這些有擦痕的木頭與玻璃的碎片遮蔽了這房間的一部分。

⭐ KEY 4

- ✪ Scorn 輕蔑、奚落 (*n.*)
- ✪ Carry 攜帶 (*v.*)
- ✪ Score 大量、許多 (*n.*)
- ✪ Scorching 灼熱的、激烈的 (*a.*)

> He has been the scorn of his colleagues since they saw him carrying scores of goods in such a scorching day.

自從他同事看到他在烈日下提著大包小包的貨物後，他就成為他同事奚落的對象。

★ KEY 5

✪ Scented 有氣味的 (*a.*)
✪ Scope 範圍、廣度 (*n.*)
✪ Samples 樣品 (*n.*)
✪ Save for 除了 (preposition)

> Having the mass production of scented dress is outside the scope of our ability, save of designing just few samples of it.

大量製作有香氛的洋裝完全超出我們的可行範圍，除了只是設計出幾樣樣本以外。

★ KEY 6

✪ Satisfied 感到滿足的 (*a.*)
✪ Scented 有氣味的 (*a.*)
✪ Roam 漫步、漫遊 (*v.*)
✪ Fanciful 想像的、奇怪的 (*a.*)

> I feel quite satisfied using a scented soap for the shower, making me feel like roaming around the street full of roses in Paris - the most fanciful city in the world.

使用有香氛的香皂洗澡讓我感到很滿意，感覺就像是漫步在開滿玫瑰的巴黎街道，而巴黎則是世界上最讓人充滿幻想的城市。

✪ **KEY 7**

- ✪ Realm 領域、界 (*n.*)
- ✪ Profound 深奧的 (*a.*)
- ✪ Rudimentary 基本的、初步的 (*a.*)
- ✪ Sacred 宗教的、不可侵犯的 (*a.*)

> The realm of religions is so philosophical and profound that makes me merely have a rudimentary grasp of Buddhism, for example that the cow is a sacred animal in India.

宗教這個領域是非常哲學且深奧的，讓我只能大概知道佛教的基礎，像是牛是印度神聖的動物。

✪ **KEY 8**

- ✪ Roundabout 繞圈子的、不直接了當的 (*a.*)
- ✪ Rupture 破裂、斷開 (*n.*)
- ✪ Roughly 概略地、粗糙地 (*adv.*)
- ✪ Execute 執行 (*v.*)

The president's roundabout way of making a presentation leads to the deep ruptures within the party, making roughly 70% percent of the members unable to execute their power.

總統兜圈子的報告方式導致了這個黨派的破裂，使得大約百分之70的成員無法執行他們的權力。

★ KEY 9

✪ Robust 強健的、結實的 (*a.*)
✪ Role 角色 (*n.*)
✪ Rotate 旋轉 (*v.*)
✪ Cumbersome 累贅的、麻煩的、沉重的 (*a.*)

The robust man plays a rather important role in our team because he can rotate the cumbersome handle gently.

這個強健的男人在我們的團隊中扮演著相當重要的角色，因為他可以輕鬆旋轉這個沉重的把手。

★ KEY 10

✪ Rigorous 嚴格的、苛刻的 (*a.*)
✪ Distinguished 卓越的、著名的 (*a.*)
✪ Revival 再生、復活 (*n.*)
✪ Resilient 彈回的、迅速恢復精力的 (*a.*)

Through rigorous examination, the distinguished scholar states that the speed of a patient's revival after having an operation represents the person's resilient capacity.

在經歷過嚴苛的檢查後，這位卓越的學者陳述，一位病人在手術過後甦醒的速度代表著一個人的復原的能力。

★ KEY 11

✪ Retrieve 重新得到、收回 (*v.*)
✪ International 國際的 (*a.*)
✪ Anonymous 作者不詳的 (*a.*)
✪ Retain 保持、保留 (*n.*)

The old man finally retrieves his suitcase ten years after he left it at the lobby of JFK international airport and appreciates the anonymous man retaining the original appearance of his suitcase.

十年後，這老人終於取回他十年前丟失在紐約JFK國際機場的皮箱，並且對於那位不知道名字，卻幫他保留行李箱原貌的那位先生感到很感激。

KEY 12

- ✪ Acquire 取得、獲得 (*v.*)
- ✪ Sophistication 複雜、精密 (*n.*)
- ✪ Sought-after 很吃香的、受歡迎的 (*a.*)
- ✪ Meaningful 有意義的 (*a.*)

> She has acquired the sophistication of handcraft, and the necklace she made is widely sought-after, making it the most meaningful moment in her life.

她已經獲取了做手工藝的精隨,而且她親手製作的項鍊非常受歡迎,這成為她人生中最有意義的時刻。

KEY 13

- ✪ Myriad 大量的、無數的 (*a.*)
- ✪ Solicit 請求、乞求 (*v.*)
- ✪ Solitary 獨居的、孤獨的 (*a.*)
- ✪ Sink 沉入 (*v.*)

> Myriad people solicit for planting more trees after knowing there is just one solitary tree growing on the mountainside, with its stem slightly and gradually sinking down into the mud.

當民眾知道只有一棵孤獨的樹生長在山上,它的莖漸漸地且輕輕地沉入泥土中,無數的民眾乞求說要種植更多的樹。

★ KEY 14

✪ Reckon 估計、認為、猜想 (*v.*)
✪ Shield 保護、遮蔽 (*v.*)
✪ Solicitation 懇請、懇求 (*n.*)
✪ Skeptical 懷疑性的 (*a.*)

> In my cases, since I am skeptical of the truthfulness of any telephone solicitation calls from banks, I reckon people must shield themselves from information theft.

以我的例子來說，因為我對於任何銀行推銷電話的真實性感到懷疑，因此我認為人們必須要保護自己免於資訊遭竊取。

★ KEY 15

✪ Snap 咬斷、拉斷 (*v.*)
✪ Segment 分割 (*n.*)
✪ Sank 沉入 (*v.*)
✪ Shallow 淺的 (*a.*)

> The branch he was standing on snapped off and a small segment of it sank down in to the shallow-end of the swimming pool.

他剛剛站在上面的樹枝斷掉了，且小部分的枝幹沉入泳池中較淺的部分。

KEY 16

- ✪ Singularity 奇異、奇妙 (*n.*)
- ✪ Spectator 觀眾、目擊者 (*n.*)
- ✪ Speculate 推測 (*v.*)
- ✪ Shiver 顫抖 (*v.*)

> The singularity of this event is that even though the spectators speculated that this man with a suspicious look murdered his mother, the police officer still believed that the young woman somewhat shivering on the floor did that.

這件事情奇妙的地方在於,雖然目擊者推測說這個擁有可疑外型的男子殺了他的母親,警察方面還是認為是那位在地上顫抖的年輕小姐做的。

KEY 17

- ✪ Switch 主換、切換 (*v.*)
- ✪ Principally 原理的、原則的 (*adv.*)
- ✪ Concentrate 集中、集結 (*v.*)
- ✪ Showcase 陳列 (*v.*)

> After she switched to the department principally concentrating on composing rather than singing, this singer finally got a chance to showcase her new songs.

在被調去著重創作歌曲而非歌唱的部門之後，這位歌手最終有機會可以展現她的新歌了。

⭐ KEY 18

- ✪ Exceedingly 極端的 (*adv.*)
- ✪ Severe 嚴厲的 (*a.*)
- ✪ Sedentary 久坐的 (*a.*)
- ✪ Secreted 分泌的 (*a.*)

The tiger mother has been exceedingly severe with her son, making him a sedentary student who may have potential secreted problems.

這位虎媽對她的兒子極端嚴厲，使她的兒子成為習慣於久坐，且可能會有潛在內分泌方面問題的學生。

⭐ KEY 19

- ✪ Scrutiny 仔細檢查、監視 (*n.*)
- ✪ Aesthetic 美學的 (*a.*)
- ✪ Sculpture 雕刻 (*n.*)
- ✪ Spectacular 驚人的 (*a.*)

In order to create a spectacular marble sculpture, the architect has to have the close scrutiny of people's preference to art and aesthetic attitude.

為了要創造出不凡的大理石雕刻，這位建築師必須要仔細觀察人們對於美的喜好與審美觀。

★ KEY 20

- ✪ Establish 創立 (*v.*)
- ✪ Aid 幫助 (*v.*)
- ✪ Subjected to 使…遭受 (*v.*)
- ✪ Abuse 侮辱、虐待 (*n.*)

Unit 12

> The language institute in which I was teaching English language was established for aiding immigrants and refugees subjected to verbal and physical abuse in acquiring required abilities to get a job.

我以前任教的語言機構之所以創立，是基於幫助遭受言語與肢體虐待的移民跟難民能夠獲取找工作必備的能力。

攻克要點III 同義詞一覽表

Severe	Synonym	Acute/ bitter/ fierce/ intense
	Antonym	Gentle/ moderate
Rigorous	Synonym	Severe/ brutal/ burdensome
	Antonym	Careless/ inexact/ negligent
Spectacular	Synonym	Wonderful/ astonishing/ impressive/
	Antonym	Expected/ plain
Sculpt	Synonym	Carve/chisel/ engrave
	Antonym	Unite/ combine
Aesthetic	Synonym	Artistic/ creative/esthetic
	Antonym	Displeasing/ unattractive
Sedentary	Synonym	Motionless/ inactive /settled
	Antonym	Activated/ mobile
Switch	Synonym	Alteration/ reversal/ transformation
	Antonym	Stagnation/ inactivity
Execute	Synonym	Carry out/ accomplish/ implement
	Antonym	Abandon/ cease
Robust	Synonym	Strong/ potent/ vigorous
	Antonym	Fragile/ incapable/ lethargic
Retrieve	Synonym	Bring back/recapture/ restore
	Antonym	Endanger/damage/ destroy

Establish	Synonym	Organize/ build/ create
	Antonym	Destroy/ prevent
Concentrate	Synonym	Intensify/ settle/ contemplate
	Antonym	Confuse/ unsettle / disregard
Showcase	Synonym	Boast/ demonstrate/ disclose
	Antonym	Conceal/ refrain
Shiver	Synonym	Shake/ tremble/ vibrate / quiver
	Antonym	Steady/still
Speculate	Synonym	Contemplate/ hypothesize / ruminate
	Antonym	Disregard/ ignore/ dismiss
Sink	Synonym	Decline/ descend/ dig
	Antonym	Ascend/ raise/ increase
Cumbersome	Synonym	Clumsy/ burdensome/ bulky
	Antonym	Easy/ convenient
Shield	Synonym	Protect/ conceal/ defend/ shelter
	Antonym	Reveal/ uncover/ disregard
Reckon	Synonym	Evaluate/ surmise/ assume
	Antonym	Disbelieve/ misunderstand
Solicit	Synonym	Promote/ require/ seek
	Antonym	Answer/ reply

攻克要點I 必考字彙表

KEY1

Sturdy 強健的 (*a.*)	Resistance 抵抗力 (*n.*)
Stringent 迫切的、嚴厲的 (*a.*)	Stealthily 悄悄地 (*adv.*)

KEY2

Predict 預測 (*v.*)	Drastic 激烈的 (*a.*)
Striking 攻擊、襲擊 (*v.*)	Stockpile 儲存 (*v.*)

KEY3

Strip 剝奪、拆卸 (*v.*)	Staunch 堅固的、忠實的 (*a.*)
Ensue 接踵而至 (*v.*)	Adversity 災難、逆境 (*n.*)

KEY4

Stabilize 使穩定 (*v.*)	Willingness 樂意 (*n.*)
Spur 刺激、鼓舞 (*v.*)	Spontaneously 自發地 (*adv.*)

KEY5

Sporadic 偶爾發生的、零星的 (*a.*)	Spell 一段時間 (*n.*)
Split 分割 (*v.*)	Source 來源 (*n.*)

KEY6

Span 廣度、全長 (*n.*)	Spawn 產卵 (*v.*)
Splendor 壯闊的景觀 (*n.*)	So far 目前 (*adv.*)

KEY7

Spark 閃爍 (*v.*)	Sparse 稀稀疏疏的 (*a.*)
Intermittent 間歇的、斷斷續續的 (*a.*)	Burst 爆裂 (*n.*)

KEY8

Tempting 誘人的 (*a.*)	Swiftly 很快地、即刻地 (*adv.*)
Relieve 釋放 (*v.*)	Tension 緊繃、壓力 (*n.*)

KEY9

Tend 趨向 (*v.*)	Teem with 充滿大量 (*v.*)
Susceptible 易受影響的、易受感動的 (*a.*)	Tailspin 深淵、混亂、困境 (*n.*)

KEY10

Tactual 觸覺的、觸覺感官的 (*a.*)	Sensation 感覺、感情 (*n.*)
Tantalize 逗弄 (*v.*)	Realm 領域 (*n.*)

KEY11

Sustenance 生計、食物來源 (*n.*)	Sustain 支援、忍受 (*v.*)
Supplant 排擠掉、替代來源 (*v.*)	Substantial 重要的 (*a.*)

KEY12

Intrude 入侵 (*v.*)	Sumptuous 奢侈的、華麗的 (*a.*)
Safeguard 保障、保護 (*v.*)	Surveillance 監督、監視 (*n.*)

KEY13

Uncertainty 不確定性 (*n.*)	Subsidiary 輔助的、次要的 (*a.*)
Approve 批准、贊成 (*v.*)	Substitute 替代方案 (*n.*)

KEY14

Uneasy 心神不寧的、不穩定的 (*a.*)	Undergo 經歷、忍受 (*v.*)
Ultimately 最終的 (*adv.*)	Trauma 外傷、損傷 (*n.*)

KEY15

Endeavor 努力、盡力 (*n.*)	Firm 堅固的 (*a.*)
Underpinning 支撐、支援 (*n.*)	Undertake 承擔 (*v.*)

KEY16

Ensure 確保 (*v.*)	Unanimity 無異議 (*n.*)
Remain 保留 (*v.*)	Unadorned 未經裝飾的、樸素的 (*a.*)

KEY17

Rebellion 謀反、叛亂 (*n.*)	Turbulent 狂暴的 (*a.*)
Trigger 引發 (*v.*)	Arrest 逮捕 (*v.*)

KEY18

Traverse 旅遊、經過 (*v.*)	Tracts 遼闊的土地 (*n.*)
Thoroughly 徹底地 (*adv.*)	Tolerate 寬容、容忍 (*v.*)

KEY19

Unsurpassed 非常卓越的 (*a.*)	Unprecedented 空前的 (*a.*)
Truism 眾所周知的事、自明之理 (*n.*)	Variation 變動 (*n.*)

KEY20

Utilitarian 實用的 (*a.*)	Appealing 吸引人的 (*a.*)
Warrant 批准、證明 (*v.*)	Underlying 潛在的、根本的 (*a.*)

攻克要點II 超給力例句

Unit 13

★ KEY 1 ♪ MP3 13

- ✪ Sturdy 強健的 (*a.*)
- ✪ Resistance 抵抗力 (*n.*)
- ✪ Stringent 迫切的、嚴厲的 (*a.*)
- ✪ Stealthily 悄悄地 (*adv.*)

> He has sturdy resistance to believe that our country is encountering a stringent economic climate that has been stealthily growing in other Asian countries for few years.

他頑強抵抗不去相信我們的國家正面臨嚴峻的經濟情勢，且此經濟危機已悄悄的在亞洲其他國家蔓延好幾年了。

★ KEY 2

- ✪ Predict 預測 (*v.*)
- ✪ Drastic 激烈的 (*a.*)
- ✪ Striking 攻擊、襲擊 (*v.*)
- ✪ Stockpile 儲存 (*v.*)

> Experts predict that there will be drastic thunderstorms striking at least twice in the following two weeks, so people have to start stockpiling foods and water.

專家預測說在接下來的兩週會有至少兩次激烈的雷暴雨襲擊我們，所以民眾必須要開始儲存食物與水。

★ KEY 3

- ✪ Strip 剝奪、拆卸 (*v.*)
- ✪ Staunch 堅固的、忠實的 (*a.*)
- ✪ Ensue 接踵而至 (*v.*)
- ✪ Adversity 災難、逆境 (*n.*)

Even though we are stripped of our right to vote for international affairs, our staunch allies are still there with us, no matter what would happen ensuing this adversity.

雖然我們被剝去我們對國際事務投票的權利，我們堅固的盟友們還是跟我們站在一起，不論在這個困境之後會發生什麼事情。

★ KEY 4

- ✪ Stabilize 使穩定 (*v.*)
- ✪ Willingness 樂意 (*n.*)
- ✪ Spur 刺激、鼓舞 (*v.*)
- ✪ Spontaneously 自發地 (*adv.*)

The way our government chooses to stabilize the price of fruits is to spur people's willingness to spontaneously go purchasing discounted fruits.

我們政府選擇使水果物價穩定的方法，就是刺激民眾自發性地去購買打折水果的意願。

★ KEY 5

✪ Sporadic 偶爾發生的、零星的 (*a.*)
✪ Spell 一段時間 (*n.*)
✪ Split 分割 (*v.*)
✪ Source 來源 (*n.*)

There have been sporadic pieces of gunfire taking place for a long spell of time between a group of students and a group split away from its source.

學生與從源頭分裂出來的群組間一些零星的擦槍走火事件已經發生了好一長段時間了。

Unit 13

★ KEY 6

- ✪ Span 廣度、全長 (*n.*)
- ✪ Spawn 產卵 (*v.*)
- ✪ Splendor 壯闊的景觀 (*n.*)
- ✪ So far 目前 (*adv.*)

> The pet frog I have had a short span of time just spawned in the pool, which is the splendor I have ever seen in my whole life so far.

我養了一小段時間的寵物青蛙剛剛在池塘中產卵了，這是一幅我人生中從沒見過的壯闊震撼的景象。

★ KEY 7

- ✪ Spark 閃爍 (*v.*)
- ✪ Sparse 稀稀疏疏的 (*a.*)
- ✪ Intermittent 間歇的、斷斷續續的 (*a.*)
- ✪ Burst 爆裂 (*n.*)

> The opinions he raised have sparked off sparse arguments and intermittent bursts of anger between these two parties.

他提出的見解使得兩派間稀稀落落的爭論以及斷斷續續的火藥味都被激活了起來。

★ KEY 8

- ✪ Tempting 誘人的 (*a.*)
- ✪ Swiftly 很快地、即刻地 (*adv.*)
- ✪ Relieve 釋放 (*v.*)
- ✪ Tension 緊繃、壓力 (*n.*)

> A full body massage is such a tempting way to swiftly relieve the tension in your muscles.

全身按摩就是個非常誘人且可以快速釋放身體肌肉緊張壓力的方法。

★ KEY 9

- ✪ Tend 趨向 (*v.*)
- ✪ Teem with 充滿大量 (*v.*)
- ✪ Susceptible 易受影響的、易受感動的 (*a.*)
- ✪ Tailspin 深淵、混亂、困境 (*n.*)

> I tend to go to bed early in a day teeming with rain in that I am so susceptible to bad weather condition that makes me feel like I am in a tailspin.

我傾向於在大雨的日子早點睡，因為我對於這種會讓我感到身陷混亂的壞天氣很敏感。

✪ Tactual 觸覺的、觸覺感官的 (*a.*)
✪ Sensation 感覺、感情 (*n.*)
✪ Tantalize 逗弄 (*v.*)
✪ Realm 領域 (*n.*)

The question pertaining to tactual sensation has long been tantalizing the world's best scientists and experts in different realms of science for a long period time.

有關觸覺的這個問題已經誘惑著世界上最好的幾個科學家以及在科學界不同領域的專家好一段時間了。

✪ Sustenance 生計、食物來源 (*n.*)
✪ Sustain 支援、忍受 (*v.*)
✪ Supplant 排擠掉、替代來源 (*v.*)
✪ Substantial 重要的 (*a.*)

Ancient people got a lot of their sustenance from hunting to sustain life, but since then, buying and selling commodities has supplanted hunting as the substantial way to get food.

古時候人們用打獵來維持生計，但從那時起，商品買賣就已取代狩獵成為人們獲取食物來源最重要的方式。

KEY 12

- ✪ Intrude 入侵 (*v.*)
- ✪ Sumptuous 奢侈的、華麗的 (*a.*)
- ✪ Safeguard 保障、保護 (*v.*)
- ✪ Surveillance 監督、監視 (*n.*)

To prevent thieves from intruding this sumptuous feast, monitors have been set to safeguard our money and personal belongings under video surveillance.

為了避免小偷們入侵這奢華的宴會，顯示器必須裝有監視器來保障錢財跟個人物品。

KEY 13

- ✪ Uncertainty 不確定性 (*n.*)
- ✪ Subsidiary 輔助的、次要的 (*a.*)
- ✪ Approve 批准、贊成 (*v.*)
- ✪ Substitute 替代方案 (*n.*)

The uncertainty of personal safety is subsidiary to this plan, meaning a substitute is required to get the plan approved.

個人安全的不確定性是此計劃所附加的，因此代表必須要有一個替代方案，這個計畫才會被批准。

Unit 13

★ KEY 14

- ✪ Uneasy 心神不寧的、不穩定的 (*a.*)
- ✪ Undergo 經歷、忍受 (*v.*)
- ✪ Ultimately 最終的 (*adv.*)
- ✪ Trauma 外傷、損傷 (*n.*)

I passed an uneasy night after undergoing the great hardship, and the sadness has been ultimately transformed into the trauma I would never recover from.

在經歷嚴重的苦難之後，我過了令人心神不寧的一夜，且這傷痛最終被轉換成我永遠也無法從中痊癒的創傷。

★ KEY 15

- ✪ Endeavor 努力、盡力 (*n.*)
- ✪ Firm 堅固的 (*a.*)
- ✪ Underpinning 支撐、支援 (*n.*)
- ✪ Undertake 承擔 (*v.*)

The endeavors her father has been making have set a firm underpinning for this company, which is about to be undertaken by the new boss.

他父親所做的努力為這個即將有新老闆接管的公司立下了堅固的基礎。

★ KEY 16

- ✪ Ensure 確保 (*v.*)
- ✪ Unanimity 無異議 (*n.*)
- ✪ Remain 保留 (*v.*)
- ✪ Unadorned 未經裝飾的、樸素的 (*a.*)

> We have to ensure that there is unanimity on remaining this apartment unadorned.

我們必須要確認大家對於維持這棟公寓未經裝修是無異議的。

★ KEY 17

- ✪ Rebellion 謀反、叛亂 (*n.*)
- ✪ Turbulent 狂暴的 (*a.*)
- ✪ Trigger 引發 (*v.*)
- ✪ Arrest 逮捕 (*v.*)

> The rebellion launched by turbulent factions was triggered by the series of police arrests.

那些狂暴的小派系引起的謀反是因一連串的警察逮捕行動所引發的。

★ KEY 18

- ✪ Traverse 旅遊、經過 (*v.*)
- ✪ Tracts 遼闊的土地 (*n.*)
- ✪ Thoroughly 徹底地 (*adv.*)
- ✪ Tolerate 寬容、容忍 (*v.*)

The influential adventurer traversed wild and mountainous tracts of land, through which he thoroughly realized how hard it would be to tolerate large amounts of ultraviolet energy.

這位有影響力的冒險家旅行過大片曠野山林，他從這趟旅行中深刻領悟到要忍受大量的紫外線是非常困難的。

★ KEY 19

- ✪ Unsurpassed 非常卓越的 (*a.*)
- ✪ Unprecedented 空前的 (*a.*)
- ✪ Truism 眾所周知的事、自明之理 (*n.*)
- ✪ Variation 變動 (*n.*)

According to the unsurpassed project the scholar presented, we are about to enter the unprecedented prosperity; however, the truism is still there denoting destiny is always subject to variation.

根據這位學者所提出的卓越計畫，我們正要進入空前的繁榮，但是大家都知道命運永遠是充滿著變數的。

★ KEY 20

- ✪ Utilitarian 實用的 (*a.*)
- ✪ Appealing 吸引人的 (*a.*)
- ✪ Warrant 批准、證明 (*v.*)
- ✪ Underlying 潛在的、根本的 (*a.*)

> The plan of providing utilitarian student accommodation is appealing to everyone attending the meeting, but statistics is still needed to warrant the underlying merits the school will get.

提供實用的學生住宿對所有來參與會議的人來說都是很吸引人的，但這還是需要數據來證明學校方面可能會因此得到的好處。

Unit 13

Unsurpassed	Synonym	Supreme/ incomparable
	Antonym	Inferior
Unprecedented	Synonym	Exceptional / extraordinary
	Antonym	Common/ customary
Tolerate	Synonym	Allow/indulge/ abide
	Antonym	Deny/ disallow/abstain
Subsidiary	Synonym	Supplementary/ secondary
	Antonym	Chief/ main
Intrude	Synonym	Interrupt/ interfere/ invade
	Antonym	Erase/ please
Sumptuous	Synonym	Luxurious/ splendid/ deluxe
	Antonym	Economical/ destitute
Traverse	Synonym	Cross over/ pass through
	Antonym	Stay/ back up
Appealing	Synonym	Attractive/ engaging
	Antonym	Repulsive
Warrant	Synonym	Guarantee/ justify/ approve
	Antonym	Deny/ disallow/ refuse
Safeguard	Synonym	Protect/ defend/ ensure
	Antonym	Destroy/ endanger
Endeavor	Synonym	Aim/ effort
	Antonym	Inactivity/ passivity

Underlying	Synonym	Fundamental/ basic/ elemental
	Antonym	Secondary
Turbulent	Synonym	Chaotic/ quarrelsome
	Antonym	Agreeable/ gentle
Trigger	Synonym	Bring about/ cause/ generate
	Antonym	Destroy/ prevent
Ensure	Synonym	Guarantee/assure/ safeguard
	Antonym	Endanger/ injure
Susceptible	Synonym	Affected/ impressionable/ responsive
	Antonym	Insensitive
Stringent	Synonym	Rigid/ tight/ demanding
	Antonym	Amenable/ calm
Sustain	Synonym	Maintain/ bolster/ preserve
	Antonym	Hinder/ obstruct
Supplant	Synonym	Displace/ replace
	Antonym	Surrender
Tantalize	Synonym	Provoke/ entice
	Antonym	Assist/ encourage

Unit 13

攻克要點I 必考字彙表

KEY1

Participant 參與者 (n.)

Overt 明顯的 (a.)

Overlook 沒注意到 (v.)

Outrage 凌辱、觸犯 (v.)

KEY2

Incorporate 合併 (v.)

Conservative 保守的 (a.)

Blend 使混合 (v.)

Empirical 以經驗為依據的 (a.)

KEY3

Impose 施加影響、把⋯強加於 (v.)

Bizarre 奇異的 (a.)

Restrictions 限制、約束 (n.)

Assemblage 集合、裝配 (n.)

KEY4

Adherent 擁護者、追隨者 (n.)

Surrounding 附近的 (a.)

Absorb 吸收 (v.)

Rapidly 快速地 (adv.)

KEY5

Erratic 不穩定的、奇怪的 (a.)

Eradicate 根除、滅絕 (v.)

Thoroughly 徹底地 (adv.)

Transient 短暫的、瞬間的 (a.)

KEY6

Drastically 激烈地、徹底地 (adv.)

Duplicate 複製品 (n.)

Reveal 透露、顯示 (v.)

Dispute 爭論 (n.)

KEY7

Distinguish 識別、辨認出 (v.)

Distinction 區別、差別 (n.)

Discrepant 有差異的 (a.)

Dispositions 性情 (n.)

KEY8

Continual 持續不斷的 (a.)

Interruptions 阻礙、打擾 (n.)

Doom 末日 (v.)

Countervailing 補償、抵銷 (a.)

KEY9

Constellation 燦爛的一群；星座 (n.)

Convert 轉變、轉換 (v.)

Consistent 一致的 (a.)

Interior 室內的 (a.)

KEY10

Contemplate 沉思、深思熟慮 (v.)

Deluxe 豪華的 (a.)

Detractor 誹謗者 (n.)

Debate 辯論 (v.)

KEY11

Inveterate 根深的、成癖的 (a.)

Chisel 雕 (v.)

Exquisite 精緻的、敏銳的 (a.)

Resemblance 相似處 (n.)

KEY12

Beckon 向…示意、召喚 (v.)

Cautiously 小心地 (adv.)

Bulk 大批 (n.)

Brittle 易碎的 (a.)

KEY13

Channel 引導、付出 (v.)

Be inclined to 傾向於 (a.)

Boost up 增加、推進 (v.)

Boast 吹牛 (v.)

KEY14

Beforehand 預先、事先 (*adv.*)　　Burgeon 萌芽、急速成長 (*v.*)

Bring about 引起 (*v.*)　　Chaotic 混亂的 (*a.*)

KEY15

Nocturnal 夜的 (*a.*)　　appealing 有吸引力的 (*a.*)

Zoologist 動物學家 (*n.*)　　Withstand 抵抗、經得起 (*v.*)

KEY16

Agilely 靈活地、敏捷地 (*adv.*)　　Wield 運用 (*v.*)

Unprecedented 空前的 (*a.*)　　Excellence 優秀、卓越 (*n.*)

KEY17

Fateful 宿命的、重大的 (*a.*)　　Irreparable 不能修補的 (*a.*)

Disguise 假裝、隱藏 (*v.*)　　Empire 帝國 (*n.*)

KEY18

Liberal 慷慨的、寬大的 (*a.*)　　Intrinsic 本質的 (*a.*)

Ingenious 聰明、靈敏的 (*a.*)　　Genuine 真誠的、誠懇的 (*a.*)

KEY19

Urge 催促 (*v.*)　　Preserve 保存 (*v.*)

Heritage 遺產、傳統 (*n.*)　　Found wanting 需要改進的 (*a.*)

KEY20

Disentangle 解開 (*v.*)　　Domestic 家庭的 (*a.*)

Refuse 拒絕 (*v.*)　　Dictate 命令 (*v.*)

攻克要點II 超給力例句

★ **KEY 1** ♪ MP3 14

✪ Participant 參與者 (*n.*)
✪ Overlook 沒注意到 (*v.*)
✪ Overt 明顯的 (*a.*)
✪ Outrage 凌辱、觸犯 (*v.*)

> The participant's behavior that he overlooked an overt point that might invoke another set of problems, extremely outraged his administrator.

這位參與者忽略了一個很明顯且會導致其他問題產生的一點，這樣的行為嚴重的惹怒了他的負責人。

★ **KEY 2**

✪ Incorporate 合併 (*v.*)
✪ Blend 使混合 (*v.*)
✪ Conservative 保守的 (*a.*)
✪ Empirical 以經驗為依據的 (*a.*)

He attempts to incorporate other scholars' opinions into his paper and to blend conservative and modern thoughts together to elaborate his teaching practices, based on empirical evidence.

他嘗試著合併其他學者的意見並放入他的論文中，並且試著混合保守與現代的想法進一步以經驗主義為基礎來闡釋他的教學實踐。

KEY 3

✪ Impose 施加影響、把…強加於 (*v.*)
✪ Restrictions 限制、約束 (*n.*)
✪ Bizarre 奇異的 (*a.*)
✪ Assemblage 集合、裝配 (*n.*)

The government has imposed new restrictions to the Internet usage to ensure information security; it is, however, totally bizarre to see an assemblage of alarming messages popping up on your computer screen.

政府頒布並實施網路使用的限制來確保資訊安全，然而看到一堆警告視窗在你的電腦螢幕上跳出來時，是一件令人感到很奇怪的事。

KEY 4

✪ Adherent 擁護者、追隨者 (*n.*)
✪ Absorb 吸收 (*v.*)
✪ Surrounding 附近的 (*a.*)
✪ Rapidly 快速地 (*adv.*)

> Adherents of this city reform movement suggest absorbing surrounding villages into the rapidly growing city.

城市改良運動的擁護者建議把周圍的鄉村都給吸進這個快速成長的城市。

KEY 5

✪ Erratic 不穩定的、奇怪的 (*a.*)
✪ Thoroughly 徹底地 (*adv.*)
✪ Eradicate 根除、滅絕 (*v.*)
✪ Transient 短暫的、瞬間的 (*a.*)

> The erratic schedule thoroughly eradicates the transient happiness I have ever had since I started working in this company.

這個不穩定的行程徹底的毀了自從我進這公司以來所擁有的短暫快樂。

Unit 14

✪ Drastically 激烈地、徹底地 (*adv.*)
✪ Duplicate 複製品 (*n.*)
✪ Reveal 透露、顯示 (*v.*)
✪ Dispute 爭論 (*n.*)

The examination drastically reveals that this is just a duplicate rather than the original one, and the exact cause of this accident is still in dispute.

這檢查全然地揭露這只是一個複製品而不是原作，並且造成這個意外的確切原因還在爭論當中。

✪ Distinguish 識別、辨認出 (*v.*)
✪ Distinction 區別、差別 (*n.*)
✪ Discrepant 有差異的 (*a.*)
✪ Dispositions 性情 (*n.*)

The two best friends are so alike that no one can even distinguish one from the other, yet their parents can still tell the distinction from their discrepant dispositions.

這兩個好朋友實在是太相似了，以致於沒有人可以區分他們兩個，但是他們的父母親還是可以從他們不相同的性情看出差別。

★ KEY 8

- ✪ Continual 持續不斷的 (*a.*)
- ✪ Interruptions 阻礙、打擾 (*n.*)
- ✪ Doom 末日 (*v.*)
- ✪ Countervailing 補償、抵銷 (*a.*)

> Due to the lack of ability to cope with continual interruptions, the project was doomed from the start without any countervailing advantages.

由於缺乏處理持續不斷的阻礙的能力，這個計畫從一開始就註定失敗且沒有任何可以補償的優勢。

★ KEY 9

- ✪ Constellation 燦爛的一群；星座 (*n.*)
- ✪ Convert 轉變、轉換 (*v.*)
- ✪ Consistent 一致的 (*a.*)
- ✪ Interior 室內的 (*a.*)

> A constellation of talented carpenters converted the room from a walk-in closet to a kitchen with its design being consistent with the interior design of the entire apartment.

一群天才般的工匠們把這個房間從一個可走進的衣櫥轉變為廚房，其設計與整棟公寓的室內設計相一致。

★ KEY 10

✪ Contemplate 沉思、深思熟慮 (*v.*)
✪ Deluxe 豪華的 (*a.*)
✪ Detractor 誹謗者 (*n.*)
✪ Debate 辯論 (*v.*)

The architect is standing there contemplating how delicate this deluxe chandelier is but simultaneously thinking that how come there are still detractors debating about the truthfulness of this magnificent work.

這位建築師站著，靜靜的沉思這個如此細緻豪華的吊燈，但也同時想著為什們還會有誹謗者對於這個傑作的真實性做辯論。

★ KEY 11

✪ Inveterate 根深的、成癖的 (*a.*)
✪ Chisel 雕 (*v.*)
✪ Exquisite 精緻的、敏銳的 (*a.*)
✪ Resemblance 相似處 (*n.*)

The inveterate sculptor chiseled the regular stone into an exquisite statue that has a certain degree of resemblance to another work.

雕刻成癖的雕刻師把這個平凡無奇的石頭雕刻成一個精緻且有一定程度上與其他作品相似的雕像。

★ KEY 12

- ✪ Beckon 向…示意、召喚 (*v.*)
- ✪ Cautiously 小心地 (*adv.*)
- ✪ Bulk 大批 (*n.*)
- ✪ Brittle 易碎的 (*a.*)

> She beckons to me asking me to cautiously carry the bags because the grapes she got in bulk are as brittle as thin glasses.

她示意我過來要我小心地提著袋子，因為她買的一大袋葡萄就跟玻璃一樣的脆弱。

★ KEY 13

- ✪ Channel 引導、付出 (*v.*)
- ✪ Be inclined to 傾向於 (*a.*)
- ✪ Boost up 增加、推進 (*v.*)
- ✪ Boast 吹牛 (*v.*)

> Even though we all know every member channels their energies into this project, he is still inclined to boast of his success focusing on how "he", rather than the whole team, boosts up the productivity of the team.

縱使我們都清楚每一個成員都對這個計畫付出了很多的心力，這位先生還是傾向於吹噓他的成功且關注在「他」如何促進團隊的生產力，而不是整個團隊。

★ KEY 14

✪ Beforehand 預先、事先 (*adv.*)
✪ Burgeon 萌芽、急速成長 (*v.*)
✪ Bring about 引起 (*v.*)
✪ Chaotic 混亂的 (*a.*)

Scholars have been aware of the problem beforehand that the burgeoning population must be one of the main reasons bringing about the chaotic situation in developing countries.

學者們已經事先察覺到問題，這問題指出人口急速成長是導致開發中國家混亂情勢的其中一個主因。

★ KEY 15

✪ Nocturnal 夜的 (*a.*)
✪ Widely appealing 有吸引力的 (*a.*)
✪ Zoologist 動物學家 (*n.*)
✪ Withstand 抵抗、經得起 (*v.*)

Nocturnal creatures, such as owls are widely appealing to some zoologists because it is even more effortless for them to withstand attacks and wind.

夜行性動物例如貓頭鷹，對於動物學家來說是非常有吸引力的，因為對貓頭鷹來說，抵抗攻擊及強風是輕而易舉的事。

★ KEY 16

✪ Agilely 靈活地、敏捷地 (*adv.*)
✪ Wield 運用 (*v.*)
✪ Unprecedented 空前的 (*a.*)
✪ Excellence 優秀、卓越 (*n.*)

> The emperor agilely and flexibly wielded authority and power to push the country to an unprecedented level of excellence.

這國王靈活及彈性地運用他的權威跟權力把這個國家推到一個空前的盛世。

★ KEY 17

✪ Fateful 宿命的、重大的 (*a.*)
✪ Irreparable 不能修補的 (*a.*)
✪ Disguise 假裝、隱藏 (*v.*)
✪ Empire 帝國 (*n.*)

> The fateful decision has caused an irreparable harm to this country, and no one can possibly disguise the fall of the empire.

Unit 14

這個重大的決定已經對這個國家造成不可挽回的傷害，沒有人可以隱藏這個國家即將衰亡的事實。

★ KEY 18

✪ Liberal 慷慨的、寬大的 (*a.*)
✪ Intrinsic 本質的 (*a.*)
✪ Ingenious 聰明、靈敏的 (*a.*)
✪ Genuine 真誠的、誠懇的 (*a.*)

> She has a liberal attitude to relationship, thinking that a man's intrinsic worth arises from how ingenious and genuine he is, rather than how much he owns.

她對於情感關係保持著寬容的態度，並認為說一個男人的自身價值不在於他有多富有，而在於他聰明與誠懇的態度。

★ KEY 19

✪ Urge 催促 (*v.*)
✪ Preserve 保存 (*v.*)
✪ Heritage 遺產、傳統 (*n.*)
✪ Found wanting 需要改進的 (*a.*)

> The States urges us to work even harder to preserve our architectural heritage in that the heritage protection project we presented was found wanting.

美國方面催促我們要在保存我們的建築遺產上多下點功夫，因為我們對遺產保護的計畫並不夠周全。

★ KEY 20

✪ Disentangle 解開 (*v.*)
✪ Domestic 家庭的 (*a.*)
✪ Refuse 拒絕 (*v.*)
✪ Dictate 命令 (*v.*)

> The poor little boy is attempting to disentangle himself from domestic violence because he refuses to be dictated by his parents anymore.

這個可憐的小男孩試圖把他自己從家暴中抽離出來，因為他拒絕再被他的父母所命令了。

Dictate	Synonym	Govern/guide/ impose
	Antonym	Disallow/ mismanage
Refuse	Synonym	Deny/ decline/ turn down
	Antonym	Accept/ allow
Domestic	Synonym	Indigenous/ internal /national
	Antonym	Alien/ foreign
Disentangle	Synonym	Disconnect/ detach / emancipate
	Antonym	Attach/ connect
Contemplate	Synonym	Consider/ ponder/ propose
	Antonym	Disregard/ Discard
Urge	Synonym	Encourage/ advocate/ compel
	Antonym	Disapprove/ discourage
Intrinsic	Synonym	Basic/ elemental /underlying
	Antonym	Acquired/ learned
Ingenious	Synonym	Clever/ brilliant / intelligent
	Antonym	Dull/ foolish
Disguise	Synonym	Deceive/cloak/ conceal
	Antonym	Disclose/expose
Irreparable	Synonym	Irreversible/ irreplaceable
	Antonym	Fixable/ replaceable
Fateful	Synonym	Deadly/ calamitous/ catastrophic/
	Antonym	Blessed/ fortunate

Agile	Synonym	Buoyant/ frisky
	Antonym	Depressed/ dull
Wield	Synonym	Control/ use/ exert/ employ
	Antonym	Ignore/misuse
Eradicate	Synonym	Abolish/ eliminate/ exterminate
	Antonym	Bear/ ratify/ construct
Chaotic	Synonym	Anarchic/ disorganized/ turbulent
	Antonym	Harmonized/ ordered/ systematic
Bring about	Synonym	Accomplish/ achieve/ generate
	Antonym	Destroy/ fail/ halt
Burgeoning	Synonym	Bloom/ prosper/ sprout
	Antonym	Decline/ decrease/ diminish
Incline	Synonym	Tend toward/ bend/ impel
	Antonym	Prevent/ depress/ suppress
Boost	Synonym	Improve/advance/ promote
	Antonym	Decrease/ hinder/ discourage
Boast	Synonym	Brag/ bombast
	Antonym	Humility/ modesty

Unit 14

攻克要點I 必考字彙表

KEY1
Rigid 堅硬的 (*a.*)	Attempt 嘗試 (*v.*)
Delve 探究、搜索、挖掘 (*v.*)	Combat 戰鬥 (*v.*)

KEY2
Exuberant 繁茂的、豐富的、興高采烈活躍的 (*a.*)	Commencement 畢業典禮 (*n.*)
Interrupt 打斷、妨礙 (*v.*)	Diligent 勤奮的 (*a.*)

KEY3
Pedantic 學究式的、迂腐的 (*a.*)	Endure 忍受 (*v.*)
Discrete 不連續的、離散的 (*a.*)	Equivalent 相等的、同等的 (*a.*)

KEY4
Indulge 遷就、放任 (*v.*)	Relinquish 放棄、撤出 (*v.*)
Permanently 永久地 (*adv.*)	Deprive 剝奪、使喪失 (*v.*)

KEY5
Conform 符合、使一致 (*v.*)	Cogent 世人信服的 (*a.*)
Comprehensively 全面地 (*adv.*)	Enhance 增高 (*v.*)

KEY6

Contemporary 當代的 (*a.*)	Conscious 有意識的、知覺的 (*a.*)
Deliberately 刻意地 (*adv.*)	Discrepancy 差異 (*n.*)

KEY7

Pretentious 自命不凡的 (*a.*)	Precipitous 陡峭的、急躁的 (*a.*)
Significance 重要性 (*n.*)	Debate 爭論、辯論 (*n.*)

KEY8

Commercial 商業化的 (*a.*)	Propaganda 宣傳活動 (*n.*)
Invigorate 賦予精神、鼓舞 (*v.*)	Exponential 指數的、快速增長的 (*a.*)

KEY9

Revolution 革命 (*n.*)	Acceleration 加速、促進 (*n.*)
Appalling 駭人可怕的 (*a.*)	Rampant 猛烈的、猖獗的 (*a.*)

KEY10

Fundamental 基本的 (*a.*)	Assumption 推測 (*n.*)
Supply 提供 (*n.*)	Escalating 逐步擴大 (*a.*)

KEY11

Discriminate 區別 (*v.*)	Difference 不同 (*n.*)
Disparage 貶低、毀謗 (*v.*)	Optical 視覺的 (*a.*)

KEY12

Impetus 推動力、衝力 (*n.*)	Reward 獎賞、報酬 (*n.*)
Debunk 揭穿；暴露 (*v.*)	Flourish 繁榮、興盛 (*v.*)

KEY13

Formidable 強大的、艱難的 (*a.*)	Historic 有歷史性的 (*a.*)
Witness 目擊到 (*v.*)	Depict 描繪 (*v.*)

Unit 15

KEY14

Obviously 明顯地 (*adv.*)	Confusing 令人困惑的 (*a.*)
Perplex 使困惑 (*v.*)	Infer 推論 (*v.*)

KEY15

Even though 縱使 (*conj.*)	Gather 集合、聚集 (*v.*)
Judge 評論 (*v.*)	Dominate 支配、控制 (*v.*)

KEY16

Ensure 確保 (*v.*)	Gain 取得 (*v.*)
Conversely 相反地 (*adv.*)	Discard 拋棄 (*v.*)

KEY17

Affect 影響 (*v.*)	Deal with 處理 (*v.*)
Dilemma 困境 (*n.*)	Uncertainty 不確定 (*n.*)

KEY18

Harness 使用 (*v.*)	Subconsciously 下意識地 (*adv.*)
Adjust 調整 (*v.*)	Regulate 管理 (*v.*)

KEY19

Intruder 入侵者 (*n.*)	Ancestor 祖先 (*n.*)
Elevation 海拔 (*n.*)	Dwellings 居住地 (*n.*)

KEY20

Traumatic 創傷的 (*a.*)	Resist 抵抗 (*v.*)
Interact 相互作用 (*v.*)	Connections 關聯 (*n.*)

攻克要點 II 超給力例句

★ **KEY 1** ♪ MP3 15

⚙ Rigid 堅硬的 (*a.*)
⚙ Attempt 嘗試 (*v.*)
⚙ Delve 探究、搜索、挖掘 (*v.*)
⚙ Combat 戰鬥 (*v.*)

> Faced with rigid environmental issues, experts have been attempting to delve into the latest research to find out possible ways to combat these threatening phenomena.

面對生硬難解決的環境議題時，專家已經嘗試去探究最新的研究來找出可能的方法去打擊這些有威脅性的現象。

★ **KEY 2**

⚙ Exuberant 繁茂的、豐富的、興高采烈活躍的 (*a.*)
⚙ Commencement 畢業典禮 (*n.*)
⚙ Interrupt 打斷、妨礙 (*v.*)
⚙ Diligent 勤奮的 (*a.*)

Unit 15

Exuberant crowds and parents rush into the Franklin arena in which the commencement of the year of 2015 is held; however, it completely interrupts students who have been unceasingly diligent in the pursuit of their future in the nearby library.

歡騰的群眾們及家長們擁入舉辦2015畢業典禮的富蘭克林運動場，這同時打斷了正在附近圖書館不停地用功、追求他們未來的學生們。

★ KEY 3

- ✪ Pedantic 學究式的、迂腐的 (*a.*)
- ✪ Endure 忍受 (*v.*)
- ✪ Discrete 不連續的、離散的 (*a.*)
- ✪ Equivalent 相等的、同等的 (*a.*)

It is so hard for this pedantic scholar to endure discrete opinions and thoughts raised by other researchers in that he does not think people are equivalent.

對於這賣弄學問、迂腐的學者來說，要忍受來自其他研究者的不同意見跟想法是非常困難的，因為他不認為人是相等的。

★ KEY 4

- ✪ Indulge 遷就、放任 (*v.*)
- ✪ Relinquish 放棄、撤出 (*v.*)
- ✪ Permanently 永久地 (*adv.*)

✪ Deprive 剝奪、使喪失 (*v.*)

> This murderer was raised by strangers who had indulged him in the ways they would have never done with their children, making him relinquish his education, family, and his future and permanently deprive him of this society.

這個殺人犯是被陌生人以一種不會對自己孩子教養的一種放任方式來放任他做任何事撫養長大的，這樣使得這位殺人犯放棄了他的教育、家庭、以及他的未來，並且永久使他脫離這個社會。

★ KEY 5

✪ Conform 符合、使一致 (*v.*)
✪ Cogent 世人信服的 (*a.*)
✪ Comprehensively 全面地 (*adv.*)
✪ Enhance 增高 (*v.*)

> These changes, conforming to the requirements and the plan we set, were cogent and could comprehensively enhance our productivity at work.

這個有符合我們所設定的要求與計畫的改變，是可以使人信服且可以全面提升我們的工作生產力的。

★ KEY 6

✪ Contemporary 當代的 (*a.*)

✪ Conscious 有意識的、知覺的 (*a.*)

✪ Deliberately 刻意地 (*adv.*)

✪ Discrepancy 差異 (*n.*)

> The contemporary world is a race-conscious society in which people, such as humanitarians and any other types of volunteers are deliberately trained to understand the discrepancies between races and to make individuals accept the differences between themselves and others.

現在的世界是個有種族意識的社會，其中人們例如人道主義者及其他的自願者被刻意的訓練要去了解不同種族間的差異，並且要讓個人接受他們與其他人的不同處。

⭐ KEY 7

✪ Pretentious 自命不凡的 (*a.*)

✪ Precipitous 陡峭的、急躁的 (*a.*)

✪ Significance 重要性 (*n.*)

✪ Debate 爭論、辯論 (*n.*)

> Those pretentious governors soon regreted the precipitous reactions they have had at the earlier of significance international conference, and no one could possibly help them escape from the coming debate.

我們那些自命不凡的政府官員們馬上就後悔他們在早先重要的國際會議中所做的那些急躁的回應，並且沒有人可以幫助他們逃離即將到來的爭論。

★ KEY 8

✪ Commercial 商業化的 (*a.*)
✪ Propaganda 宣傳活動 (*n.*)
✪ Invigorate 賦予精神、鼓舞 (*v.*)
✪ Exponential 指數的、快速增長的 (*a.*)

> This commercial propaganda eventually invigorated industrialized reforms, giving rise to exponential population growth.

這商業化的宣傳活動最後鼓舞了工業化的改革，並導致了如快速成長的人口。

★ KEY 9

✪ Revolution 革命 (*n.*)
✪ Acceleration 加速、促進 (*n.*)
✪ Appalling 駭人可怕的 (*a.*)
✪ Rampant 猛烈的、猖獗的 (*a.*)

Even though we all know that Industrial Revolution has already caused appalling living conditions because of the rampant changes, it still contributes to an acceleration of the population growth.

即使我們都知道工業革命是因為過於猛烈的改變導致可怕的生活環境，其依舊有助於促進人口快速成長。

⭐ KEY 10

✪ Fundamental 基本的 (*a.*)
✪ Assumption 推測 (*n.*)
✪ Supply 提供 (*n.*)
✪ Escalating 逐步擴大 (*a.*)

The fundamental assumption to the population growth in human history is that the increasing raise of food supply led to the escalating population growth.

對於人類歷史上人口成長基本的推測是，因為食物供給的增加導致人口加速成長。

⭐ KEY 11

✪ Discriminate 區別 (*v.*)
✪ Difference 不同 (*n.*)
✪ Disparage 貶低、毀謗 (*v.*)

✪ Optical 視覺的 (*a.*)

> This system can discriminate any micro differences, even colors of eyes, but somehow it may disparage children with certain optical diseases.

這個系統可以區別任何些微的差異，甚至是眼睛的顏色，但是可能或多或少它會貶低患有視覺疾病的孩童們。

⭐ **KEY 12**

✪ Impetus 推動力、衝力 (*n.*)
✪ Reward 獎賞、報酬 (*n.*)
✪ Debunk 揭穿；暴露 (*v.*)
✪ Flourish 繁榮、興盛 (*v.*)

> This reward is an impetus that has movie makers come and share their creations and whomever the best director goes to, no one would debunk the decision and keep flourishing movie industry and their career.

這獎賞是作為一個推動力去讓電影工作者分享他們的創意，不論最佳導演獎落誰家，沒有人會指出這個決定的不對，並且會繼續使電影產業以及他們的事業蓬勃發展。

⭐ **KEY 13**

✪ Formidable 強大的、艱難的 (*a.*)

✪ Historic 有歷史性的 (*a.*)

✪ Witness 目擊到 (*v.*)

✪ Depict 描繪 (*v.*)

It is such a formidable and historic moment yet even people who have been living here for a life time might not have witnessed it; however, they still can see from the cave painting depicting the battle in greater details than any other documents.

這是個如此強大且富有歷史性的時刻，即使一輩子都居住在這的人也可能沒有親眼目睹過；然而，他們還是可以從比任何其他的資料都還要仔細描繪戰爭細節的洞穴壁畫中窺知一二。

⭐ KEY 14

✪ Obviously 明顯地 (*adv.*)

✪ Confusing 令人困惑地 (*a.*)

✪ Perplex 使困惑 (*v.*)

✪ Infer 推論 (*v.*)

Obviously, those questions are quite confusing, and the given instructions perplex all the students even more, letting them hardly infer the meanings.

很明顯地，這些問題令人感到困惑，加上所給的指示使所有的學生更加疑惑，讓大家都很難去推測意思。

★ KEY 15

- ✪ Even though 縱使 (*conj.*)
- ✪ Gather 集合、聚集 (*v.*)
- ✪ Judge 評論 (*v.*)
- ✪ Dominate 支配、控制 (*v.*)

> Even though all required information has been thoroughly and accurately gathered, we still cannot judge whether or not he was able to dominate most part of America back in 1800s.

即使所有必需的資訊都已經完全且準確地收集好了，我們還是無法評論他是否能在19世紀支配大部分的美洲。

★ KEY 16

- ✪ Ensure 確保 (*v.*)
- ✪ Gain 取得 (*v.*)
- ✪ Conversely 相反地 (*adv.*)
- ✪ Discard 拋棄 (*v.*)

> Before making any decision, you definitely have to ensure what you intend to gain from this and, conversely, what you might discard from this.

在做任何決定之前，你一定要確定你想要從中取得的東西，並且相反的來說，你有可能會因此而拋棄的東西。

★ KEY 17

✪ Affect 影響 (*v.*)
✪ Deal with 處理 (*v.*)
✪ Dilemma 困境 (*n.*)
✪ Uncertainty 不確定 (*n.*)

Changes that uncertainties contribute to may affect the way you deal with the dilemma.

在不確定下造成的改變可能會影響你處理困境的方式。

★ KEY 18

✪ Harness 使用 (*v.*)
✪ Subconsciously 下意識地 (*adv.*)
✪ Adjust 調整 (*v.*)
✪ Regulate 管理 (*v.*)

The innovative medical therapy can be harnessed specifically for patients to subconsciously adjust their breathing rates and further, regulate the levels of carbon dioxide.

這個創新的醫學治療法可特別使用於讓病人潛意識地自行調整他們的呼吸頻率，並且進一步的管理二氧化碳的程度。

KEY 19

✪ Intruder 入侵者 (*n.*)
✪ Ancestor 祖先 (*n.*)
✪ Elevation 海拔 (*n.*)
✪ Dwellings 居住地 (*n.*)

> Two thousand years ago, as intruders moved in, our ancestors were forced to move their fields to the lower elevations and then they; thus, formed the largest communal dwellings in this region.

兩千年前，當入侵者移來時，我們的祖先就被迫把他們的家園移到低海拔的區域並且建造了那個地區中最大的公有居住地。

KEY 20

✪ Traumatic 創傷的 (*a.*)
✪ Resist 抵抗 (*v.*)
✪ Interact 相互作用 (*v.*)
✪ Connections 關聯 (*n.*)

> Thousands of people dwelling in this town were traumatic and; thus, resisted to interact with people coming from other towns who were extremely willing to assist them in restoring connections with the world.

住在這個城鎮的數千民眾受到創傷，因此不願意與從其他城鎮來幫助他們恢復跟這個世界做連結的人交流。

Unit 15

Traumatic	Synonym	Alarming/ atrocious/ appalling
	Antonym	Comforting/ pleasing
Conscious	Synonym	Attentive/ aware / informed
	Antonym	Careless/ doubtful/ dubious
Pretentious	Synonym	Conceited/ snobbish/ pompous
	Antonym	Genuine/ moderate/ modest
Invigorate	Synonym	Stimulate/ excite/ energize
	Antonym	Bore/ discourage/ dissuade
Harness	Synonym	Exploit/ utilize/ tame
	Antonym	Allow/ detach/ liberate
Dilemma	Synonym	Crisis/ difficulty/ predicament
	Antonym	Solution/ benefit/ advantage
Ensure	Synonym	Guarantee/ assure/ insure
	Antonym	Endanger/ injure/ deny
Gain	Synonym	Acquire/ achieve/ attain
	Antonym	Decline/ decrease/ depart
Discard	Synonym	Get rid of/ abandon/ dispose of
	Antonym	Accept/ allow/ approve
Gather	Synonym	Assemble/ cluster/ congregate
	Antonym	Disperse/ scatter/ dissemble
Judge	Synonym	Assess/ conclude/ criticize
	Antonym	Ignore/ hesitate/ disregard

Dominate	Synonym	Command/ control/ dictate
	Antonym	Lose/ neglect / mismanage
Infer	Synonym	Conclude/ ascertain/ deduce
	Antonym	Abstain/ disbelieve
Perplex	Synonym	Complicate/ compound/ baffle
	Antonym	Clarify/ enlighten
Relinquish	Synonym	Abandon/abdicate/quit
	Antonym	Assert/ claim/ continue
Debate	Synonym	Argue/ discuss/ contest/ deliberate
	Antonym	Agree/ endorse
Witness	Synonym	Observe/ attend/ notice
	Antonym	Ignore/ neglect/ overlook
drastic	Synonym	Extreme/ severe/ harsh/ radical
	Antonym	Calm/ mild
Flourish	Synonym	Grow/ prosper/ bloom
	Antonym	Decrease/ fail/ lesson
Indulge	Synonym	Spoil/ satisfy
	Antonym	Deprive/dissatisfy

Unit 16

攻克要點I 必考字彙表

KEY1

Consider 考慮、認為 (*v.*)

Financial 財政 (*a.*)

Influential 有影響力的 (*a.*)

Transition 過度、轉變 (*n.*)

KEY2

Achieve 達成 (*v.*)

Challenge 挑戰 (*n.*)

Cooperation 合作 (*n.*)

Pivotal 樞軸的、關鍵的 (*a.*)

KEY3

Incorrect 不正確的 (*a.*)

Submitted 提交 (*v.*)

Modified 修正 (*v.*)

Review 考察、評論 (*n.*)

KEY4

Hand out 分發 (*v.*)

Ensure 確保 (*v.*)

Diagram 圖表 (*n.*)

Familiar 熟悉的、常見的 (*a.*)

KEY5

Explanation 解釋、說明 (*n.*)

Suspect 懷疑、猜想 (*v.*)

Extinction 滅絕 (*n.*)

According to 根據 (*preposition*)

KEY6

Demonstrate 展示、論證 (*v.*)

Considerable 大量的、可觀的 (*a.*)

Accomplish 完成 (*v.*)

Controversy 爭論、論戰 (*n.*)

KEY7

No matter 不論 (*conj.*)	Candidate 候選者 (*n.*)
Opponent 對手、反對者 (*n.*)	Contradict 反駁、牴觸 (*v.*)

KEY8

Qualified 有資格的 (*a.*)	Evidence 證明 (*v.*)
Migrate 遷移 (*v.*)	Survive 存活 (*v.*)

KEY9

Treat 對待 (*v.*)	Force 強迫 (*v.*)
Unstable 不穩定的 (*a.*)	Endure 忍受 (*v.*)

KEY10

Infer 作推論 (*v.*)	Elaborate 闡述 (*v.*)
Viewpoints 觀點 (*n.*)	Associated 使有關連 (*v.*)

KEY11

Summarize 總結、摘要 (*v.*)	Interpret 闡釋 (*v.*)
Solution 解決方法 (*n.*)	Crisis 危機 (*n.*)

KEY12

Documentary 紀錄的 (*a.*)	Expose 揭露、曝光 (*v.*)
Disappear 消失 (*v.*)	Opportunity 機會 (*n.*)

KEY13

Examination 檢查 (*n.*)	Respiratory 呼吸的 (*a.*)
Reveal 透露 (*v.*)	Contain 包含 (*v.*)

KEY14

Convey 傳遞 (*v.*)	Extraordinary 非凡的 (*a.*)
Alternative 替代的 (*a.*)	Affect 影響 (*v.*)

KEY15

Surpass 凌駕、超越 (*v.*)	Aspects 面向 (*n.*)
Problematic 有問題的 (*a.*)	Fantastic 幻想的、奇妙的 (*a.*)

Unit 16

KEY16

Prescript 命令、法規 (*n.*)	Manipulate 操作 (*v.*)
Decompose 分解 (*v.*)	Float 漂浮 (*v.*)

KEY17

Schema 輪廓、概要 (*n.*)	Sedentary 久坐的 (*a.*)
Chronic 慢性的 (*a.*)	Sensitive 敏感的 (*a.*)

KEY18

Uptake 攝取 (*n.*)	Cultivate 培養 (*v.*)
Exploit 利用 (*v.*)	Visual 視覺的 (*a.*)

KEY19

Crouch 捲曲、蹲 (*v.*)	Scrutinize 詳細檢查 (*v.*)
Wreck 殘骸 (*n.*)	Vanish 消失不見 (*v.*)

KEY20

Procedure 過程 (*n.*)	Precipitation 降水 (*n.*)
Primary 主要的 (*a.*)	Features 特色 (*n.*)

攻克要點 II 超給力例句

★ KEY 1 ♪ MP3 16

✪ Consider 考慮、認為 (*v.*)
✪ Influential 有影響力的 (*a.*)
✪ Financial 財政 (*a.*)
✪ Transition 過度、轉變 (*n.*)

> Mr. Chen, considered to be a tremendously influential push to the financial and economic situations in China, has been attempting to the transition of the current state to a new page in the following few years.

陳先生被認為是中國經濟財政有影響力的推手，他嘗試著要在接下來的幾年把現況轉變為新的一頁。

★ KEY 2

✪ Achieve 達成 (*v.*)
✪ Cooperation 合作 (*n.*)
✪ Challenge 挑戰 (*n.*)
✪ Pivotal 樞軸的、關鍵的 (*a.*)

Since people have already achieved their goals in food and water supplies, cooperation between people and the outside world would be the next upcoming challenge that is pivotal for human survival as well.

因為人們已經達成對於食物與水供給的目標，人們與外在世界的合作將會是下個即將到來的挑戰，這個挑戰對於人類生存也至關重要。

⭐ KEY 3

- ✪ Incorrect 不正確的 (*a.*)
- ✪ Modified 修正 (*v.*)
- ✪ Submitted 提交 (*v.*)
- ✪ Review 考察、評論 (*n.*)

The information was incorrect, so the file needs to be modified and then submitted again for a further review.

因為資訊不正確，所以文件必須要修正，然後再次提交作進一步地評論。

⭐ KEY 4

- ✪ Hand out 分發 (*v.*)
- ✪ Diagram 圖表 (*n.*)
- ✪ Ensure 確保 (*v.*)
- ✪ Familiar 熟悉的、常見的 (*a.*)

The teacher hands out a piece of diagram and then has students do the comprehension questions, to ensure students are all familiar with the geographical features of Southern Europe.

老師發下一張圖表並讓學生作答，來確保學生都熟悉南歐的地理特色。

★ **KEY 5**

✪ Explanation 解釋、說明 (*n.*)
✪ Extinction 滅絕 (*n.*)
✪ Suspect 懷疑、猜想 (*v.*)
✪ According to 根據 (*preposition*)

The expert pointed out the explanation they recently gained regarding the extinction of large mammals in North Africa; nevertheless, a large amount of audience still suspected him of giving out false information, according to New York Times.

根據紐約時報，這位專家提出最近取得的解釋，說明北非大型哺乳類的滅亡，然而一大部分的觀眾懷疑他提出的是假訊息。

★ **KEY 6**

✪ Demonstrate 展示、論證 (*v.*)

✪ Accomplish 完成 (v.)

✪ Considerable 大量的、可觀的 (a.)

✪ Controversy 爭論、論戰 (n.)

> The assistant professor is demonstrating how this hypothesis has formed and how arduous it was for scholars to accomplish it, but still, considerable controversy is there presenting the opposite thoughts.

這位助理教授正在展示這個假說是如何建構的,以及對於學者來說有多難去完成這項工作。但是,不少持相反想法的爭論依舊存在。

⭐ KEY 7

✪ No matter 不論 (conj.)

✪ Candidate 候選者 (n.)

✪ Opponent 對手、反對者 (n.)

✪ Contradict 反駁、牴觸 (v.)

> No matter what each candidate says in this forum, there are always opponents contradicting the options they present.

不論每一位候選人在這場論壇中說了什麼,總是會有反對者牴觸他們的言論。

KEY 8

✪ Qualified 有資格的 (*a.*)
✪ Evidence 證明 (*v.*)
✪ Migrate 遷移 (*v.*)
✪ Survive 存活 (*v.*)

> We need someone qualified to evidence that large mammals indeed had migrated from inner lands to coastal areas for the purpose of gaining water sources and that they had the ability to survive in a variety of habitats.

我們需要有資格的人士來證明大型的哺乳類動物的確曾經為了獲取水資源從內陸地區遷移至沿海地區，並且去證明牠們有能力可以存活在各類型的棲息地。

KEY 9

✪ Treat 對待 (*v.*)
✪ Force 強迫 (*v.*)
✪ Unstable 不穩定的 (*a.*)
✪ Endure 忍受 (*v.*)

> How we treat our environment, or saying, the Earth, will end up forcing us to accept the unstable temperatures and to endure the reducing variety of foods available.

我們如何對待我們的地球，終究會使我們必須要被迫去接受這樣不穩定的氣溫，並且忍受種類越來越少的食物。

 **KEY 10**

✪ Infer 作推論 (*v.*)
✪ Elaborate 闡述 (*v.*)
✪ Viewpoints 觀點 (*n.*)
✪ Associated 使有關連 (*v.*)

> The instruction is asking you to infer what the article actually means and then to elaborate your viewpoints and perspectives associated with climate change and global warming.

這個指示要求你對於這篇文章的內容作推論，並且闡述氣候變遷與全球暖化相關的觀點及看法。

KEY 11

✪ Summarize 總結、摘要 (*v.*)
✪ Interpret 闡釋 (*v.*)
✪ Solution 解決方法 (*n.*)
✪ Crisis 危機 (*n.*)

> The reporter is asked to briefly summarize the solutions the president interpreted to the nuclear crisis.

記者被要求簡短地摘要總統所闡述的有關核子危機的解決方法。

KEY 12

- ✪ Documentary 紀錄的 (*a.*)
- ✪ Expose 揭露、曝光 (*v.*)
- ✪ Disappear 消失 (*v.*)
- ✪ Opportunity 機會 (*n.*)

> This documentary film exposes how the extinction of dinosaurs happened and how this ancient city disappeared, offering opportunities for people to know more about the history of the Earth.

這部紀錄片揭露出恐龍滅絕是如何發生的，還有古城市是如何消失的，並提供機會給民眾來更加地了解地球的歷史。

KEY 13

- ✪ Examination 檢查 (*n.*)
- ✪ Respiratory 呼吸的 (*a.*)
- ✪ Reveal 透露 (*v.*)
- ✪ Contain 包含 (*v.*)

> The examination set for the purpose of knowing why some people would get the respiratory diseases reveals that their blood contains certain types of chemical materials that may lead to some disorders of the heart and blood vessels and further affect transport of oxygen in our blood.

這個檢查主要是要了解為什麼有一些民眾會得到呼吸方面的疾病，其檢查發現他們的血液中還有一些特定會導致心臟功能運作失常，以及血液輸送氧氣不順的化學物質。

⭐ KEY 14

- ✪ Convey 傳遞 (*v.*)
- ✪ Extraordinary 非凡的 (*a.*)
- ✪ Alternative 替代的 (*a.*)
- ✪ Affect 影響 (*v.*)

> The expert is conveying how extraordinary the theory is and how alternative energy sources may affect Earth's atmosphere.

這位專家正在傳輸這個理論有多特別，以及替代能源如何能影響地球大氣。

⭐ KEY 15

- ✪ Surpass 凌駕、超越 (*v.*)
- ✪ Aspects 面向 (*n.*)
- ✪ Problematic 有問題的 (*a.*)
- ✪ Fantastic 幻想的、奇妙的 (*a.*)

> She has been trying to surpass her sister in any aspects in that she has been always regarded as the problematic one, while her sister has always been the fantastic one.

她已經試圖要在各方面超越她姊姊，因為她總是被認為是有問題的那個，而她姊姊總是被認為是好的那個。

★ KEY 16

✪ Prescript 命令、法規 (*n.*)
✪ Manipulate 操作 (*v.*)
✪ Decompose 分解 (*v.*)
✪ Float 漂浮 (*v.*)

> He got a prescript which is having him analyze how long it would take for a rock to decompose and float into the ocean, by manipulating this statistics application.

他接獲一個命令要讓他使用統計軟體分析岩石要多久時間會分解並浮流到大海。

★ KEY 17

✪ Schema 輪廓、概要 (*n.*)
✪ Sedentary 久坐的 (*a.*)
✪ Chronic 慢性的 (*a.*)
✪ Sensitive 敏感的 (*a.*)

> He presented a schema indicating that if people are sedentary all the time, chronic diseases will come and dry skin will become sensitive through changing of the seasons.

他提出一個概要，其中指出如果久坐的話慢性病會找上你，且乾性肌膚會因為季節變化而變得敏感。

⭐ KEY 18

- ✪ Uptake 攝取 (*n.*)
- ✪ Cultivate 培養 (*v.*)
- ✪ Exploit 利用 (*v.*)
- ✪ Visual 視覺的 (*a.*)

> To increase your nutrient absorption, experts suggest cultivating good eating habits and exploiting visual aids, such as changing plates into white or other light colors, for nutrient uptake to occur.

為了能夠增加養分的攝取，專家建議要培養良好的飲食習慣，並且可利用視覺上的幫助，例如改變盤子的顏色為白色或是其他淡色系。

⭐ KEY 19

- ✪ Crouch 捲曲、蹲 (*v.*)
- ✪ Scrutinize 詳細檢查 (*v.*)
- ✪ Wreck 殘骸 (*n.*)
- ✪ Vanish 消失不見 (*v.*)

He crouched down for the sake of scrutinizing in details why plane wrecks from an aviation accident had vanished in the defensive trench.

他蹲下來為了能夠更仔細地檢查為什麼飛機失事的殘骸在防護溝渠中會不見。

★ KEY 20

- ✪ Procedure 過程 (*n.*)
- ✪ Precipitation 降水 (*n.*)
- ✪ Primary 主要的 (*a.*)
- ✪ Features 特色 (*n.*)

The chapter that you have to pay more attention to is chapter four, the procedures for a scientific project, steps of water cycle-the primary mechanism for transporting water from the air to the surface of the Earth- types of precipitation, and the geographical features of Southern Europe.

你需要花多一點心思在第四章，其有關科學專題的製作流程、水循環的過程（把水從空中運輸到地球表面的主要機制）、降水的種類以及南歐的地理特色。

攻克要點III 同義詞一覽表

Vanish	Synonym	Disappear/ evaporate/ fade
	Antonym	Improve/ solidify / appear
Migrate	Synonym	Immigrate/ shift
	Antonym	Remain/stay
Scrutinize	Synonym	Examine/ analyze/investigate
	Antonym	Forget/ ignore/ neglect
Elaborate	Synonym	Amplify/ comment/ clarify
	Antonym	Abridge/ compress/condense
Suspect	Synonym	Suspected/ dubious/ problematic
	Antonym	Innocent/ trust
Cultivate	Synonym	Breed/ fertilize/ prepare
	Antonym	Abandon/ destroy
Unstable	Synonym	Changeable/ erratic/ insecure
	Antonym	Certain/ dependable/ constant
Infer	Synonym	Conclude/ ascertain/ assume
	Antonym	Abstain/ disbelieve
Reveal	Synonym	Disclose/ affirm/ acknowledge
	Antonym	Conceal/ dispute/ hide
Contain	Synonym	Include/ hold/ enclose/ consist of
	Antonym	Exclude
Interpret	Synonym	Define/ clarify/ decipher
	Antonym	Confuse/ obscure

Sensitive	Synonym	Conscious/ delicate/ emotional
	Antonym	Calm/ ignorant/ unaware
Influential	Synonym	Effective/ Authoritative/ dominant
	Antonym	Inconspicuous/ subordinate
Surpass	Synonym	Beat/ exceed/ outperform
	Antonym	Fall behind/ lose/ surrender/
Manipulate	Synonym	Employ/ wield/ manage
	Antonym	Destroy
Alternative	Synonym	Substitute/ surrogate/ back-up
	Antonym	Obligation/ force
Convey	Synonym	Communicate/ impart/ transmit
	Antonym	Conceal/ cover/ withhold
Problematic	Synonym	Ambiguous/ dubious/ precarious
	Antonym	Certain/ decided/ undoubted
Expose	Synonym	Reveal/ disclose/ uncover/ unmask
	Antonym	Secret/ withhold /suppress
Disappear	Synonym	Vanish/ cease/ dissolve/ escape
	Antonym	Begin/ appear/ coagulate

攻克要點I 必考字彙表

KEY1

Expound on 解釋、詳細述說 (*v.*)	Maturity 成熟 (*n.*)
Prediction 預測 (*n.*)	Depletion 消耗、用盡 (*n.*)

KEY2

Instrumental 可作為手段的、儀器的 (*a.*)	Mount 上升 (*v.*)
Persistence 堅持、持續 (*n.*)	Provocation 激怒、挑撥 (*n.*)

KEY3

Didactic 教誨的、說教的 (*a.*)	Discordant 不調和的、不悅耳的 (*a.*)
Misleading 誤導 (*adj.*)	Discrimination 差別、歧視 (*n.*)

KEY4

Establish 創建、制定 (*v.*)	Deprecate 反對、抨擊 (*v.*)
Divergent 分歧的 (*a.*)	Deter 制止、使斷念 (*v.*)

KEY5

Rumor 謠言 (*n.*)	Detach 分離 (*v.*)
Propagate 傳播、使普及、繁殖 (*v.*)	Throughout 徹頭徹尾、在所有各處 (*adv.*)

KEY6

Property 財產、所有權 (*n.*)	Agent 仲介人 (*n.*)
Magnificent 華麗的、高尚的 (*a.*)	Meticulous 一絲不苟的 (*a.*)

KEY7

Optimistic 樂觀的 (*a.*)	Expand 擴大 (*v.*)
Reform 改革、改良 (*v.*)	Ramify 分支、分派 (*v.*)

KEY8

Integration 整合性 (*n.*)	Racial 種族的 (*a.*)
Religious 宗教性的 (*a.*)	Evoke 喚起、引起 (*v.*)

KEY9

Intuition 直覺 (*n.*)	Invoke 祈求、懇求 (*v.*)
Tend 趨向 (*v.*)	Compromise 妥協、折衷 (*v.*)

KEY10

Isolated 孤立的 (*a.*)	Protest 主張、抗議 (*v.*)
Estimation 預計 (*n.*)	Erupt 爆發 (*v.*)

KEY11

Sincere 真誠的 (*a.*)	Execute 執行 (*v.*)
Integrity 正直 (*n.*)	Perilous 危險的 (*a.*)

KEY12

Investigator 調查者 (*n.*)	Inquire 詢問 (*v.*)
Resign 辭職 (*v.*)	Instigate 唆使、煽動 (*v.*)

KEY13

Rhetorical 符合修辭學的 (*a.*)	Ritual 儀式 (*n.*)
Address 致詞、演說 (*v.*)	Restrict 限制 (*v.*)

Unit 17

KEY14

Undertake 承擔、接受 (v.)	Strengthen 加強、變堅固 (v.)
Resolve 決心 (n.)	Ultimate 終極的 (a.)

KEY15

Inform 告知 (v.)	Judgment 審判、判決 (n.)
Ethical 倫理的 (a.)	Expect 期待 (v.)

KEY16

Subtle 微妙的、敏感精細的 (a.)	Superficial 表面的 (a.)
Scratch 抓、刮痕 (n.)	Sweep 掃除、肅清 (v.)

KEY17

Render 給予、歸還 (v.)	Thematic 主題的 (a.)
Tactic 戰術、戰略 (n.)	Achieve 達成 (v.)

KEY18

Symmetrical 對稱的 (a.)	Dominant 主要支配的 (a.)
Renaissance 文藝復興 (n.)	Redundant 多餘的、過多的 (a.)

KEY19

Witness 證人、目擊者 (n.)	Testify 證明、作證 (v.)
Insist 堅持 (v.)	Remote 遙遠的 (a.)

KEY20

Inflammatory 煽動性的、發炎的 (a.)	Response 回應 (n.)
Reject 拒絕 (v.)	Immune 免疫的、不受影響的 (a.)

攻克要點II 超給力例句

★ KEY 1 ♪ MP3 17

✪ Expound on 解釋、詳細述說 (*v.*)
✪ Maturity 成熟 (*n.*)
✪ Prediction 預測 (*n.*)
✪ Depletion 消耗、用盡 (*n.*)

> My professor is expounding on the progress of intelligence from childhood to maturity; on the other hand, that the professor is making a prediction to when food and fruits will be getting less due to soil depletion.

我的教授正在詳述從小時候到成熟階段智力的發展狀況；另一方面來看，另一位教授正在預測食物與水果何時會因為土壤的耗盡而越來越少。

★ KEY 2

✪ Instrumental 可作為手段的、儀器的 (*a.*)
✪ Mount 上升 (*v.*)
✪ Persistence 堅持、持續 (*n.*)
✪ Provocation 激怒、挑撥 (*n.*)

Psychologists claim that there are ways instrumental for you to develop patience, for instance the following two ways: mounting that takes patience and persistence, and not responding to provocation.

心理學家指出現在有很多方法可以幫助你去培養你的耐心，例如以下兩種方法： 需要耐心與堅持的爬山，以及對於他人的挑釁不做出回應。

★ KEY 3

- ✪ Didactic 教誨的、說教的 (*a.*)
- ✪ Discordant 不調和的、不悅耳的 (*a.*)
- ✪ Misleading 誤導 (*adj.*)
- ✪ Discrimination 差別、歧視 (*n.*)

This didactic song is set out to unveil the discordant memories the singer had in her childhood and to expose the misleading thoughts people might have pertaining to racial discrimination.

這個富教育意義的歌曲是為了要揭開他在小時候有的一些不好的回憶，且暴露出人們可能會對種族歧視有些誤解。

★ KEY 4

- ✪ Establish 創建、制定 (v.)
- ✪ Deprecate 反對、抨擊 (v.)
- ✪ Divergent 分歧的 (a.)
- ✪ Deter 制止、使斷念 (v.)

> This organization is established for the purpose of deprecating death penalty, whereas the rest of the people with divergent interpretations about it in this country stand on the side of using death penalty to deter crime.

這個團體創建的目的是要抨擊死刑，然而這個國家內持不同意見的其他人卻站在使用死刑來制止犯罪的立場。

★ KEY 5

- ✪ Rumor 謠言 (n.)
- ✪ Detach 分離 (v.)
- ✪ Propagate 傳播、使普及、繁殖 (v.)
- ✪ Throughout 徹頭徹尾、在所有各處 (adv.)

> The rumor that he attempts to detach himself from the political party he belongs to has already been widely propagated throughout the nation.

有關於他嘗試要自己脫離整個黨派的這個謠言已經廣泛的被傳播至整個國家了。

✪ Property 財產、所有權 (*n.*)
✪ Agent 仲介人 (*n.*)
✪ Magnificent 華麗的、高尚的 (*a.*)
✪ Meticulous 一絲不苟的 (*a.*)

The top property agent is introducing the magnificent interior design painted with meticulous care to her prospective client.

這位頂尖的房屋仲介正在向她的預期客戶介紹這美輪美奐且作工精細的室內設計。

✪ Optimistic 樂觀的 (*a.*)
✪ Expand 擴大 (*v.*)
✪ Reform 改革、改良 (*v.*)
✪ Ramify 分支、分派 (*v.*)

This optimistic business woman is trying very badly to expand her business connection, just as how the railway system was reformed to ramify throughout the States.

這位樂觀的女商人非常努力地嘗試要擴張她的商業交流，這就像是鐵路系統改良成能夠於全美縱橫交錯著。

KEY 8

✪ Integration 整合性 (*n.*)
✪ Racial 種族的 (*a.*)
✪ Religious 宗教性的 (*a.*)
✪ Evoke 喚起、引起 (*v.*)

> To achieve the integration, having people of different racial and religious groups gather together, we have to evoke the bright side people already had instead of the dark side.

為了達成整合，也就是說讓不同種族及宗教的人民能夠聚集在一起，我們必須要喚起人們已擁有的光明面而不是黑暗面。

KEY 9

✪ Intuition 直覺 (*n.*)
✪ Invoke 祈求、懇求 (*v.*)
✪ Tend 趨向 (*v.*)
✪ Compromise 妥協、折衷 (*v.*)

> He tends to figure out a solution using his intuition instead of invoking aids of people mastering in this field, indicating that he is a person not willing to collaborate and compromise.

他傾向靠他的直覺去解決問題，而不是向這行的專家尋求幫助，也就是說他不是個願意合作與妥協的人。

★ KEY 10

✪ Isolated 孤立的 (*a.*)
✪ Protest 主張、抗議 (*v.*)
✪ Estimation 預計 (*n.*)
✪ Erupt 爆發 (*v.*)

Feeling isolated by their government, villagers living nearby the biggest volcano protest that they must receive a statement of estimation regarding when and to what extent the volcano will erupt.

感覺到被政府隔離，居住在這最大的火山旁的村民們抗議說，他們必須要收到預測聲明，得知火山何時噴發，以及噴發會到什麼程度。

★ KEY 11

✪ Sincere 真誠的 (*a.*)
✪ Execute 執行 (*v.*)
✪ Integrity 正直 (*n.*)
✪ Perilous 危險的 (*a.*)

Politicians are supposed to be sincere and execute plans with integrity, or both the people and country will be pushed to a perilous situation.

政治家必須要真誠且正直的去執行計畫，否則人民以及國家將會被推向一個危險的局面。

KEY 12

✪ Investigator 調查者 (*n.*)
✪ Inquire 詢問 (*v.*)
✪ Resign 辭職 (*v.*)
✪ Instigate 唆使、煽動 (*v.*)

> Investigators are inquiring why the cabinet members were forced to resign their positions because they thought probably someone had instigated them to perform this action.

調查者正在查詢為什麼內閣成員會被強迫辭掉他們的職位，因為他們覺得之前可能有人唆使他們這麼做。

KEY 13

✪ Rhetorical 符合修辭學的 (*a.*)
✪ Ritual 儀式 (*n.*)
✪ Address 致詞、演說 (*v.*)
✪ Restrict 限制 (*v.*)

> Having a rhetorical speech is a part of this traditional ritual and the access to the stage at which the captain is addressing his thanks to his people will be restricted then.

有個符合修辭學的演講是傳統儀式的一部分，而那個有個將軍正在致詞感謝他的人民的舞台是被限制通行的。

✪ Undertake 承擔、接受 (*v.*)
✪ Strengthen 加強、變堅固 (*v.*)
✪ Resolve 決心 (*n.*)
✪ Ultimate 終極的 (*a.*)

> He undertakes the responsibility that is strengthening her resolution of reaching an ultimate success she wants in her career.

他接受了加強這位小姐想要達到她事業最終成功的決心這樣的責任。

★ KEY 15

✪ Inform 告知 (*v.*)
✪ Judgment 審判、判決 (*n.*)
✪ Ethical 倫理的 (*a.*)
✪ Expect 期待 (*v.*)

> Teachers have to inform students the importance of keeping their behaviors and judgments ethical as people would expect.

老師必須要告知學生們做出合乎道德的行為與批判的重要性，就像社會上人們所期待的一樣。

★ KEY 16

- ✪ Subtle 微妙的、敏感精細的 (*a.*)
- ✪ Superficial 表面的 (*a.*)
- ✪ Scratch 抓、刮痕 (*n.*)
- ✪ Sweep 掃除、肅清 (*v.*)

My mother can tell the subtle differences between these two tables, even the superficial scratch in that she attentively sweeps every furniture, stairway, and appliance every day.

我媽媽可以察覺出這兩張桌子間些微差異，即使是很表面的刮痕，因為她每天都仔細的擦拭家裡每一件家具、階梯以及家電用品。

★ KEY 17

- ✪ Render 給予、歸還 (*v.*)
- ✪ Thematic 主題的 (*a.*)
- ✪ Tactic 戰術、戰略 (*n.*)
- ✪ Achieve 達成 (*v.*)

This genius renders a thematic tactic to his boss for successfully achieving a particular goal he set few years ago.

這個天才給予他的老闆一個富有主題性的戰略，為了能成功地達成他幾年前所設立的目標。

✪ Symmetrical 對稱的 (*a.*)
✪ Dominant 主要支配的 (*a.*)
✪ Renaissance 文藝復興 (*n.*)
✪ Redundant 多餘的、過多的 (*a.*)

Symmetrical design was not dominant during the period of Renaissance due to the fact that people thought of it as being redundant and dull.

對稱的設計並沒有稱霸文藝復興時期是因為當時人們認為對稱不必要而且很無聊。

✪ Witness 證人、目擊者 (*n.*)
✪ Testify 證明、作證 (*v.*)
✪ Insist 堅持 (*v.*)
✪ Remote 遙遠的 (*a.*)

Even though some witnesses testified that they had seen a man with a knife wandering around the array of scooters, the suspect still insisted that he in a store remote from the spot.

一些目擊者作證說他們有看到一名持刀的男人在一排機車附近晃蕩，但這名嫌疑犯堅稱說他當時在離案發現場很遠的一間商店裡。

 **KEY 20**

✪ Inflammatory 煽動性的、發炎的 (*a.*)

✪ Response 回應 (*n.*)

✪ Reject 拒絕 (*v.*)

✪ Immune 免疫的、不受影響的 (*a.*)

> Her body starts having an inflammatory response due to transplant rejection, meaning the transplanted tissue is rejected by the recipient's immune system.

這個女孩的身體因為移植排斥開始有發炎反應，移植排斥也就是指移植過來的組織被接受移植者自身的免疫系統所拒絕。

攻克要點III 同義詞一覽表

Reject	Synonym	Deny/ dismiss/ refuse
	Antonym	Accept/ admit/ allow
Ultimate	Synonym	Preeminent/ utmost/ superlative
	Antonym	Lowest/ inferior/ secondary
Subtle	Synonym	Exquisite/ faint / indirect
	Antonym	Ignorant/ open/ harsh
Remote	Synonym	Distant/ inaccessible
	Antonym	Close/ approachable
Achieve	Synonym	Accomplish/ attain/ enact
	Antonym	Abandon/ forfeit/ depart
Rhetorical	Synonym	Wordy/ oratorical/ articulate
	Antonym	Concise
Instigate	Synonym	Influence/ provoke/ foment/ incite
	Antonym	Deter/ discourage/ dissuade
Testify	Synonym	Announce/ assert/ affirm
	Antonym	Conceal/ deny/ contradict
Symmetrical	Synonym	commeasurable/ equal/ proportional
	Antonym	Asymmetrical/ disproportioned
Render	Synonym	Contribute/ deliver/ provide
	Antonym	Take/ withhold/ deny
Dominant	Synonym	Superior/ controlling/ assertive
	Antonym	Auxiliary/ extra/ incapable

Witness	Synonym	Attend/ notice/ perceive
	Antonym	Ignore/ neglect/ overlook
Perilous	Synonym	Dangerous/ delicate/ hazardous
	Antonym	Calm/ certain/ secure/ stable
Superficial	Synonym	Cursory/ frivolous/ trivial
	Antonym	Thoughtful/ detailed
Undertake	Synonym	Attempt/ engage in/ commence/ initiate
	Antonym	Cease/ complete
Ethical	Synonym	Moral/ righteous / humane
	Antonym	Immoral/ improper/ unethical
Redundant	Synonym	Excessive/ repetitious/ unnecessary
	Antonym	Needed/ necessary/ essential
Scratch	Synonym	Laceration/ blemish
	Antonym	Perfection
Sweep	Synonym	Clean/ broom/ mop
	Antonym	dirty
Inform	Synonym	Advise/ brief/ instruct/ notify
	Antonym	Deceive/ conceal/ withhold

Unit

攻克要點I 必考字彙表

KEY1

Immediately 立即地 (*adv.*)

Exhibition 展覽 (*n.*)

Dominant 佔優勢的 (*a.*)

Hypothesis 假說 (*n.*)

KEY2

Acknowledge 承認 (*v.*)

Concentrations 濃縮、集中 (*v.*)

Considerable 相當的、可觀的 (*a.*)

Literature 文學 (*n.*)

KEY3

Signatures 簽名 (*n.*)

Nonetheless 然而 (*adv.*)

Discernible 可識別的 (*a.*)

Ratify 批准、認可 (*v.*)

KEY4

Waste 浪費 (*n.*)

Decayed 腐朽 (*v.*)

Detrimental 有害的 (*a.*)

Obviously 明顯地 (*adv.*)

KEY5

Invade 闖入 (*v.*)

Instigate 教唆 (*v.*)

Plunder 搶奪、掠奪 (*v.*)

Disrupt 破壞 (*v.*)

KEY6

Presence 存在、現存 (*n.*)

Inhospitable 不適合居住的 (*a.*)

Hostile 敵對的 (*a.*)

Creatures 生物 (*n.*)

KEY7

Relatively 相對地 (*adv.*)	Scant 少的 (*a.*)
Ultraviolet 紫外線 (*n.*)	Radiation 輻射 (*n.*)

KEY8

Injurious 有害的 (*a.*)	Suffer 受痛苦 (*v.*)
Iniquitous 不正的、不法的 (*a.*)	Untenable 不能維持的 (*a.*)

KEY9

Pompous 傲慢的、自大的 (*a.*)	Resemble 相似 (*v.*)
Incipient 初期的 (*a.*)	Election 選舉的 (*n.*)

KEY10

Meteorite 隕石 (*n.*)	Controversial 有爭議的 (*a.*)
Origin 來源 (*n.*)	Contaminate 汙染 (*v.*)

KEY11

Assort 分類、配合 (*v.*)	Conspicuous 顯著的 (*a.*)
Attempt 嘗試 (*v.*)	Attention 注意力 (*n.*)

KEY12

Planet 星球 (*n.*)	Slightly 一點點地 (*adv.*)
Spin 旋轉 (*v.*)	Condense 使濃縮、縮短 (*v.*)

KEY13

Cryptically 神秘地、涵義模糊地 (*adv.*)	Blend in 調和、滲入 (*v.*)
Surrounding 周圍的 (*a.*)	Camouflage 偽裝 (*n.*)

KEY14

Feasible 可行的 (*a.*)	Gestures 姿態、手勢 (*n.*)
Ritual 因儀式而行的 (*a.*)	Conceal 隱藏 (*v.*)

KEY15

Trigger 觸發、引起 (*v.*)	Headache 頭痛 (*n.*)
Routine 例行的 (*a.*)	Sufficient 足夠的 (*a.*)

KEY16

Strictures 狹窄 (*n.*)	Impose 強加 (*v.*)
Inspire 鼓舞、使啟發 (*v.*)	Inquiry 查詢、調查 (*n.*)

KEY17

Deem 認為 (*v.*)	Strategies 策略 (*n.*)
Restrain 限制 (*v.*)	Illegal 非法的 (*a.*)

KEY18

Accordingly 因此 (*adv.*)	Military 軍隊的 (*a.*)
Exempt 免除 (*v.*)	Chronic 慢性的 (*a.*)

KEY19

Desolated 荒蕪的 (*a.*)	Chunk 塊 (*n.*)
Continent 大陸 (*n.*)	Thrive 使欣欣向榮 (*v.*)

KEY20

Primary 主要的 (*a.*)	In tandem with 同…合作 (*adv.*)
Metropolitan 大都市的 (*a.*)	Rapidly 快速地 (*adv.*)

攻克要點 II 超給力例句

★ KEY 1 ♪ MP3 18

✪ Immediately 立即地 (*adv.*)
✪ Dominant 佔優勢的 (*a.*)
✪ Exhibition 展覽 (*n.*)
✪ Hypothesis 假說 (*n.*)

> This product would immediately make this company dominant in the computer exhibition of the year, but it is still a hypothesis.

這個產品會使這家公司成為今年電腦展上的主角，但這還只是假設而已。

★ KEY 2

✪ Acknowledge 承認 (*v.*)
✪ Considerable 相當的、可觀的 (*a.*)
✪ Concentrations 濃縮、集中 (*v.*)
✪ Literature 文學 (*n.*)

> Scholars acknowledge that there were considerable cultural activities taking place during the Middle Ages that basically concentrated on classical literature.

學者承認在中世紀時曾經有大量的文化活動發生且大量集中於古典文學。

✪ Signatures 簽名 (*n.*)
✪ Discernible 可識別的 (*a.*)
✪ Nonetheless 然而 (*adv.*)
✪ Ratify 批准、認可 (*v.*)

People would place their signatures in a rather not discernible spot, such as in the back or at the corner to make it imperceptible if they did not want to take any possible responsibility; nonetheless, the Senate might not ratify the treaty.

當人們不想要負責任的時候，人們會簽名簽在較不容易識別的區域，例如在背面或是在角落讓它變得不易辨識，然而，議院可能不會批准這個條約。

✪ Waste 浪費 (*n.*)
✪ Detrimental 有害的 (*a.*)
✪ Decayed 腐朽 (*v.*)
✪ Obviously 明顯地 (*adv.*)

His greatest concern is the fact that chemical wastes would be detrimental to our environment, and some decayed plants and animal matters might also be obviously harmful to our land.

他對於化學廢棄物有可能會對環境造成危害，以及一些腐朽的植物與動物也明顯對我們的土地有害存有很大的顧慮。

★ KEY 5

- ✪ Invade 闖入 (*v.*)
- ✪ Plunder 搶奪、掠奪 (*v.*)
- ✪ Instigate 教唆 (*v.*)
- ✪ Disrupt 破壞 (*v.*)

The invading army, instigated by other gangs to plunder this village, has disrupted each family member's dream and right to live in the world.

被其他幫派教唆闖入並掠奪這個村莊的闖入者，已經破壞了住在這個村莊的每一個家庭的夢，跟生存在這個世界上的權力。

★ KEY 6

- ✪ Presence 存在、現存 (*n.*)
- ✪ Hostile 敵對的 (*a.*)
- ✪ Inhospitable 不適合居住的 (*a.*)

✪ Creatures 生物 (*n.*)

> Scholars point out that there has not been any convincing evidence for the presence of life on this recently discovered basin located at the biggest desert in Africa, due to its hostile and inhospitable living conditions for any form of creatures.

學者指出對於最近發現的，因為其嚴酷且不適合任何生物居住的生存條件，位於非洲最大沙漠中的盆地是否有生命的存在依舊缺乏令人信服的相關證據。

⭐ KEY 7

✪ Relatively 相對地 (*adv.*)
✪ Scant 少的 (*a.*)
✪ Ultraviolet 紫外線 (*n.*)
✪ Radiation 輻射 (*n.*)

> This national park has a relatively scant portion of forests, indicating that it cannot completely block the ultraviolet radiation the Sun emits.

這個國家公園擁有相對少量的森林，也就是說它無法完全阻擋來自太陽光照射的紫外線輻射。

★ KEY 8

✪ Injurious 有害的 (*a.*)
✪ Suffer 受痛苦 (*v.*)
✪ Iniquitous 不正的、不法的 (*a.*)
✪ Untenable 不能維持的 (*a.*)

> It is an untenable argument that the child who has suffered through iniquitous bully that may be injurious to one's cognitive development can become a psychologically mature grown-up.

關於遭受過不法且認知發展霸凌的孩子，其心靈會變成熟的論調是站不住腳的。

★ KEY 9

✪ Pompous 傲慢的、自大的 (*a.*)
✪ Resemble 相似 (*v.*)
✪ Incipient 初期的 (*a.*)
✪ Election 選舉的 (*n.*)

> The pompous way the presidential candidate adopts to talk about her goals and achievements resembles how her mentor does und having a speech is still at the incipient stage of the final election.

這個總統候選人談論她的目標及成就時那種傲慢自大的方式與她的導師相同，且這個演講還只是在最終選舉的初期階段而已。

★ KEY 10

✪ Meteorite 隕石 (*n.*)
✪ Controversial 有爭議的 (*a.*)
✪ Origin 來源 (*n.*)
✪ Contaminate 汙染 (*v.*)

> It's still a controversial issue regarding the biological origin of the carbon element found in this meteorite and whether the element has been contaminated by Earth.

關於在這個隕石中所發現的碳元素來源，以及是否這元素有被地球所污染依舊是個富爭議的議題。

★ KEY 11

✪ Assort 分類、配合 (*v.*)
✪ Conspicuous 顯著的 (*a.*)
✪ Attempt 嘗試 (*v.*)
✪ Attention 注意力 (*n.*)

The collection of Egyptian antiquities assorted according to their geographical origins was placed in a very conspicuous spot in this museum, attempting to drive more attention to it.

依照地理來源所分類的古埃及系列被放置在很明顯的區域，以嘗試取得更多的注意力。

★ KEY 12

- ✪ Planet 星球 (*n.*)
- ✪ Slightly 一點點地 (*adv.*)
- ✪ Spin 旋轉 (*v.*)
- ✪ Condense 使濃縮、縮短 (*v.*)

This newly-found planet is believed to be slightly smaller than Earth and consists of the spinning, condensing cloud of gas the Sun is composed of as well.

這個新發現的星球被認為體積稍小於地球，而且是由跟組成太陽一樣的旋轉與壓縮的氣體與塵埃所組成的。

★ KEY 13

- ✪ Cryptically 神秘地、涵義模糊地 (*adv.*)
- ✪ Blend in 調和、滲入 (*v.*)
- ✪ Surrounding 周圍的 (*a.*)

Unit 18

✪ Camouflage 偽裝 (*n.*)

> This secrete creature is known for its capability to cryptically color itself, called camouflage, meaning it is able to blend into the surrounding environment.

這個神祕的生物是因為牠可以神秘地以顏色來偽裝牠自己而有名，也就是說牠可以把牠自己與周遭的環境融合在一起。

⭐ KEY 14

✪ Feasible 可行的 (*a.*)
✪ Gestures 姿態、手勢 (*n.*)
✪ Ritual 因儀式而行的 (*a.*)
✪ Conceal 隱藏 (*v.*)

> There are other feasible actions, such as singing, dancing, other special gestures, or wearing ritual costumes that can be relied on to conceal the prayer's human identity.

其他可行的動作像是唱歌、跳舞以及其他的手勢，或是穿著儀式的服飾可被用來隱藏祈禱者的人類身分。

⭐ KEY 15

✪ Trigger 觸發、引起 (*v.*)
✪ Headache 頭痛 (*n.*)
✪ Routine 例行的 (*a.*)

✪ Sufficient 足夠的 (*a.*)

His bad eating habit triggers his headache and stomach problems; hence, living a routine lifestyle and having sufficient sleeping are quite necessary.

他不好的飲食習慣觸發了他的頭痛及一些腸胃問題，因此規律的生活型態跟充足的睡眠是非常必要的。

★ KEY 16

✪ Strictures 狹窄 (*n.*)
✪ Impose 強加 (*v.*)
✪ Inspire 鼓舞、使啟發 (*v.*)
✪ Inquiry 查詢、調查 (*n.*)

The effect of Humanism assists people to break free from the mental strictures imposed by certain religions, inspires free inquiry, and further motivates people to have their own thoughts and creations.

人道主義幫助人民從特定宗教造成的心理限制走出來， 鼓舞自由的詢問且激勵人們有他們自己的想法與創意。

★ KEY 17

✪ Deem 認為 (*v.*)

✪ Strategies 策略 (*n.*)
✪ Restrain 限制 (*v.*)
✪ Illegal 非法的 (*a.*)

> Attacks, such as small-scale robberies or highly-organized hijacking are deemed as major threats to our society so that there are strategies proposed to restrain those illegal crimes.

小型的攻擊像是搶奪或高組織性的劫機都被認為對我們社會有很大的威脅，所以有策略被提出來抑制非法的犯罪。

★ KEY 18

✪ Accordingly 因此 (*adv.*)
✪ Military 軍隊的 (*a.*)
✪ Exempt 免除 (*v.*)
✪ Chronic 慢性的 (*a.*)

> Accordingly, the government announces that military service could be exempted if you have foreign passports or any chronic disease.

因此，政府發聲明說如果你持有外國護照或是有慢性疾病的話，兵制是可以被免除的。

★ KEY 19

- ✪ Desolated 荒蕪的 (*a.*)
- ✪ Chunk 塊 (*n.*)
- ✪ Continent 大陸 (*n.*)
- ✪ Thrive 使欣欣向榮 (*v.*)

> The biggest desert in the world, used to be a desolated chunk of land situated in the inner Asia continent, is now thriving under the reign of emperor.

在亞洲大陸內陸這個世界最大的沙漠，之前是個荒蕪的大陸，現在因為皇帝的統治，已經變得欣欣向榮。

★ KEY 20

- ✪ Primary 主要的 (*a.*)
- ✪ In tandem with 同⋯合作 (*adv.*)
- ✪ Metropolitan 大都市的 (*a.*)
- ✪ Rapidly 快速地 (*adv.*)

> The effect of Urban Heat Island normally and primarily occurs in tandem with metropolitan development and rapidly develops in densely populated centers.

熱島效應主要與都市發展相呼應，且快速發展於主要都市及人多的中心。

Unit 18

Desolated	Synonym	Bare/ barren/ isolated
	Antonym	Inhabited/ populated
Exempt	Synonym	Excuse/ relieve/ exonerate
	Antonym	Hold/ keep/ incarcerate
Impose	Synonym	Enforce/ demand/ appoint
	Antonym	Overlook/ prevent/ displace
Inspire	Synonym	Encourage/ stimulate/ arouse
	Antonym	Depress/ discourage
Inquiry	Synonym	Asking/ inspection/ examination
	Antonym	Ignorance/ answer
Trigger	Synonym	Cause to happen/ bring about/ generate
	Antonym	Destroy/ end/ prevent
Sufficient	Synonym	Adequate/ satisfactory/ample
	Antonym	Insufficient/ deficient/ inadequate
Feasible	Synonym	Possible/doable/ practicable
	Antonym	Implausible/ impossible/ impractical
Spin	Synonym	Twist/ spiral/ circuit
	Antonym	Stagnation/ inaction
Conceal	Synonym	Hide/ disguise/ bury/ camouflage
	Antonym	Disregard/ uncover/ unwrap

Camouflage	Synonym	Conceal/ cover up/ cloak
	Antonym	Reveal/ uncover/ show
Pompous	Synonym	Arrogant/ egotistic / bombastic
	Antonym	Humble/ kind/ modest
Condense	Synonym	Compress/ curtail/ shorten
	Antonym	Extend/ increase/ lengthen
Resemble	Synonym	Parallel/ simulate/ coincide/ approximate
	Antonym	Contradict/ contrast / deviate
Incipient	Synonym	Developing/ embryonic/ commencing
	Antonym	Grown/ developed/ mature
Indigenous	Synonym	Domestic/ primitive / aboriginal
	Antonym	Alien/ foreign
Controversial	Synonym	Contentious/dubious/ disputed
	Antonym	Certain/ definite
Assort	Synonym	Categorize/ class/ classify/ group
	Antonym	scatter
Iniquitous	Synonym	Evil/ sinful/ wicked
	Antonym	Decent/ ethical/ virtuous
Untenable	Synonym	Indefensible
	Antonym	Defensible/ excusable

Unit 18

攻克要點I 必考字彙表

KEY1

Muscular 肌肉強壯的、有利的 (*a.*)	Elongate 使延長 (*v.*)
Adapted to 適應於 (*v.*)	Prey 被捕食者 (*n.*)

KEY2

Fossils 化石 (*n.*)	Carnivorous 食肉類的 (*a.*)
Fragile 脆弱的 (*a.*)	Slightly 輕微的、一點點 (*adv.*)

KEY3

Geothermal 地熱 (*n.*)	Tectonic plates 板塊 (*n.*)
Conjoin 使結合、使連接 (*v.*)	Crust 殼 (*n.*)

KEY4

Ubiquitous 普及的、到處存在的 (*a.*)	Aquatic 水生的 (*a.*)
Habitats 棲息地、居住地 (*n.*)	Absorb 吸收 (*v.*)

KEY5

Elaborate 精緻的 (*a.*)	Exceptional 非凡的 (*a.*)
Sculpture 雕塑 (*n.*)	Relief 浮雕 (*n.*)

KEY6

Exquisite 精緻的、細膩的 (*a.*)	Political 政治的 (*a.*)
Religious 宗教的 (*a.*)	Symbol 象徵 (*n.*)

KEY7

Invention 創作 (*n.*)	Thicken 加厚 (*v.*)
Conducive to 有益於、有助於 (*a.*)	Transport 運輸 (*n.*)

KEY8

Accelerate 加速、加快 (*v.*)	Incrementally 增量地 (*adv.*)
Boost up 增強 (*v.*)	Efficiency 效率 (*n.*)

KEY9

Distinctive 有區別性的、與眾不同的 (*a.*)	Contrast 對比 (*n.*)
Polar 極的 (*a.*)	Dry 乾的 (*a.*)

KEY10

Halting 使停止 (*v.*)	Barely 幾乎不 (*adv.*)
Figure out 想出 (*v.*)	Conquer 征服 (*v.*)

KEY11

Mimic 模仿 (*v.*)	Abundant 豐富的 (*a.*)
Tremendously 異常地、巨大地 (*adv.*)	Master 駕馭 (*v.*)

KEY12

Critics 評論家 (*n.*)	Deprecate 抨擊、反對 (*v.*)
Hinder 阻止 (*v.*)	Release 釋放 (*v.*)

KEY13

Efforts 努力 (*n.*)	Convince 使信服 (*v.*)
Futile 細瑣的、無用的 (*a.*)	Ineffective 無效的 (*a.*)

Unit 19

KEY14

Inevitably 不可避免的 (*adv.*)	Contend 鬥爭、競爭 (*v.*)
Giving rise to 引起、導致 (*v.*)	Elimination 消除 (*n.*)

KEY15

Eventually 最終地 (*adv.*)	Entrench 防護、保護 (*v.*)
Frequently 頻繁地 (*adv.*)	Yield 被迫放棄 (*v.*)

KEY16

Apparently 明顯地 (*adv.*)	Contain 含有 (*v.*)
Capacious 寬廣的 (*a.*)	Extraordinary 非凡的 (*a.*)

KEY17

Hostile 有敵意的 (*a.*)	Innovations 創新 (*n.*)
Restricted 限制 (*v.*)	Consolidate 鞏固、使聯合 (*v.*)

KEY18

Intricate 錯綜複雜的 (*a.*)	Confine to 限制於 (*v.*)
Designate 指派 (*v.*)	Ludicrous 可笑的、荒唐的 (*a.*)

KEY19

Attack 攻擊 (*v.*)	Arrest 逮捕 (*v.*)
Intruder 入侵者 (*n.*)	Delineate 描繪 (*v.*)

KEY20

Imminent 逼近的、即將到來的 (*a.*)	Emergency 緊急事件 (*n.*)
Mitigate 減輕 (*v.*)	Disaster 災害 (*n.*)

攻克要點 II 超給力例句

★ KEY 1 ♪ MP3 19

✪ Muscular 肌肉強壯的、有利的 (*a.*)
✪ Elongate 使延長 (*v.*)
✪ Adapted to 適應於 (*v.*)
✪ Prey 被捕食者 (*n.*)

> The organ, tongue is capable of doing various muscular movements, for instance that in some animals, such as frogs, it can be elongated and can be adapted to capturing insect prey.

舌頭這個器官可以做很多項的肌肉運動，例如有些動物的舌頭像是青蛙，是可以被延長且適於捕食昆蟲的。

★ KEY 2

✪ Fossils 化石 (*n.*)
✪ Carnivores 食肉類的 (*a.*)
✪ Fragile 脆弱的 (*a.*)
✪ Slightly 輕微、一點點 (*adv.*)

Through the examination of a fossil of a carnivorous plant, scientists have gotten some interesting findings even though the soft parts of it were slightly fragile.

經過檢查食肉類植物化石後，雖然這些化石比較軟的部分有一點點脆弱，科學家還是有得到一些有趣的發現。

⭐ KEY 3

- ✪ Geothermal 地熱的 (*adj.*)
- ✪ Tectonic plates 板塊 (*n.*)
- ✪ Conjoin 使結合、使連接 (*v.*)
- ✪ Crust 殼 (*n.*)

Geothermal energy can mostly be perceived in areas where tectonic plates conjoin, and where the earth crust is thinner than it is in other regions.

地熱的能量通常可以在板塊相接的地方，以及地球板塊相較於其他地方較薄的部分被發現。

⭐ KEY 4

- ✪ Ubiquitous 普及的、到處存在的 (*a.*)
- ✪ Aquatic 水生的 (*a.*)
- ✪ Habitats 棲息地、居住地 (*n.*)
- ✪ Absorb 吸收 (*v.*)

Algae are ubiquitous throughout the world, being the most common in aquatic habitats, and are categorized based on the diversified light wavelengths the seawater absorbs.

藻類普及於全世界且最常見於水生棲息地，並且以受水體吸收的多樣光波長來做分類的基礎。

KEY 5

✪ Elaborate 精緻的 (*a.*)
✪ Exceptional 非凡的 (*a.*)
✪ Sculpture 雕塑 (*n.*)
✪ Relief 浮雕 (*n.*)

People living in this ancient village have developed an elaborate and exceptional tradition of sculpture and relief carving.

住在這古老村莊的人民發展出雕塑與浮雕這樣精緻又非凡的傳統。

KEY 6

✪ Exquisite 精緻的、細膩的 (*a.*)
✪ Political 政治的 (*a.*)
✪ Religious 宗教的 (*a.*)
✪ Symbol 象徵 (*n.*)

This vase, known as a political and religious symbol, shows the exquisite sense of design and the power of the king.

這個花瓶被認為是政治與宗教的象徵，展現了細膩的設計與這個國王的權力。

⭐ KEY 7

- ✪ Invention 創作 (*n.*)
- ✪ Thicken 加厚 (*v.*)
- ✪ Conducive to 有益於、有助於 (*a.*)
- ✪ Transport 運輸 (*n.*)

This creative invention that could be conducive to transport both in water and land is widely known for its thickened structures and being light-weighted.

這個充滿創作感的發明因為他厚實的結構，且極度輕盈，並有助於陸上與水上的運輸，而廣為人知。

⭐ KEY 8

- ✪ Accelerate 加速、加快 (*v.*)
- ✪ Incrementally 增量地 (*adv.*)
- ✪ Boost up 增強 (*v.*)
- ✪ Efficiency 效率 (*n.*)

This program accelerates the process of editing text and images and incrementally boosts up your working efficiency and accuracy.

這個程式加快了文字與圖片的修正，且增量地升高你的工作效率與準確性。

★ KEY 9

✪ Distinctive 有區別性的、與眾不同的 (*a.*)
✪ Contrast 對比 (*n.*)
✪ Polar 極的 (*a.*)
✪ Dry 乾的 (*a.*)

The most distinctive aspect of the earth is the contrast between its polar zones and the dry deserts.

地球極區與乾燥沙漠區的對比是地球與眾不同的一面。

★ KEY 10

✪ Halting 使停止 (*v.*)
✪ Barely 幾乎不 (*adv.*)
✪ Figure out 想出 (*v.*)
✪ Conquer 征服 (*v.*)

Most second language learners speak halting English with a heavy accent, so people can barely understand them; however, they will be ended up figuring out a way to perfectly pronounce words and conquering it.

大部分的第二語言學習者說英文時會停頓，並伴隨著很重的口音，導致聽的人幾乎無法理解他們，但是這些學習者最後還是會悟出可以完美發音的方法並征服它。

★ KEY 11

- ✪ Mimic 模仿 (*v.*)
- ✪ Abundant 豐富的 (*a.*)
- ✪ Tremendously 異常的、巨大的 (*adv.*)
- ✪ Master 駕馭 (*v.*)

Try to mimic the way people use their languages and there are abundant learning materials online that can be tremendously helpful for you to master a new language.

試著去模仿人們使用這個語言的方式，而且網路上有很多豐富的資源可以用來幫你去駕馭這個語言。

★ KEY 12

- ✪ Critics 評論家 (*n.*)
- ✪ Deprecate 抨擊、反對 (*v.*)

✪ Hinder 阻止 (*v.*)
✪ Release 釋放 (*v.*)

> The music critic deprecates this album as the worst album of the year with hindering the singer's plan of releasing her new songs.

這位音樂評論家砲轟這個專輯是今年最爛的專輯,並阻撓這位歌手要出新歌的計畫。

⭐ KEY 13

✪ Efforts 努力 (*n.*)
✪ Convince 使信服 (*v.*)
✪ Futile 細瑣的、無用的 (*a.*)
✪ Ineffective 無效的 (*a.*)

> He made efforts to convince his friends not to spend too much time on playing games but that was futile and completely ineffective.

他努力地說服他朋友別花太多時間在玩遊戲上面,但是結果完全無效。

⭐ KEY 14

✪ Inevitably 不可避免的 (*adv.*)
✪ Contend 鬥爭、競爭 (*v.*)

Unit 19

✪ Giving rise to 引起、導致 (*v.*)
✪ Elimination 消除 (*n.*)

As time went by, the government inevitably had to contend with those people who thought they had the right to talk to the president, giving rise to the elimination of such peace in the country.

隨著時間的流逝，政府無可避免地必須要和這些認為有權利跟總統講話的人民鬥爭，這導致了這個國家消失的和平。

★ **KEY 15**

✪ Eventually 最終地 (*adv.*)
✪ Entrench 防護、保護 (*v.*)
✪ Frequently 頻繁地 (*adv.*)
✪ Yield 被迫放棄 (*v.*)

Eventually, those people were strongly entrenched by the power of government and frequently yielded their powers to it.

最終這些人受到政府的保護，並且屢次地放棄並向政府給予他們的權力。

★ KEY 16

✪ Apparently 明顯地 (*adv.*)
✪ Contain 含有 (*v.*)
✪ Capacious 寬廣的 (*a.*)
✪ Extraordinary 非凡的 (*a.*)

Apparently, this apartment contains a capacious storage space that makes it an extraordinary choice for families with children.

很明顯地因為這個公寓包含一個很大的儲藏空間，所以對有小孩的家庭來說是個不錯的選擇。

★ KEY 17

✪ Hostile 有敵意的 (*a.*)
✪ Innovations 創新 (*n.*)
✪ Restricted 限制 (*v.*)
✪ Consolidate 鞏固、使聯合 (*v.*)

People living here are hostile to technological innovations that may threaten their traditions and are restricted to communicate with outsiders for the sake of consolidating the safety system.

為了鞏固他們的安全系統，居住在這裡的人們對於會危及他們傳統的科技創新帶有敵意，而且被限制不能與外來者交流。

★ KEY 18

- ✪ Intricate 錯綜複雜的 (*a.*)
- ✪ Confine to 限制於 (*v.*)
- ✪ Designate 指派 (*v.*)
- ✪ Ludicrous 可笑的、荒唐的 (*a.*)

> Due to the intricate process of obtaining the membership, candidates were particularly confined to stay in designated rooms and then take ludicrous tests.

因為取得會員的這個步驟很複雜，所以候選人必須要待在一個指定的房間，然後進行很荒唐的測試。

★ KEY 19

- ✪ Attack 攻擊 (*v.*)
- ✪ Arrest 逮捕 (*v.*)
- ✪ Intruder 入侵者 (*n.*)
- ✪ Delineate 描繪 (*v.*)

> This young man said he was attacked and arrested by an unknown intruder and was delineating how the intruder looked like with a portrait.

這個年輕人說他被一位不知名的入侵者攻擊並逮捕，他正描繪這個入侵者的長相。

KEY 20

✪ Imminent 逼近的、即將到來的 (*a.*)
✪ Emergency 緊急事件 (*n.*)
✪ Mitigate 減輕 (*v.*)
✪ Disaster 災害 (*n.*)

People were facing imminent death after the earthquake even though emergency funds were being provided to mitigate the effect of the disaster.

在地震過後，人們面臨了立即的死亡，即使已提供緊急的資金協助來減輕災害的傷亡。

攻克要點III 同義詞一覽表

Mitigate	Synonym	Diminish/ lighten/ allay/ alleviate
	Antonym	Agitate/ aggravate/ intensify
Imminent	Synonym	Impending/ immediate/ at hand
	Antonym	Distant/ avoidable/ escapable
Delineate	Synonym	Define/ depict/ outline/ describe
	Antonym	Confuse/ distort
Capacious	Synonym	Ample/ extensive
	Antonym	Small/ squeezed/ tiny
Convince	Synonym	Prove/ persuade
	Antonym	Dissuade/ discourage
Consolidate	Synonym	Combine / concentrate/ strengthen
	Antonym	Decrease/ disperse
Futile	Synonym	Pointless/ impractical
	Antonym	Effective/ fruitful/ productive
Hostile	Synonym	Adverse/ contentious / inhospitable
	Antonym	Aiding/ agreeable/ favorable
Arrest	Synonym	Capture/ detain/ apprehend
	Antonym	Liberate/ release
Attack	Synonym	Assault/ assail/ ambush
	Antonym	Aid/ assist/ guard

Intricate	Synonym	Complicated/ complex/ convoluted
	Antonym	Direct/apparent
Exceptional	Synonym	Extraordinary/ notable
	Antonym	Common/ inconsequential
Conquer	Synonym	Crush/ overthrow/ defeat
	Antonym	Release/ surrender/ yield
Deprecate	Synonym	Depreciate/ belittle
	Antonym	Approve/ commend/ compliment
Abundant	Synonym	Ample/ plentiful/ bountiful
	Antonym	Depleted/ insufficient
Elongate	Synonym	Lengthen/ extend
	Antonym	Shorten/ abbreviate/ curtail
Fragile	Synonym	Breakable/ delicate/ brittle
	Antonym	Strong/ durable
Accelerate	Synonym	Expedite/ stimulate/ hasten
	Antonym	Cease/ delay/ halt
Exquisite	Synonym	Admirable/ delicate/ impeccable
	Antonym	Careless/ flawed/ imperfect
Ubiquitous	Synonym	Omnipresent/ universal / pervasive
	Antonym	Rare/ scarce

攻克要點Ⅰ 必考字彙表

KEY1
Astonishing 令人驚喜的 (*a.*)	Civilization 文明 (*n.*)
Emerge 出現 (*v.*)	Approximately 大約 (*adv.*)

KEY2
Origin 起源 (*n.*)	Remain 保留 (*v.*)
Obscure 難解的、含糊的 (*a.*)	Related 相關的 (*a.*)

KEY3
Rival 對手 (*n.*)	Contact 接觸 (*v.*)
Retain 保留 (*v.*)	Distinct 清楚的、不同的 (*a.*)

KEY4
Plow 犁 (*n.*)	Oxen 公牛 (*n.*)
Invent 發明 (*v.*)	Enable 使…成為可能 (*v.*)

KEY5
Assume 推測 (*v.*)	Perceive 察覺 (*v.*)
Natural selection 自然選擇 (*n.*)	Gradual 逐漸的 (*a.*)

KEY6
Pervasive 廣泛的，普遍的 (*a.*)	Recognize 認識 (*v.*)
Connote 暗示、表示 (*v.*)	Root 根 (*n.*)

KEY7

Dialect 方言 (*n.*)	Evolve 演化 (*v.*)
Restrain 限制 (*v.*)	Isolate 隔離 (*v.*)

KEY8

Stratification 階層化 (*n.*)	Nutrients 養分 (*n.*)
Constant 不斷的 (*a.*)	Shallow 淺的 (*a.*)

KEY9

Fungi 真菌類 (*n.*)	Reef 礁 (*n.*)
Resilient 有回復力的 (*a.*)	Bleach 漂白 (*v.*)

KEY10

Numerous 廣大的 (*a.*)	Texture 質地 (*n.*)
Accessories 飾品 (*n.*)	Unique 獨有的 (*a.*)

KEY11

Sculptures 雕刻 (*n.*)	Marble 大理石 (*n.*)
Granite 花崗岩 (*n.*)	Acid 酸 (*a.*)

KEY12

Weathering 風化 (*n.*)	Humid 潮濕的 (*a.*)
Tropical 熱帶的 (*a.*)	Mechanical 機械的 (*a.*)

KEY13

Planet 星球 (*n.*)	Manifest 顯現 (*v.*)
Evidence 證據 (*n.*)	Atmosphere 大氣 (*n.*)

KEY14

Harsh 嚴苛的 (*a.*)	Preexisting 先前存在的 (*a.*)
Microorganisms 微生物 (*n.*)	Adapted to 適應於 (*v.*)

KEY15

Canal 運河、渠道 (*n.*)	Irrigation 灌溉 (*n.*)
Coastal 海岸的 (*a.*)	Deserts 沙漠 (*n.*)

KEY16

Consume 消耗 (*v.*)	A great amount 大量 (*adv.*)
Maintain 維持 (*v.*)	Figure 體型 (*n.*)

KEY17

Enormously 大地 (*adv.*)	Mammal 哺乳類 (*n.*)
Breed 養育 (*v.*)	Bear 負荷 (*v.*)

KEY18

Require 需要 (*v.*)	Quantities 數量 (*n.*)
Particular 特別的 (*a.*)	Prefer 比較喜歡 (*v.*)

KEY19

Defensive 防禦的 (*a.*)	Frighten off 嚇退 (*v.*)
Ostensible 表面的 (*a.*)	Alarming 驚嚇 (*a.*)

KEY20

A wide array of 大量 (*n.*)	Decorative 裝飾性的 (*a.*)
Tranquility 寂靜 (*n.*)	Horn 角 (*n.*)

攻克要點II 超給力例句

★ KEY 1　♪ MP3 20

- ✪ Astonishing　令人驚喜的 (*a.*)
- ✪ Civilization 文明 (*n.*)
- ✪ Emerge 出現 (*v.*)
- ✪ Approximately 大約 (*adv.*)

It is such an astonishing fact that human civilization has emerged into the light of history approximately three thousand years ago.

人類文明始於約三千年前的歷史中，是個令人驚喜的事實。

★ KEY 2

- ✪ Origin 起源 (*n.*)
- ✪ Remain 保留 (*v.*)
- ✪ Obscure 難解的、含糊的 (*a.*)
- ✪ Related 相關的 (*a.*)

The origin of this civilization remains obscure because the languages they use are not quite related to any other known tongues in the world.

這個文明的起源依舊很模糊，因為他們所使用的語言跟其他世界上所知的語言並沒有關聯。

KEY 3

- ✪ Rival 對手 (*n.*)
- ✪ Contact 接觸 (*v.*)
- ✪ Retain 保留 (*v.*)
- ✪ Distinct 清楚的、不同的 (*a.*)

> For about twenty years, although the two rival centers in the Middle East region had contacted with each other from their earliest beginning, they still retained their distinct characters.

雖然這競爭的兩方於大約二十年前在中東地區就開始相互接觸，他們還是保有他們清楚且明顯不同的特性。

KEY 4

- ✪ Plow 犁 (*n.*)
- ✪ Oxen 公牛 (*n.*)
- ✪ Invent 發明 (*v.*)
- ✪ Enable 使…成為可能 (*v.*)

> About five thousand years ago, plow that oxen can pull was invented by Egyptian and Mesopotamian farmers, enabling more and more people to give up farming and then move to cities.

大約五千年前，牛所拉的犁田工具是被美索布達米雅以及埃及農夫所發明的，使得更多的人放棄農耕朝大都市發展。

★ KEY 5

- ✪ Assume 推測 (*v.*)
- ✪ Perceive 察覺 (*v.*)
- ✪ Natural selection 自然選擇 (*n.*)
- ✪ Gradual 逐漸的 (*a.*)

> Darwin assumed that it would not have been possible to perceive natural selection due to the fact that it was too slow and gradual in general.

達爾文推測說自然選擇是不容易被察覺的，因為一般來說它太慢而且是逐漸變化的。

★ KEY 6

- ✪ Pervasive 廣泛的，普遍的 (*a.*)
- ✪ Recognize 認識 (*v.*)
- ✪ Connote 暗示、表示 (*v.*)

✪ Root 根 (*n.*)

> The study claims that this pervasive painting is widely recognized in European countries, connoting the drawing skill of human beings may share the same root.

研究指出這普遍流傳的畫作在歐洲國家廣為人知，表示說人類的繪畫技巧是有相同來源的。

⭐ KEY 7

✪ Dialect 方言 (*n.*)
✪ Evolve 演化 (*v.*)
✪ Restrain 限制 (*v.*)
✪ Isolate 隔離 (*v.*)

> Dialects may evolve into a new language if they are restrained in a particular area for long, especially isolated districts or islands.

如果方言長期被限制於特定的區域，特別指被隔離的區域或是島嶼，它們可以演化成新的語言。

⭐ KEY 8

✪ Stratification 階層化 (*n.*)
✪ Nutrients 養分 (*n.*)
✪ Constant 不斷的 (*a.*)

✪ Shallow 淺的 (*a.*)

The stratification of the nutrients may not be formed because of the constant mixing of the shallow sea.

因為淺海水體不斷的混合，養分的階層化可能不容易形成。

★ **KEY 9**

✪ Fungi 真菌類 (*n.*)
✪ Reef 礁 (*n.*)
✪ Resilient 有回復力的 (*a.*)
✪ Bleach 漂白 (*v.*)

Due to the natural protection from certain types of fungi living in co-existence, some reefs remain healthy under damage and appear to be more resilient to coral bleaching than others.

因為受到特定共存的菌類的天然的保護，一些礁可以在損害下維持健康，而且可以在珊瑚白化中，相較於其他未受到菌類保護的，更有復原力。

★ **KEY 10**

✪ Numerous 廣大的 (*a.*)
✪ Texture 質地 (*n.*)
✪ Accessories 飾品 (*n.*)

✪ Unique 獨有的 (*a.*)

There are numerous styles of clothing in China related to the Asian history with their texture and accessories having unique meanings.

中國存有大量不同形式且關於亞洲歷史的服飾，其中他們的質地與飾品都有的獨特的意義。

★ KEY 11

✪ Sculptures 雕刻 (*n.*)
✪ Marble 大理石 (*n.*)
✪ Granite 花崗岩 (*n.*)
✪ Acid 酸 (*a.*)

Some buildings and sculptures made of marble and granite are more likely to be damaged by acid rain than those made by others.

使用花崗岩與大理石所製成的建築物與雕刻，相較於用其他材料製造的，比較容易被酸雨所毀壞。

★ KEY 12

✪ Weathering 風化 (*n.*)
✪ Humid 潮濕的 (*a.*)
✪ Tropical 熱帶的 (*a.*)

✪ Mechanical 機械的 (*a.*)

Chemical weathering may be more likely to take place and be more effective in humid tropical climate, while mechanical weathering may occur in sub-Arctic climates.

化學風化可能更易發生於潮濕的熱帶氣候，而機械性風化比較容易發生在亞北極區。

★ KEY 13

✪ Planet 星球 (*n.*)
✪ Manifest 顯現 (*v.*)
✪ Evidence 證據 (*n.*)
✪ Atmosphere 大氣 (*n.*)

Scientists have announced that the surface of the planet Mars manifests evidence of having ancient water and volcanoes, and it has an atmosphere with seasons and weather changing.

科學家指出火星的表面顯現了曾有水與火山存在的證據，火星的大氣有季節與氣候的變換。

★ KEY 14

✪ Harsh 嚴苛的 (*a.*)

✪ Preexisting 先前存在的 (*a.*)
✪ Microorganisms 微生物 (*n.*)
✪ Adapted to 適應於 (*v.*)

> We are still not sure whether life could start in such a harsh environment as on Mars even though preexisting Martian microorganisms could have adapted to the environment with high acidity and saltiness.

雖然先前就存在過火星微生物可以適應的高酸性、高鹽分的惡劣環境，我們現在始終不太確定到底火星上嚴酷的環境能否有生命的存在。

⭐ KEY 15

✪ Canal 運河、渠道 (*n.*)
✪ Irrigation 灌溉 (*n.*)
✪ Coastal 海岸的 (*a.*)
✪ Deserts 沙漠 (*n.*)

> The canal has been a national-scale irrigation project carrying water from the wet coastal areas to the dry central deserts.

這個貫通國家的灌溉渠道把水從潮濕的沿海區域帶進乾燥的中部沙漠。

★ KEY 16

- ✪ Consume 消耗 (*v.*)
- ✪ A great amount 大量
- ✪ Maintain 維持 (*v.*)
- ✪ Figure 體型 (*n.*)

> One of the reasons why it might be quite difficult for huge sized animals to live is that they need to consume a great amount of food to maintain the sizable figure.

大型動物比較不容易生存的其中一個原因是他們需要消耗大量的食物去維持牠們相對大的體型。

★ KEY 17

- ✪ Enormously 大的 (*adv.*)
- ✪ Mammal 哺乳類 (*n.*)
- ✪ Breed 養育 (*v.*)
- ✪ Bear 負荷 (*v.*)

> Sauropods are enormously huge than the biggest mammals on modern Earth, and due to their breeding characteristic, they can only bear one descendant at a time, according to Scientific American.

根據《科學人》，這種長頸龍比現在地球上最大的哺乳類動物還要大得多，而且由於牠的繁殖特色，牠一次只可以養育一個後代。

✪ Require 需要 (*v.*)
✪ Quantities 數量 (*n.*)
✪ Particular 特別的 (*a.*)
✪ Prefer 比較喜歡 (*v.*)

We all know that she requires large quantities of vegetal food to lose weight fast, but we have no idea as to what particular types of food or vegetable she prefers in the diet.

我們都知曉她需要大量的蔬菜來快速減重，但我們卻不知道她在減重中比較偏向於哪些特別的食物或是蔬菜。

★ KEY 19

✪ Defensive 防禦的 (*a.*)
✪ Frighten off 嚇退 (*v.*)
✪ Ostensible 表面的 (*a.*)
✪ Alarming 驚嚇 (*a.*)

Psychologists claim that this defensive behavior has well been known for being used to frighten off potential hunters as an ostensible alarming act.

心理學家指出這個防禦行動被廣泛認知為一種表面上的警示行為，用於嚇退可能的狩獵者。

KEY 20

✪ A wide array of 大量 (*n.*)
✪ Decorative 裝飾性的 (*a.*)
✪ Tranquility 寂靜 (*n.*)
✪ Horn 角 (*n.*)

A wide array of decorative items representing tranquility are widely applied to the surface of their traditional clothing, such as feathers, pearls, horns, or teeth.

大量帶有寧靜意義的裝飾品像是羽毛、珍珠角或牙齒被廣泛使用在傳統服飾上。

Unit 20

攻克要點III 同義詞一覽表

Ostensible	Synonym	Plausible/ avowed/ professed
	Antonym	Improbable/ obscure
Restrain	Synonym	Confine/ constrain
	Antonym	Aid/allow/ assist
Require	Synonym	Demand/ call for
	Antonym	Disallow/ give
Particular	Synonym	Specific/ exact/ peculiar
	Antonym	Ambiguous/ ordinary
Prefer	Synonym	Go for/ choose/ adopt
	Antonym	Refuse/ reject
isolate	Synonym	Confine/ detach/ disconnect
	Antonym	Attach/ combine/ connect
Consume	Synonym	Absorb/ devour/deplete
	Antonym	fill
Maintain	Synonym	Continue/ control/ keep
	Antonym	Abandon/ destroy
Harsh	Synonym	Rough/ crude
	Antonym	Calm/ easy
Adapt	Synonym	Acclimate/ accommodate/ conform
	Antonym	Neglect/ refuse
Manifest	Synonym	Demonstrate/ illustrate
	Antonym	Conceal/ hide

Evidence	Synonym	Clue/ confirmation
	Antonym	Denial/ concealment
Humid	Synonym	Dank/ moist/ wet
	Antonym	Dehydrated/ arid/ dry
Connote	Synonym	Imply/ signify/ denote
	Antonym	Conceal/ hide
Perceive	Synonym	Discern/ distinguish/ observe
	Antonym	Disbelieve/ disregard/ ignore
Numerous	Synonym	Abundant/ plentiful/ diverse
	Antonym	Little/ miniature
Unique	Synonym	Exclusive/ particular/ rare
	Antonym	Common/ normal
Resilient	Synonym	Flexible/ bouncy/ volatile
	Antonym	Delicate/ weak/ rigid/ stuff
Shallow	Synonym	Flat/trivial/ depthless
	Antonym	Deep/full
Constant	Synonym	Ceaseless/ continual/ continuous
	Antonym	Broken/ ceasing/ discontinuous

題目篇

1. Overgrazing was one of the _____ factors contributing to the extinction of certain kinds of animals.
   A. primary
   B. reluctant
   C. expected
   D. staunch

2. There are still proponents attempting to be the support of those _____ and barely accessible articles.
   A. concrete
   B. abstract
   C. feasible
   D. flexible

3. I just could not imagine how _____ this test would be even though I have gotten a bunch of comprehensive reading materials from my friends.
   A. easy
   B. complex
   C. stable
   D. severe

Unit 21

4. The drawings found in this cave depicted that the attack of an adjacent country fully _____ the defenses of the village.
   A. decimated
   B. established
   C. stimulated
   D. pacified

5. People nowadays are supposed to _____ and be thankful for what our ancestors did to make our life even more convenient.
   A. contradict
   B. acknowledge
   C. revoke
   D. shift

6. The chemical pollutants released from this array of plants, have been _____ to be detrimental to human body.
   Affirmed is in the closest meaning to this word.
   A. justified
   B. attested
   C. solicited
   D. disproved

7. Scientists just found there will be a huge, _____ explosion taking place in our solar system. *Inescapable* is in the closest meaning to this word.
   A. underlying
   B. inevitable
   C. potential
   D. substantial

8. This inauspicious sign will _____ the success of this upcoming presentation.
   A. inhibit
   B. facilitate
   C. urge
   D. trigger

9. This lethal disease _____ this child from breathing and walking.
   A. hinders
   B. encourages
   C. permits
   D. remedies

10. We have to _____ in what we believe is right and what we have in nature.

    A. cease

    B. prolong

    C. persist

    D. halt

11. He took a _____ journey through the hostile territory around the Middle East area.

    A. perilous

    B. definite

    C. secure

    D. predominant

12. This world is a _____ where people have to fight a war for peace.

    A. normality

    B. standard

    C. paradox

    D. phenomenon

13. The government should have a well-prepared program to protect this _____ forest that has never been subjected to logging or development.
    A. pristine
    B. affected
    C. monotonous
    D. obscure

14. Scientists from around the world are still _____ for the cause of the decimation.
    A. replying
    B. ignoring
    C. probing
    D. invading

15. Regardless of the ranking, our chemistry department has a good reputation, but the school's science facilities are _____ lacking a bit.
    A. relatively
    B. invariably
    C. definitely
    D. inevitably

16. You have to be constantly keeping a _____ eye on everything and being energetic to your work.
    A. inattentive
    B. wary
    C. incautious
    D. harsh

17. This brilliant 5-year old child impressed the audience with his concise, _____ answers to the host's questions.
    A. pertinent
    B. improper
    C. irrelevant
    D. groundless

18. The grounds he provided to explain why he murdered his wife were _____ .
    Unconvincing is in the closest meaning to this word.
    A. convincing
    B. believable
    C. implausible
    D. dispensable

19. A few modifications need to be made to prevent the project from being _____ .
    A. aborted
    B. continued
    C. carried on
    D. disintegrated

20. The ancient city _____ by high waves was full of endangered reptiles.
    A. uncovered
    B. engulfed
    C. underwhelmed
    D. distributed

Unit 21 解答表

1. A	6. B	11. A	16. B
2. B	7. B	12. C	17. A
3. B	8. A	13. A	18. C
4. A	9. A	14. C	19. A
5. B	10. C	15. A	20. B

NOTE

1. The former CEO has _____ herself of most of her responsibilities and has already delegated someone to take over all her works.
   A. divested
   B. given
   C. offered
   D. endowed

2. This young scientist intensely _____ himself to the study of physics in college with his best endurance and endeavor.
   A. devotes
   B. refrains
   C. withholds
   D. disassemble

3. The purpose of this task is to _____ how fast the certain amount of salt and sugar would evenly diffuse and dissolve in water.
   A. assemble
   B. neglect
   C. figure out

D. disband

4. Mount Olympus has long been well-known for being the _____ place of the gods.
   A. dwelling
   B. moving
   C. departing
   D. erratic

5. Research studies into finding alternative energy sources have been _____ by this funding increase.
   A. dictated
   B. stimulated
   C. halted
   D. dissuaded

6. Standing at the _____ of a new page of his life, he has to make effort to pursue the goal he set.
   A. disposition
   B. threshold
   C. conclusion
   D. completion

7. He attempts to make his company the most
   prosperous and _____ business in Asia.
   A. inferior
   B. poor
   C. unsurpassed
   D. dispensable

8. Because of the corruption issue occurring between
   faculties and governors, the university _____ the
   committee and started having an intense scrutiny of
   the members involved.
   A. disbanded
   B. assembled
   C. encouraged
   D. ignited

9. The impressive interior designs _____ this church
   and made this a magnificent achievement.
   A. adorned
   B. disfigured
   C. spoiled
   D. induced

10. Running a _____ business involves a great deal of patience, speed, perseverance, and creativity.
    A. impoverished
    B. prosperous
    C. lacking
    D. harsh

11. The lawyer designated to deal with this case said that the suspect already knew the _____ of what he had done.
    A. consequence
    B. begging
    C. source
    D. hazard

12. Research studies indicate that the stone with a strange shape found at the largest basin in South Africa was _____ with Latin inscription by a brutal captain from France.
    A. neglected
    B. engraved
    C. dislodged
    D. exceeded

Unit 22

13. He was struggling with all kinds of _____ taking place in this life.
    A. adversity
    B. assistance
    C. benefit
    D. evidence

14. He was _____ of having an affair with another woman.
    A. accused
    B. applauded
    C. approved
    D. contrived

15. She was quite _____ because not everyone approved of the events she had hosted.
    A. beneficial
    B. upset _____
    C. comforted
    D. content

16. According to the recently revealed studies about Moon, there may be no underground supplies that could be used for lunar inhabitants due to the possible fact that the interior Moon is essentially _____ water.

A. devoid of

B. full

C. augmented

D. vigorous

17. The hospital's operating rooms are full of the latest medical _____ that could be especially helpful for doctors to save people and increase surgical strength and experiences.

Appliance is in the closest meaning to this word.

A. apparatus

B. vehicle

C. zenith

D. threshold

18. Nowadays a large number of people in Korea were appalled at the misconduct of their president on _____ the scandal even though they had voted for her.

Dealing with is in the closest meaning to this word.

A. dodging

B. abstaining

C. tackling

D. transforming

19. The audience of The Ellen Show definitely cherishes every opportunity they _____ to win free flight tickets, free presents, and money donated by other organizations.

Acquire is in the closest meaning to this word.

A. decline

B. gain

C. diminish

D. trigger

20. Researchers and scientists have been _____ in searching for a cure for the SARS, AIDS, and Ebola virus due to lacking funding by the academy.

Hamper is in the closest meaning to this word.

A. handicapped

B. allowed

C. facilitated

D. substituted

Unit 22 解答表

1. A	6. B	11. A	16. A
2. A	7. C	12. B	17. A
3. C	8. A	13. A	18. C
4. A	9. A	14. A	19. B
5. B	10. B	15. B	20. A

★ NOTE

1. The speaker _____ the vague allegations, claiming that the statement was untrue.
   A. denied
   B. accepted
   C. allowed
   D. burgeoned

2. The incident happening at a critical point in the campaign forces the Britain authorities to consider an airlift if the situation becomes even more _____ in the next few hours.
   A. ancient
   B. uncontrollable
   C. manageable
   D. moderate

3. The American government has been continuing their efforts to _____ a supply line from enemy raids after an agreement to a cease-fire was approved.
   A. secure
   B. endanger
   C. insecure
   D. appear

4. Before _____ replacement, we have to investigate the possible reasons why all the chairs, books, and tables are all damaged and lost.
   A. hindering
   B. dispatching
   C. impeding
   D. aggravating

5. Since the speaking you had was too _____ and general, the girls, apparently, were not amused and would not join the upcoming party in your apartment.
   A. vague
   B. distinct
   C. explicit
   D. ample

Unit 23

6. A proposal outlining how global warming would be controlled in the following years was submitted and instantly voted through, _____ by enthusiastic applause.

A. abandoned

B. altered

C. accompanied

D. disregarded

7. There is little or even no _____ to adopt this method due to the fact that the scientific assumption the global warming theory is based on was questioned by Dr. Chen.

A. prevention

B. incentive

C. hindrance

D. alarm

8. These two counties acceded to try to settle their _____ by negotiation.

A. disputes

B. agreement

C. concord

D. sustenance

9. The instructors have the project well executed and hope that their efforts will _____ a sense of responsibility in both children and parents and affect their lives.
   A. substitute
   B. instill
   C. take out
   D. uproot

10. The prosecutors of this gang _____ to overthrow the government.
    A. neglected
    B. conspired
    C. disagreed
    D. took

11. The patient is so happy in that all his symptoms have already been _____ .
    A. relieved
    B. aggravated
    C. agitated
    D. sustained

12. Due to increased risk of MERS infections, the presidential candidate announced that at least three countries are going to _____ Korean imports to a maximum of twenty percent of their markets.

A. assist

B. restrict

C. develop

D. soak

13. He was accused of _____ cutting a branch off the tree.

A. deliberately

B. unintentionally

C. singularly

D. unwittingly

14. The superstar was taking a sip of her coffee while _____ a painting hung on the wall.

Neatening is in the closest meaning to this word.

A. straightening up

B. shielding

C. disarranging

D. dispersing

15. She started using furniture polish to _____ her favorite sofa back to its original look.
    A. destroy
    B. restore
    C. decline
    D. refine

16. My mom was _____ against the wall feeling tired after doing household chores.
    A. disregarding
    B. leaning
    C. reserving
    D. straightening

17. Since Korea is celebrating the one hundredth anniversary of the birth of Emperor Lee, the person in charge of Central Bank decides to _____ the interest rates by five percent.
    A. lower
    B. elevate
    C. increase
    D. rotate

Unit 23

18. We can tell from this year's budget for AIDS prevention that probably the government's initiative to help AIDS patients has been _____ .
Lacking is in the closest meaning to this word.
A. inadequate
B. abundant
C. sufficient
D. sacred

19. Our government needs to make a revision of how we take care of our elders due to the fact that supplies of food and medicines are _____ and to ensure that all of them are safely settled down.
A. insufficient
B. adequate
C. sufficient
D. remote

20. School of Education is deemed as one of the outstandingly equipped and _____ schools in this university.
A. prestigious
B. insignificant
C. ordinary
D. scorching

Unit 23 解答表

1. A	6. C	11. A	16. B
2. B	7. B	12. B	17. A
3. A	8. A	13. A	18. A
4. B	9. B	14. A	19. A
5. A	10. B	15. B	20. A

NOTE

Unit 23

Unit 24

1. Right in the conference, researchers are proposing that nowadays Taiwan still _____ the traditional ways of celebrating Lunar Chinese New Year.
   A. retains
   B. abandons
   C. excludes
   D. ruptures

2. The copy of the itinerary in which their honey moon location are listed seems _____ so they decide to discuss with an attorney they have enough faiths in.
   A. imprecise
   B. definite
   C. accurate
   D. rigorous

3. Aluminum is the most _____ metallic element in the Earth's crust.
   A. abundant
   B. depleted
   C. insufficient
   D. scant

4. Aluminum has been found to be _____ to human bodies, especially for abdomen that contains a twenty feet long small intestine.

   Poisonous is in the closest meaning to this word.

   A. fatal

   B. blessed

   C. harmless

   D. radical

5. Volcanic _____ and debris avalanches always accompany other natural disasters, such as earthquake and tsunami.

   A. trickle

   B. eruptions

   C. realm

   D. ramification

6. With its extraordinary size and power, a mountain is believed to be the _____ storehouse of national resources.

   A. miniature

   B. vast

   C. bounded

   D. renowned

Unit 24

7. The frozen archives have been _____ gradually and give scientists unprecedented views of the history of earth's crust.
   A. disclosed
   B. concealed
   C. denied
   D. recurred

8. Sounds waves, like other types of frequencies, are _____ in an undulating manner.
   A. transmitting
   B. gathering
   C. holding
   D. reserving

9. The reason why the Sun always appears in the polar regions of the Moon is that the Moon's axis of _____ is almost perpendicular to the surface of its orbit around the Sun.
   A. pledge
   B. rotation
   C. stagnation
   D. repercussion

10. The presidential candidate's illuminations of her viewpoints on a number of _____ issues left many supporters in confusion.
    Questionable is in the closest meaning to this word.
    A. certain
    B. controversial
    C. undisputed
    D. prosperous

11. The analysis of ways to deal with global warming needs to be considered deeply to see which method could be properly adopted and more economically _____ .
    Achievable is in the closest meaning to this word.
    A. feasible
    B. implausible
    C. impractical
    D. prevailing

12. According to the psychological studies, many doctors claimed that people with a lot of phobias may be _____ as having unusually high stress levels.
    Defined is in the closest meaning to this word.
    A. characterized
    B. confused
    C. mixed up
    D. protruded

13. Scientists said that the criminal propensities of the family may _____ over several generations because children may be forced to do what they are not intended to do by their parents.
    A. pursue
    B. extend
    C. abbreviate
    D. cease

14. The article says that scientists are collecting ice cores by driving a _____ tube deep into the miles thick ice sheets of glaciers, a large body of ice moving slowly down a slope or valley.
    Unfilled is in the closest meaning to this word.
    A. hollow
    B. honest
    C. solid
    D. radical

15. According to the book discussing the role of slaves played in the nation's history, we know that one _____ cause of the Civil War was for the emancipation of all slaves in the South.
    Basic is in the closest meaning to this word.
    A. pronounced
    B. underlying

C. secondary

D. plausible

16. Since the temperature is getting higher, by mid-
morning, the fog that has _____ this village just
evaporates and the land covered with an exceptional
amount of snow appears right in front of us.
Cloak is in the closest meaning to this word.
A. postulated
B. enshrouded
C. disclosed
D. exposed

17. Some prestigious scientists believe that the evolution
of the universe basically depends on a series of
_____ , which is also essential in the formation of
galaxy and planets.
Blast is in the closest meaning to this word.
A. implosion
B. explosions
C. predicament
D. proximity

18. The funding increase has been _____ those research studies to find alternative energy sources, making scientists perform a more strenuous work on their experiment.
    A. dissuading
    B. stimulating
    C. discouraging
    D. prolonging

19. Situated close to the Atlantic Ocean, France has a _____ climate with temperatures ranging from fifteen to thirty Celsius degrees so that people from Greenland and Alaska would escape a cold polar region by vacationing down south.
    A. prohibitive
    B. temperate
    C. harsh
    D. excessive

20. The reason why people decided to settle down in England is that the constitution _____ religious tolerance.
    Assure is in the closest meaning to this word.
    A. guarantees
    B. injures
    C. contradicts
    D. precedes

Unit 24 解答表

1. A	6. B	11. A	16. B
2. A	7. A	12. A	17. B
3. A	8. A	13. B	18. B
4. A	9. B	14. A	19. B
5. B	10. B	15. B	20. A

★ NOTE

1. General causes for primary lung cancer can include
   _____ , the establishment of a pathogen in its host
   after invasion, or exposure to chemical toxins such as
   insecticides.
   Epidemic is in the closest meaning to this word.
   A. sterility
   B. infections
   C. sanitation
   D. pigment

2. _____ , known as the transmission of some qualities
   from ancestors to descendants through the genes,
   might be one of the deciding factors in why some
   individuals may become clinically obese.
   Inheritance is in the closest meaning to this word.
   A. Nature
   B. Heredity
   C. Acquirement
   D. Objective

3. He was _____ by our instructor to figure out the ways to better educate retarded children, such developing a surveillance system to track records and analyzing every action they have in the lab.
Consigned is in the closest meaning to this word.
A. obscured
B. commissioned
C. discharged
D. dismissed

4. Abundant supplies of water and foods on this _____ island would make the establishment of a self-sustaining community much more feasible.
Confined is in the closest meaning to this word.
A. isolated
B. incorporated
C. mingled
D. disintegrated

5. Exercising would be the best way to protect our _____ organs and keep them working properly because it increases bone mass and is extremely significant to keep healthy and strong bones.
Inside is in the closest meaning to this word.
A. external
B. Internal
C. outer
D. dissipated

6. His favorite book, a classic of the mystery genre, _____ him toward a literary career.

A. diffused

B. inclined

C. dissuaded

D. prevented

7. Even though we have already known the potential _____ of age on a woman's fertility, scientists committed to fertility research claim that this is the first time a strong association has been found between age and male fertility.

Brunt is in the closest meaning to this word.

A. impact

B. failure

C. stillness

D. dispute

8. The study seems to overwhelmingly indicate that a critical period does exist by which second language learning must _____ in order to offer learners the possibilities to achieve native-like capabilities.

Initiate is in the closest meaning to this word.

A. dictate

B. commence

C. complete

D. conclude

9. The idol is having an interview in which she spoke with
_____ about the recent scandal; however, folks feel
she is still attempting to hide something, just as how
snakes camouflage in the sand or rocks.
Frankness is in the closest meaning to this word.

   A. unfairness   B. candor

   C. dishonesty   D. solicitation

10. Five days after Montgomery civil rights activists Rose
Park refused to _____ the city's rules mandating
segregation on buses, black residents launched a
bus boycott.
Comply is in the closest meaning to this word.

   A. obey

   B. decline

   C. disregard

   D. stockpile

11. There will be something happening to strike us,
according to the records that allow researchers to
_____ the impact of vital events from volcanic
eruptions to global warming.
Forecast is in the closest meaning to this word.

   A. conserve

   B. misunderstand

   C. predict

   D. ignore

Unit 25

12. A _____ trait to owls is that they can rotate their heads and necks as much as 270 degrees and to the blue whales is that they can dive down really deep into the ocean for long periods of time.

Exclusive is in the closest meaning to this word.

A. unique

B. normal

C. ordinary

D. conspicuous

13. Animals _____ a backbone as a distinguishing anatomical feature are known as vertebrates, including mammals, birds, reptiles, amphibians, and fishes.

Acquiring is in the closest meaning to this word.

A. possessing

B. lacking

C. abandoning

D. contemplating

14. Earthquake performs shaking or trembling of the earth that could be either volcanic or tectonic in origin and may cause tsunami to be generated when the seafloor abruptly _____ and vertically displaces the overlaying water.

Contorts is in the closest meaning to this word.

A. deforms

B. repairs

C. assists

D. contrives

15. He soon becomes a leader but feeling like rather overwhelmed in the _____ environment of the big city.
    Dynamic is in the closest meaning to this word.
    A. vibrant   B. apathetic
    C. dispirited   D. considerable

16. Vomiting, the process of disgorging the contents of the stomach through the mouth, sometimes happens when a person _____ a large amount of food and then intentionally vomits or has diarrhea for the purpose of avoiding weight gain.
    Devour is in the closest meaning to this word.
    A. accumulates
    B. constructs
    C. consumes
    D. collaborates

17. The business owner wary of _____ investors will be more likely to believe defensive investors who are less likely to make any mistakes.
    Combative is in the closest meaning to this word.
    A. aggressive
    B. complaisant
    C. calm
    D. unsurpassed

18. A large number of buildings in Tokyo, Japan, from as far as eighteen miles from the epicenter of the earthquake measuring 8.5 magnitudes, suffered _____ damage.

    Large-scale is in the closest meaning to this word.

    A. exclusive   B. extensive

    C. limited   D. versatile

19. Equation is usually a formal statement of the _____ or equivalence of mathematical or logical expressions, such as A + B = C, or an expression representing a chemical reaction quantitatively by means of chemical symbols.

    A. vagary

    B. equality

    C. dissimilarity

    D. difference

20. It was not until the end of the Civil War that the eternal succession of wars between opposing groups of citizens _____ in the United States of America.

    Terminate is in the closest meaning to this word.

    A. ceased

    B. persevered

    C. carried on

    D. unleashed

Unit 25 解答表

1. B	6. B	11. C	16. C
2. B	7. A	12. A	17. A
3. B	8. B	13. A	18. B
4. A	9. B	14. A	19. B
5. B	10. A	15. A	20. A

NOTE

附錄：Background Knowledge

1. Biology 生物學 (Entomology 昆蟲學/ Botany 植物學/ Zoology 動物學)

生物學的部分包含昆蟲學、植物學、以及動物學三部分。其中主要會出現的背景是昆蟲的身體構造以及他們如何適應環境與保護自己免受獵食者的危害、生物群落以及食肉類植物。

(1) ENTOMOLOGY 昆蟲學 Entomology is the study concerned with INSECTS (昆蟲). Experts who specialize in insects and ARTHROPODS (節肢動物) are called ENTOMOLOGISTS (昆蟲學家)

ANATOMY OF AN INSECT 昆蟲身體構造

★ Insects are a class of INVERTABRATES (無脊椎動物), with a EXOSKELETON (外骨骼), three pairs of jointed legs, a three-part body- consisting of HAED (頭部), THORAX (胸腔), ABDOMEN (腹部), compound eyes, and one pair of ANTENNAE (觸角). Exoskeleton is the outer covering of an insect which does not grow with an insect. The exoskeleton-shedding process called MOLTING (脫皮) happens when the outer cover becomes too tight and needs to be shed. The head part consists of mouthparts, compound eyes, and antennae. Almost all insects smell with their antennae (some of them taste and hear with antennae), mostly located between their compound eyes.

★ Adapted to modes of feeding, insects have different types of mouthparts. CHEWING (咀嚼) insects such as DRAGONFLIES (蜻蜓), TERMITES (白蟻), and BETTLES (甲蟲), have two MANDIBLES (下顎), one on each side of the head. The other type is called SUCKING (吸食) insects, such as MOSQUITOES (蚊子) with mouthparts used to pierce food items to enable sucking up internal fluids or blood.

ANTS

★ Ants form colonies, which consist mostly of STERILE (不育的) female ants building up castes of WORKERS (工蜂), some fertile males called DRONES (雄蜂), and one or more fertile females called QUEENS (女王蜂).

BEES

★ A bee colony consists of one QUEEN (女王蜂), thousands of WORKERS (工蜂), and hundreds of DRONES (雄蜂). Bees live in HIVES (蜂群), which is composed of multiple HONEYCOMBS (蜂巢). The beehive's internal structure is packed up densely with six-sided COMPARTMENTS (小隔間) called CELLS (蜂房). The survival of a bee hive depends on the SCOUT BEES (偵查蜂). They are sent out to look for a constant supply of NECTAR (花蜜) for their hive. They use a dance to locate where the food is in relation to the sun and to indicate the distance of the food based on how fast they dance.

HOW ANIMALS PROTECT THEMSELVES

★ The ways animals blend with their surroundings as to render them like the items and colors adjacent to them are called CAMOUFLAGE (偽裝). PROTECTIVE COLORATION (保護色) makes animals hard to be seen and disguises them as something else. For example, the CHAMELEON (變色龍) is green surrounded by leaves but turns down to be brown while moving slowly on the ground. WARNING COLORATION (警戒色) functions as warning to defense against predators.

(2) BOTANY 植物學

★ BIOMES 生物群落. Biomes are natural communities of plants, animals, and other organisms. There are types of biomes in the world, such as TUNDRA (凍原) TAIGA 針葉樹林, TEMPERATE CONIFEROUS/DECIDUOUS FOREST (溫帶節毬果/落葉 林), CHAPARRAL (叢林), DESERT (沙漠), SAVANNA (熱帶大草原), TROPICAL RAIN FOREST (熱帶雨林), and more.

THE STRUCTURE OF FORESTS 樹林分層

★ There are various STRATA (分層) of plants in every forest, consisting of five basic forest strata, from the lowest to the highest, the forest floor, the HERB (草本) layer, the SHRUB layer (矮樹層), the understory, and the CANOPY (樹冠層).

CARNIVOROUS PLANTS 食肉植物

★ CARNIVOROUS PLANTS (食肉植物) are insect-eating plants normally growing in an area where certain supplies of minerals are insufficient, such as NITROGEN (氮氣), making them adapt for obtaining needed nutrients.

★ Not only do carnivorous plants trap for gaining needed minerals, they also PHOTOSYTHESIZE (光合作用) to manufacture their own food.

★ The most well-known carnivorous plants include PITCHER PLANT (豬籠草) and VENUS'S-FLYTRAP (捕蠅草).

(3) ZOOLOGY 動物學

★ ZOOLOGY (動物學) is the branch of biology dealing with the animal kingdom. ZOOLOGISTS (動物學家), also known as animal scientists or animal biologists, research on everything related to the animal kingdom, including the structure, EMBRYOLOGY (胚胎學), EVOLUTION (進化), CLASSIFICATION (分類), habits, and more.

CAMOUFLAGE (偽裝)

★ The way animals blending themselves with their surroundings is called CAMOUFLAGE (偽裝). Animals can choose to perform any of the following ways to resemble their surroundings: PROTECTIVE COLORATION (保護色), WARNING COLORATION (警戒色), or MIMICRY (擬態).

PROTECTIVE COLORATION (保護色)

★ Animals change their colors to be like where they are, for example, a dark MOTH (蛾) laying against the dark bark of a tree to be invisible.

WARNING COLORATION (警戒色)

★ The other type of protective coloration is WARNING COLORATION (保護色), serving to warn potential predators of the harm that could come from attacking or eating them. Normally the insects are brightly colored, for example, like LADYBUGS (瓢蟲) and BUMBLEBEES (大黃蜂). The warning coloration reminds their intended predators they taste bad.

MIMICRY (擬態)

★ MIMICRY (擬態) means the resemblance of one species to another in its surroundings for concealment and protection. For instance, green insects act like green leaves.

2. POLITICS 政治學

★ Delegates from 12 colonies met in the First Continental Congress (第一次大陸會議) in the Philadelphia.The DECLARATION OF INDEPENDENCE (獨立宣言) was officially declared in the SECOND CONTINENTAL CONGRESS (第二次大陸會議) and adopted to form the United States of America. Legislature of the America is bicameral legislature, which possesses two separate chambers, the SENATE (參議院) and the HOUSE OF REPRESENTITIVES (眾議院).

3. ECOLOGY (生態學) 生態學主要注意的是兩生物體間的關聯以及替代能源的議題

★ ECOLOGY(生態學) is the study of interaction between living organisms and the environment.

FOOD WE (CHAIN) (食物鏈)

★ PRODUCER (生產者) converts light energy into chemical energy and stores it in their cells. HERBIVORES (草食類) is the primary consumers that eat producers. The secondary consumers is CARNIVORES (肉食類). OMNIVORES (雜食類) consume both plants and animals. DECOMPOSERS (分解者) get energy from decayed plants and animals and give it to DETRIVORES (食腐者).

SYMBIOSIS(共生現象)

★ SYMBIOSIS(共生現象) is an interaction between two or more different biological species living together and can be used to explain any association between two living organisms.Biologists classified symbiosis into the following three forms: COMMENSALISM (共生關係)、 MUTUALISM (互利共生)、 PARASITISM (寄生關係)

ALTRUISM (利他主義)

★ ALTRUISM (利他主義) is the principle of concern for the welfare of others..

ALTERNATIVE ENERGY (替代能源)

★ WATER POWER (水力發電) / SOLAR ENERGY (太陽能) / WIND POWER (風力發電) / TIDAL ENERGY (潮汐能源). SPRING TIDES (朔望潮) are SEMIDIURNAL TIDES (半日潮) happening when sun, earth, and moon are in line, occurring at times of FULL

MOON (滿月) and NEW MOON (新月). On the other hand, NEAP TIDES (小潮) are semidiurnal tides happening when the sun, earth, and moon forms a right angle with earth located in the middle.

GEOTHERMAL POWER (地熱)

★ GEOTHERMAL POWER (地熱) occurs whenever steam is made with water coming in contact with hot rocks underneath the surface of the earth.

4. ASTROLOGY 占星術　ASTRONOMY 天文學

天文學的部分主要注意的是宇宙的擴張理論、八大行星、冥王星以及小行星帶的英文。並且對於星體演化過程中各個過程的名詞做強調。

ASTRONOMY 天文學

★ ASTRONOMY (天文學) is the study of the UNIVERSE (宇宙), including COSMOLOGY (宇宙學), the study of CELESTIAL BODIES (天體), and observations and theories of the SOLAR SYSTEM (太陽系).

ASTRONOMER 太空人

★ Astronomers are the groups of experts using tools, for example, TELESCOPES (望遠鏡), SPECTROGRAPHS (光譜儀), and computers, to observe and analyze the changes the astronomical objects have.

THE BIG BANG THEORY 大霹靂理論

★ THE BIG BANG THEORY (大霹靂理論) is the modern theory, indicating the EXPANSION (擴張) of the universe is the key part of the beginning of our universe.

★ The "BIG BANG" indicates the huge EXPLOSION (爆炸) the universe began with. The universe was composed of intense RADIATION (輻射) and PARTICLES (例子) after that huge explosion. In time, those particles broke apart into huge CLUMPS (塊), forming the GALAXIES (銀河系), with groups of CLUSTERS (群). The clumps formed STARS (星體) in the galaxies and part of them became the sun and other astronomical objects in our SOLAR SYSTEM (太陽系).

GALAXIES 銀河系

★ GALAXY(銀河系) is an uneven-distributed system in space, held together by GRAVITY (重力), with stars, gas, and dust in it.

★ Our SOLAR SYSTEM (太陽系) is within the galaxy called THE MILKY WAY (銀河系). Some of the galaxies are SPIRAL (螺旋狀) and some are OVAL (卵形的), ELLIPTICAL (橢圓狀), or irregular (不規則狀的).

THE HOBBLE SPACE TELESCOPE (HST) 哈伯望遠鏡

★ THE HOBBLE SPACE TELESCOPE (哈伯望遠鏡) is the REFLECTING (反射式) telescope that orbits around the EARTH (地球) and transmits back the clearest images of any OPTICAL (光學的) telescopes.

REDSHIFT 紅移/ BLUESHIFT 藍移

★ REDSHIFT (紅移) is a stretching of the WAVELENGTHS (波長) while BLUESHIFT (藍移) is the COMPRESSION (壓縮) of wavelengths.A REDSHIFT (紅移) occurs whenever an object emitting the radiation moves away from an observer, while BLUESHIFT (藍移) occurs whenever an object moves toward the observer.

STELLAR EVOLUTION 星的演化

★ NEBULA (星雲), PROTOSTAR (原始星), RED GIANT (紅巨星), SUPERGIANT (超巨星). SUPERGIANT (超巨星), SUPERNOVA (超新星), NEUTRON STAR (中子星), BLACK HOLE (黑洞). PANETARY NEBULA (行星星雲), WHITE DWARF (白矮星), BLACK DWARF (黑矮星).

CEPHEID VARIABLE STARS 造父變星

★ A CEPHEID VARIABLE STARS (造父變星) is a star, extremely luminous and the very distant one that can be observed and measured. Cepheid variable stars have been one of the most valuable methods used to determine how far away these galaxies are and the distance determination of the universe.

BLACK HOLE (黑洞)

★ BLACK HOLES (黑洞) are tremendously massive and dense that no light, even nothing, can escape it because of its immense gravitational pull.

★ The GRAVITAITONLA FORCE (引力) is too strong to let the OUTWARD FORCE (外擴力) resist it; thus, the CORE (核心) of the star keeps COLLAPSING (崩解). EINSTEIN'S GENERAL THEORY OF REALIVITVY (愛因斯坦的 廣義相對論) has been used to explain the light and matter under such huge gravitational forces.

THE SOLAR SYSTEM 太陽系

★ The planets in the SOLAR SYSTEM (太陽系) can be categorized into two groups: THE TERRESTRIAL PLANETS (類地行星) and THE JOVIAN PLANETS (類木行星).

★ The Terrestrial Planets: MERCURY (水星), VENUS (金星), EARTH (地球) and MARS (火星). The Jovian Planets : JUPITER (木星), SATURN (土星), URANUS (天王星), and NEPTUNE (海王星).

REVOLVE 公轉/ ROTATE 自轉

★ As the Earth REVOLVES (公轉), moving in a circle around the sun, it SPINS (旋轉) on its AXIS (地軸). The spinning movement of the Earth is called ROTATION (自轉).

★ The Earth's axis is TILTED (傾斜) 23.5degrees, which creates the seasons of the Earth.

MOON 月亮, 衛星

★ Moon refers to the natural SATELLITES (衛星) of other planets in the solar system.

★ The large areas of the surface of the moon were formed by the volcanic eruptions and METEORS (流星) bumping. The surface of the moon has been covered with CRATERS (火山口、隕石坑)

COMETS 彗星

★ A COMET (彗星) is composed of a solid CORE (核), surrounded by a cloudy atmosphere called COMA (慧髮), and one or two TAILS (尾). Comets are rocky and icy bodies. Ice begins to BOIL (沸騰、氣化) when a comet approaches the sun and the comet will be releasing dust and gas from the NUCLEUS CORE (核心).

METEORS 流星

★ METEORS are also known as SHOOTING STARS (流星). The streaks of light appearing in the sky are METEORS (流星), which consist of bits of rock, called METEOROIDS (流星體) . If the bits of rock land on the Earth, they are known as METEORITES (隕石).

6. MATHEMATICS 數學

數學主要是各形狀的名稱

★ MATHEMATICS is the study of topics, such as quantity (numbers), space, and structure.

★ SYMMETRY(對稱)、VERTICAL(垂直的)、HORIZONTAL (水平的)、TRIANGLE (三角形) 、CUBE(立方體)、CIRCLE(圓形)、COLUMN(圓柱狀物) 、ELLIPSE (橢圓形)、POLYGON(多角形)、RECTANGLE(長方形) 、SQUARE(正方形)

7. HISTORY (of the United States of America) 歷史

歷史的部分主要著重在美國歷史，包括誰以及如何發現美洲大陸，早期歷史以及望後受英國殖民統治下的反抗，接著講到１８世紀人民為了美國獨立所做的努力，及最後的美國南北戰爭。

COLUMBUS 哥倫布

★ COLUMBUS (哥倫布) was an Italian navigator or explorer who completed four voyages across the Atlantic ocean. Columbus is remembered for his discovery of "NEW WORLD" (新世界) in 1492. He assumed that it was the FAR EAST (遠東) he had been searching for while the islands he had arrived were located in the CARIBBEAN SEA (加勒比海). He then came to be considered as the "discoverer of America" in American popular culture.

PURITANS PILIGRIMS---PROTESTANTS 清教徒

★ Separating from the CHURCH OF ENGLAND (英國國教) owning to their opposition to it, a group of SEPARATISTS (分離派) came to settle in NEW ENGLAND (新英格蘭) district. PILGRIMS (清教徒) settled in PLYMOUTH COLONY (普里茅斯殖民地) and formed the first governing document of Plymouth colony, called THE MAYFLOWER COMPACT (五月花號盟約), which drew up with fair and equal laws, for the general good of the settlement.

THE BOSTON TEA PARTY 波士頓茶事件

★ THE BOSTON TEA PARTY (波士頓茶事件) was a political PROTEST (抗議), a resistance movement against the tea act passed by the BRITISH PARLIAMENT (英國國會) in1773 that reaffirmed their right to tax the colonists and offered the EAST INDIA COMPANY (東印度公司) an unfair advantage in the tea trade. The Boston Tea Party was a key event in the growth of the American Revolution.

TEA HISTORY美國 喝茶歷史

★ THREE KINDS OF IMPORTED TEA (三種種類的進口茶)：GREEN TEA/

UNFERMENTED 綠茶(未發酵茶葉)、BLACL OR FERMENTED TEA 紅茶(發酵茶葉)和 OOLONG/SEMIFERMENTED 烏龍茶(半發酵茶業)

THE REVOLUTIONARY WAR (1775~1783) 美國獨立戰爭

★ The FIRST CONTINENTAL CONGRESS (第一次大陸會議), held in Philadelphia, as a result, reaffirmed British Parliament had the power over colonial affairs, while DELEGATES (代表) from 12 colonies asked to cease all trade with Britain unless they repealed certain laws.

★ The SECOND CONTINENTAL CONGRESS (第二次大陸會議), on July 4, 1776, adopted the DECLARATION OF INDEPENDENCE (獨立宣言), which was written by THOMAS JEFFERSON (湯瑪士傑佛森，美國第三任總統), and officially declared independence of the United States of America.

THE CONSTITUTION (1787) OF THE UNITED STATES 美國憲法

COLD RUSH (1849) 淘金潮

THE CIVIL WAR (1861~1865) 南北戰爭

★ Between UNION (North) (北方聯盟) and the CONFEDERATE STATES OF AMERICA (South) (南部邦聯). ABRAHAN LINCOLN (亞伯拉罕林肯), known as the GREAT EMANCIPATOR (解放者), issued the EMANCIPATION PROCLAMATION (解放宣言) to free the slaves.

7. ARTS 藝術

藝術的部分從史前藝術講起，希臘與埃及的藝術歷史，接著是中世紀的藝術發展，從哥德式到寫實主義，最後談到現在藝術從印象派到最後的行動藝術。

PREHISTORIC PAINTING 史前

★ A MURALS (壁畫) is regarded as a piece of artwork painted directly on the wall that early humans applied to record events of their daily life. FRESCO paintings (濕壁畫) are a kind of murals applied to a walled covered with LIME PLASTER (石膏) with water-based PIGMENTS (顏料).

EGYPTIAN PAINTING 埃及

★ PAPYRUS SCROLLS (紙莎草紙卷軸)

★ CONVENTIONS (慣例): only the half of the eyes could be seen and the head is shown in a side view in a STARK OUTLINE(僵硬輪廓). The TORSE (軀幹) is uncomfortably twisted to the front.

GREEK PAINTING 希臘 (from 1000's B.C.)

★ Found on VASES (花瓶). The scenes were primarily from MYTHOLOGY (神話) and daily life. Painters preferred pure ornament so that normally the figures were in GEOMETRIC (幾何圖形) shapes and in black SILHOUETTE (剪影).

ROMAN PAINTING 羅馬 (from the cities of POMPEII 龐貝)

★ Roman painters REINTERPRETED (重新詮釋繪製) Greek paintings to their styles and paid more attention to the landscapes. Roman artists developed the technical INNOVATIONS (技術創新), called atmospheric PERSPECTIVE (透視畫法).

MEDIEVAL PAINTING 中世紀
★ Basically Medieval paintings included ILLUMINATED MANUSCRIPTS (圖案裝飾過的手寫稿), MURALS (壁畫), TAPESTRIES (掛毯) and MOSAICS (馬賽克) to decorate the walls.

GOTHIC ART 哥德式
★ GOTHIC ART (哥德式藝術), developing during the MEDIEVAL PERIOD (中古世紀), included SCULPTURE (雕塑), STAINED-GLASS WINDOWS (彩繪玻璃), FRESCO (濕壁畫), and ILLUMINATED MANUSCRIPTS (裝飾過的手寫稿).

THE RENAISSANCE 文藝復興
★ THE RENAISSANCE (文藝復興) can be considered as the bridge between MIDDLE AGE (中世紀) and modern history. LEONARDO DA VINCI (1452~1519) (李奧納多達文西) was one of the Florence's leading artists during the period of Renaissance.

THE HISTORY OF PAINTING (繪畫歷史)
★ GOTHIC (哥德式)>RENAISSANCE (文藝復興)>BAROQUE (巴洛克) >CLASSICISM (古典主義)>ROCOCO PAINTING (洛可可) >NEOCLASSICISM (新古典主義) >ROMANTICISM (浪漫主義) >REALISM (寫實主義)

MODERN ART 現代藝術:
★ IMPRESSIONISM (印象派)>POSTIMPRESSIONISM (後印象派)> SYMBOLISM (象徵主義) > FAUVISM (野獸派) > CUBISM (立體派) > DADAISM (達達主義) > PERFORMANCE ART (行動藝術)

★ THE HUDSON RIVER SCHOOL (1835~1870) (哈德森流派) was an art movement formed by a group of LANDSCAPE (景觀) painters to develop a romanticism-based characteristic style of landscape painting.

★ DAGUERREOTYPE (1839) (銀版照相) was the first publically announced photographic process, invented by Daguerre and introduced worldwide in 1839.

8. GEOGRAPHGY 地理
地理學主要是風化、沙漠化以及一些基本地圖用字

★ ARISTOTLE (亞里斯多德), a Greek philosopher and scientist was the first one stating that the earth was round.

★ TOPOGRAPHY/ TERRAIN (地形) is the study of the features and the surface shape of the Earth, such as PLAIN (平原), PLATEAU (高原), STRAIT (海峽), and PENINSULA (半島).

BASIC WORDS TO KNOW FOR MAP READING 基本地圖用字
★ MAP LEGEND (圖例)、ELEVATIONS (海拔高度)、THE CONTOUR LINES (等高線)、HEMISPHERE (半球)

★ LATITUDE AND LONGITUDE (經緯度): WEST LONGITURE (西經)、EAST LONGITUDE (東經)、 NORTH LATITUDE (北緯)、 SOUTH LATITUDE (南緯)、NORTH POLE (北極)、SOUTH POLE (南極)、MERIDIAN (本初子午線)、EQUATOR (赤道)

APPALACHIAN MOUNTAINS 阿帕拉契山脈: the oldest mountains in North America

TWO TYPES OF WEATHERING 風化

★ PHYSICAL WEATHING (物理風化). For example, a rock is split into small pieces due to freezing and thawing of water in rock cavities. CHEMICAL WEATHERING (化學風化): chemical changes in the composition of rock.

DESERTIFICATION 沙漠化

★ A dry land region becomes increasingly ARID (貧瘠的) and loses its bodies of water and vegetables. DESERTIFICATION (沙漠化) involves a variety of factors such as DROUGHT (乾旱) and other human activities.

STALACTITE 鐘乳石/ STALAGMITE 石筍

★ A STALACTITE (鐘乳石), an ICICLED-SHAPED (冰柱形狀) formation hanging from the ceiling, is produced by precipitation of minerals from GROUNDWATER (地下水) dripped through the CAVE (洞穴) ceiling. A STALAGMITE (石筍) is a type of rock formation growing upward from the floor of a cave due to the accumulation of CALCIUM CARBONATE (碳酸鈣) masses.

9. METEROLOGY 大氣學

大氣學是有關地球大氣以及天氣研究方面的學說。METEOROLOGY is the study of earth atmosphere

ATMOSPHERE OF EARTH 地球大氣組成

★ The atmosphere of earth primarily consists of 78% NITROGEN (氮氣) and 21% OXYGEN (氧氣) with other small amount of gases, such as ARGON (氬氣), CARBON DIOXIDE (二氧化碳), METHANE (甲烷), and OZONE (臭氧).

STRUCTURE OF ATMOSPHERE 地球大氣結構

★ TROPOSPHERE (對流層) is the lowest part where we live. STRATOSPHERE (同溫層) is the layer containing much of the ozone in the atmosphere.

★ THE OZONE LAYER (臭氧層) is placed between mesosphere and stratosphere. It has been destroyed by chemicals EMITTED (釋放) near the earth, such as CHLOROFLUOROCARBONS (CFCs) (氟氯碳化物).THE MESOSPHERE (中間層). The temperature decreases with height in this layer.

★ THE THERMOSPHERE (熱氣層).A region where the temperature increases with height. THE EXOSPHERE (外氣層)、THE MAGNETOSPHERE (磁氣圈)

GREENHOUSE EFFECT 溫室效應
Thermal radiation emitted from the Earth is absorbed by certain atmosphere greenhouse gases. GREENHOSUE EFFECT (溫室效應) insults and extremely warms the Earth.

THE KYOTO PROTOCOL 京都議定書

THE WATER CYCLE 水循環
Water cycle is the Continuous Movement (持續性的活動) of water existing on, above, and below the surface of the Earth.

★ Here are the processes of HYDROLOGIC CYCLE (水循環): PRECIPITATION (降水)、SNOWMELT RUNOFF (融雪水靜流), SURFACE RUNOFF (地表逕流)、STORAGE: INFILTRATION (滲透), GROUNDWATER FLOW (地下水流), GROUNDWATER

STORAGE（地下水儲存）、EVAPORATION（蒸發）TRANSPIRATION（蒸散）、CONDENDATION（壓縮）(clouds form)、PRECIPITATION（降水）

TYPES OF WIND 風的類型

★ THE PREVAILING WINDS（盛行風）、THE TRADE WINDS（信風）、MONSOON（季風）、THE SEASONAL WINDS（季節風）

★ DOLDRUMS（赤道無風帶）, near the EQUATOR（赤道）, a low-pressure area where the air is calm and hot. THE HORSE LATITUDES（馬緯度無風帶）are high-pressure belts of winds located at around 30 degrees from the equator. THE LOCAL WINDS TROPICAL CYCLONE（熱帶氣旋）, such as HURRICANES（颶風）and TYPHOONS（颱風）, is a rapidly ROTATING（旋轉）storm system always accompanied by strong winds and heavy rain.

TYPES OF WEATHER FRONT 鋒面種類

★ A COLD FRONT（冷鋒）、A WARM FRONT（暖鋒）、A STATIONARY FRONT（滯留鋒）、AN OCCLUDED FRONT（泅固鋒）

10. PHYSICS 物理學

HOW HEAT TRAVELS

★ CONDUCTION（傳達）、CONVECTION（對流）、RADIATION（輻射）、SOUND ACOUSTICS（聲學）、FREQUENCY（頻率）、DECIBELS (dB)（分貝）、PITCH（音高）、WAVELENTH（波長）、INTENSITY AND LOUDNESS（響度）、QUALITY（音質）

★ ELECTRICITY（電流）、STATIC ELECTRICITY（靜電）—ELECTRIC CHARGE（電荷）、CONDUCTOR（導體）、INSULATORS（絕緣體）—RESISTANCE（電阻）SUPERCONDUCTOR（超導體）—ELECTRONS（電子）、ELECTRIC LIGHTING（電燈）、INCANDESCENT LAMP（熾熱燈泡）—FILAMENT（燈絲）/ MELTING POINT（熔點）/ BULB（燈泡）、FLUORESCENT LAMP（螢光日光燈泡）

★ MAGNETISM—ATTRACTION（相吸）/ REPULSION（相斥）、CORIOLIS EFFECT（科氏例）—ROTATION / DEFLECTION（偏斜）、SURFACE TENSION（表面張力）

11. GEOLOGY (Oceanography included)

地質學是一門有關地球表面，歷史以及地貌外觀變遷的學說

★ It is the study of the planet Earth, regarding the history of the processes happening upon the rocky exterior and the study of FOSSILS（化石）. GEOLOGISTS（地質學家）are utilizing their knowledge, trying to comprehend these NATURAL HAZARDS（天災）and FORCAST（預測）the potential geological events.

INTERNAL STRUCTURE OF THE EARTH 地球構造

★ A knowledge of earth's interior is important for understanding PLATE TECTONICS（板塊構造論）. There are three parts of Earth's interior: CRUST（地殼）> MANTLE（地函）> CORE（地核）.

PLATE TECTONICS 板塊構造論

★ PLATE TECTONICS (板塊構造論) is a theory building upon the concept of CONTINENTAL DRIFT (板塊飄移), regarding PLATES (板塊) gliding over the mantle.

THE THEORY OF CONTINENTAL DRIFT 大陸飄移學說

★ THE THEORY OF CONTINENTAL DRIFT (大陸飄移學說) indicating the movement of the Earth's continents has been rejected for many years because of missing of a plausible driving force and an uncertainty of Wegener's (韋格納) estimate of the VOLECITY (速度) of continental motion.

THE MID-ATLANTIC RIDGE 大西洋中洋脊

★ THE MID-ATLANTIC RIDGE (大西洋中洋脊) is a DIVERGENT (擴張) tectonic plate - two tectonic plates moving away from each other - located along the floor of the ATLANTIC OCEAN (大西洋). The Mid-Atlantic Ridge is the place where new OCEANIC CRUST (海洋地殼) is formed through volcanic activities and gradually moves away from the ridge. SEAFLOOR SPREADING (海底擴張) occurs usually at THE MID-OCEAN RIDGE (中洋脊) and helps explain the theory of continental drift.

HOT SPOTS 熱點

★ HOT SPOTS (熱點) are volcanic regions where MAGMA (岩漿) rises from the underlying MANTLE (地函) that is ANOMALOUSLY (異常地) hotter compared with the surrounding mantle.

TECTONIC BOUNDARIES 板塊邊界

★ There are three kinds of tectonic boundaries: DIVERGENT, CONVERGENT, and TRANSFORM PLATES.

★ DIVEGENT (分離型) indicates two tectonic plates moving away from each other, places where frequent earthquakes strike along the RIFT (脊) and magma rises from the mantle. CONVERGENT (聚合型) indicates two tectonic plates coming together. It causes powerful earthquakes taking place and a chain of volcanoes formed parallel to the boundary. TRANSFORM (平移型) means two tectonic plates sliding past each other.

THE RING OF FIRE 火環帶

★ THE RING OF FIRE (火環帶) is a volcanic region located around the PACIFIC OCEAN (太平洋) where a large amount of VOLCANIC ERUPTIONS (火山噴發) and earthquakes occur.

GEYSER 間歇泉

★ GEYSER (間歇泉) is a geological event happening on the Earth surface that periodically ejects hot water and STEAM (蒸氣).

HYDROTHERMAL VENT 海底熱泉

★ HYDROTHERMAL VENT (海底熱泉), normally found near volcanically active regions, are places where geothermally heated water issues.

OCEAN CURRENTS 洋流

★ OCEAN CURRENTS (洋流) is a continuous movement of seawater generated by winds, temperature differences, and more. TIDES (潮汐) are different, which are caused by GRAVITATIONAL PULL (地球引力) of the Sun and Moon.

EUTROPHICATION 優養化

★ EUTROPHICATION (優養化) happens when the environment becomes enriched with NUTRIENTS (養分). It is considered as a problem to marine habitats because it causes ALGAL BLOOM (藻華), a rapid increase and accumulation in the population of ALGAE (海藻).

EARTHQUAKE 地震 EPICENTER (震央) is the point on the surface of the Earth that is directly above the HYPOCENTER (震源) where the earthquake originates.

EARTHQUAKE SCALE: RICHTER 芮氏規模

★ People use EARTHQUAKE SCALE: RICHTER (芮氏規模), a MAGTITUDE (震度) number, to QUANTIFY (量化) the size of an earthquake.

ROCK 岩石

★ The three main types of rock are IGENROUS (火成), SEDIMENTARY (沉積), and METAMORPHIC (變質). They are different in how they are formed. LITHIFICATION (岩化作用) is the process in which SEDIMENTS (沉積物) compact under pressure and gradually become solid rock. IGNEOUS ROCK (火成岩)、SEDIMENTARY ROCK (沉積岩)、METAMORPHIC ROCK (變質岩)、QUARTZ (石英)、LIMESTONE (石灰石)、MARBLE (大理石)、GRANITE (花崗岩)

11. ENERGY 能源

★ ALCHENY (煉金術)、PERIODIC TABLE (元素週期表)

THE STRUCTURE OF ATOMS 原子結構

★ An ATOM (原子) comprises ELECTRONS (電子) spinning around NUCLEUS (原子核) that contains PROTONS (質子) and NEUTRONS (中子)、ION (離子)、VALENCE (原子價)、ISOTOPE (同位素)

MOLECULE 分子/ COMPOUNDS 化合物

★ MOLECULES (分子) are made up of atoms and are the smallest particles in a chemical element with chemical properties of that element. COMPOUNDS (化合物): All COMPOUNDS (化合物) are molecules. A compound consists of two or more different atoms.

TRANSMUTATION 變形

★ TRANSMUTATION (變形) is the changing of one chemical element into another.

NICKEL 鎳、GOLD 金、MERCURY 水銀、POLYMER 聚合物

REFINING OIL 煉油

★ REFINING OIL (煉油) is processing and refining crude oil into a lot more useful products such as gasoline, heating oil, and more.

PETROLEUM 石油

★ PETROLEUM (石油) can be naturally occurring unprocessed CRUDE OIL (原油) and any other petroleum products that are made of refined crude oil.

Learn Smart! 054

N 倍速學會 iBT 字彙

400 魔術英語句極速提升字彙力（附 MP3 學習光碟）

作　　者	朱倩儀
發 行 人	周瑞德
執行總監	齊心瑀
企劃編輯	陳韋佑
校　　對	編輯部
封面構成	高鍾琪

內頁構成	華漢電腦排版有限公司
印　　製	大亞彩色印刷製版股份有限公司
初　　版	2016 年 1 月
定　　價	新台幣 429 元
出　　版	倍斯特出版事業有限公司
電　　話	(02) 2351-2007
傳　　真	(02) 2351-0887
地　　址	100 台北市中正區福州街 1 號 10 樓之 2
E - m a i l	best.books.service@gmail.com
網　　址	www.bestbookstw.com

港澳地區總經銷	泛華發行代理有限公司
地　　址	香港新界將軍澳工業邨駿昌街 7 號 2 樓
電　　話	(852) 2798-2323
傳　　真	(852) 2796-5471

國家圖書館出版品預行編目資料

N 倍速學會 iBT 字彙:400 魔術英語句極速提升字彙
力 / 朱倩儀著. -- 初版. -- 臺北市 : 倍斯特,
2016.01 面 ；　公分. --（Learn smart ; 54）
ISBN 978-986-91915-7-9（平裝附光碟片）
1.托福考試 2.詞彙

805.1894　　　　　　　　　　104027791